TERRAIN

HESSE CAPLINGER

TERRAIN

ISBN: 978-1-66780-504-7
eBook ISBN: 978-1-66780-505-4

CARL REINHART

Publishers

Contents

For

Lynn

TERRAIN

1995

I.

Urine against any surface makes its own sound. And here, against the wound of cleared earth—the soft red ash of Sierra Leone—it sounded flat and hollow, strangely muted, like a hot water over tea bag, like an echo choked by the throat. It furrowed a hole where it fell, as it might upon fire pit, upon snow—a proper reservoir of bushmeat and palm-wine might fuel a genuine portal of dribbling through such stuff; through clear to civilization; fresh air and reason—but Hussar was not so filled, and regardless of his imaginings, it merely punched a hot divot in the floor of the earth at his toes, and in a moment of sun, it was gone.

His shoes were dusted but for spatter. He was warm with dark canvas and kit and stamp-steel mags and drape of rifle bore, and his zipper, somehow, was live with sun beneath his fingers—raw still with trigger-touch of the M2s. The M2s lived in the spine of the Land Rover: but they, at least, should have respired to now—and would be re-fed an organ-sheet reserve of cool new belt-boxes from supply.

They had cleared Baomahun late-day yesterday, and had cleared the mines today, and they had taken the low, flat, broad plateau of the mine camp above the village for their station; and had brought up the Rovers there, and put down the gunship and the two transports, and had cleared a space on the deck for the incoming.

Kamadugu crouched in the shade and cast spells into the earth with a stick, and James Ngolo Vonjoe sat in the gate of a truck, and Inge Lange—the Swede—and Denny Smithson—the Aussie—sat at the gun-mount and pair of glasses and watched Jan Bekker and fifty Kamajors move door-to-door in the smoldering, empty village below, and Felix Graaf watched twenty-five Kamajors sweep the high fields between the plateau and the tree line at the mountain-steppe, and Erling Coevorden and Simon Van Lingen sat in lawn chairs and shorts with a satellite phone, in discussion: they were awaiting company.

That first company, when it came, was David Koning—'King David' among the *Afrikaans-Hollands*—who'd flown into Lungi from Antwerp on one of the 727s, and then by helicopter to the clearing at the mine camp, where the touch-down upset the mess being set and the tents which had been staked, and lifted all the zinc eaves like cast bed sheet—and as the helicopter retreated toward Freetown, he stooped through the wash with a parcel and his suit jacket—and he was well received. Hussar left the lumpy plateau-verge, encircling shallow streambed turned inside out with mud-pie gullies and fallow, red screen tailings, and moved to the shade of the camp—marked all over like a *Pmui* relic: with colonial geometries, and simple, vacant Calvinist industry—and stood near Kamadugu and Werner Van Der Boor in the lee of an outbuilding looted to its galvanized sheet and wood-plank.

Koning had brought gifts and tidings, and he handed them out to Coevorden and Van Lingen: bottled gin and Styrofoam and carton cigarettes and a document which they shared among them in turns. He drew it from an envelope and showed them—showed them its cover page and its concluding signatures, and poured them gin and lit them cigarettes.

"Return of the King," said Van Der Boor with a sidelong murmur. "Back from De Haas, no doubt—with land rights and a nod from Strasser. That'll be skyf and gin with mess, I wager."

"From De Haas?" said Hussar. It was 36 °C where sun fell, and Hussar was saturated with sun-fall—radiating the stuff—and still cooling the angry blue scorch from his eyes. He was watching Kamadugu rocking on his heels and drawing on the earth, and he was distracted.

"De Haas?" said Van Der Boor. "You've a stekkie, a lassie—a woman, right? She's a ring, ja?"

Hussar turned from Kamadugu to squint at Van Der Boor with a sigh.

"And dat ring, it gots a stone, ja?"

Hussar blinked a vanishing nod.

"De Haas! Don't be a tiet, mên," said Van Der Boor. "Skyf . . . and . . . gin!" repeated Van Der Boor, and poked Hussar for the measure.

Van Der Boor was large—red bearded, in full wire brush and beret he wore now, and donned the little slope of cap with the same dire dog-stake-and-chain conviction as in the Border War where he earned it; and no one since had touched its mien could not now be the same: a pendant or badge to men, but not perhaps, once received an immutable fact of self. By frame he was entry-grade large, but as a matter of psychic constitution, he was the largest metaphysical body in Bo District—save perhaps, the men in lawn chairs, thought Hussar. From another army he'd have been all self-regard and capitulation—collar pins and bluster, but here—Hussar'd been through the corporate action in Angola with him, and Freetown, and just days ago, Kono District—while being entirely less than his own estimation, the actual man and his beard and beret were size for the job—and gin and smoke and cause to sustain himself to the magnitude of his hatband, would be forever a pay in surplus.

When Koning and Coevorden and Van Lingen broke from confabulation and their gleeful suppressions, they did, as Van Der Boor predicted, bring skyf and gin for mess. There were three cartons of Dunhills and one of Belga and four bottles of Damrak turned up into Styrofoam chalices; and two packs and two cups were set out for

Jan Bekker's village return—the Kamajors would take their luck with them about tobacco and juniper, but they would be fed.

The Kamajors disdained to adventure in the buildings for their paradox of spirits, and while the Afrikaners might shade in them, they preferred to rest elsewhere—for the bats, snakes, and droppings—and so mess was under canopy and out of doors, and the trio had brought over their spoils and were in rare gay spirit there: Coevorden, a spare Rhodesian weed—a wisp with long thin lay of hair, socks, boots, and bare knees; Van Lingen, sober in delicate spectacles and heavy stubble; and Koning, in brogues and the pieces of tan suit—the jacket now over the lawn furniture—and articulating cufflinks and pealing his cuffs when there was again the paddle of helicopter on the air.

2.

What they don't have in Eckernförde is the smell. It was here waiting for them when they came, hung for them like a mist upon nocturnal moors—but one which sunlight does not lift, but festers. The people of Baomahun were waiting, too; ready there with greetings—on the road, in the fetid streambed waters and alluvial earth-cake mines, in amidst the scrub-ground like shoots of leaves—a rare and fragrant bloom—amid the village corners and squares, indoors and outdoors, at the kitchen bowl, at laundry, at bath, in obedient waiting, in animus, in hysteria, in flight; they saluted with dismembered limbs and issued welcome in fixed and swollen grimace: they were everywhere a human rubble, exploded into their constituent parts by cleaver and gun fire and a radioactive malintent whose emission broadcast to the naked eye—and to them, last night, the Company had added meaningfully to their rank. And now with them, a cohort of RUF rebels lay in their own postures of final and immergent orgasm, side-to-side and cheek-to-cheek: called to the same dream as their victims.

A persuasion of high-velocity physics, of neurochemistry, and nerve fiber conductivity, had mollified their intentions—had balmed the rebellious fervor in their souls, and now one knew them by their wares: their quieted Kalashnikovs and G3s and their ammo belts for jewelry—their dress an argot in strange, aspirational finery; almost entirely young men and boys: little posturing chieftains in playclothes and live rounds. One could only shake their head. There is no triumph in victory over the wayward—those who only months before might have been as well served with spanking and strong words.

The sound, too—neither do they have that in Eckernförde. In the barracks there are footfalls and voices, there are automobiles in the campus and the street, at the naval station—at the docks in Kiel— there are always the drone of generators and the whiff of sweet diesel on the airs, and the rasp of grinding wheel, and the cry of hoists and crane spindles. On-ship, one lives between the very piston-strike— the pulse and murmur of the draft—but here, when the Alpha jets are at home in Nigeria and the gunships are down and the M2s are not bucking in the hand—somewhere faraway Kalashnikovs are not tapping the air, but when it is still and the Company is in waiting: here, at the base of these small mountains, before the generators cackle, and when the men do not call to one another—here, now— there are birds somewhere and monkeys, in the hillside, and that faint hum of sun-touch on leaves—on scrub grass and palm frond and tree bough—inaudible as insect flight at ten paces, but charged and voluminous.

3.

Eddie Heywood sits for piano in a cramped New York, somewhere, 1943. He scoots the bench, and rests his hands, and grins slyly at the engineer. A cigarette dangles from the skin of his lip; and with a squinty head-cock against the plume, he begins with a pair of light lullaby phrases and opens out into a slow, delicate, one-handed stride. Shelly Manne and Oscar Pettiford join in unison on drums and contrabass—they follow behind; where Heywood conjures the heavens and Manne sweeps out a firmament beneath his brushes, while Pettiford casts every concrete thing to form—every cobblestone and curb and tenement house: and after a few measures Coleman Hawkins enters, too: moves upon the face of the world, descends on Mercury wings, above its firmament and pavings: breathes tenor sax like pipe tobacco; eternal, consoling as cognac and collared sweaters—the sound of blue-burning malt-and-cherry smoke; the sound of faith, and creation.

It was this image rolled out before Hussar; this image of "Sweet Lorraine," incarnate and playing before his eyes as the Land Rover jostled from rut to gouge, crown to gully. It had been a day's investment to reach this downward attitude of road, or path, or whatever it might be called from moment to moment. They had begun at the northeastern base of Kangari—climbed to late-morning until the road gave up to a vagary of footways, which needed four hours work in spades and chainsaws to lever through—and now at last they had made the crest and rocked and crashed down-grade at the head of the convoy of Rovers, where Hussar hung from the handles of the M2s, clutched to the pair of grips which roused them—two great, chain-fed bassoons which played only in the notes of bark and breath; and this image of music issued out before him. He heard it needle-in-groove above the minor key whine of drive-gear and of tires. It slipped like a transparency before him, where Manne swept their very road into being, made way through Pettiford's forest in bass-string-boughs and shade, and the sun met them low and autumnal, in shafts and hot shards, through afternoon canopy.

The radios were silent as they fell downhill toward Baomahun. Viggo De Bruyn brought up the rear, led from there in chase—led with instructions which had been given and would not be repeated in broadcast—led with silence of affirmation. Van Der Boor had the wheel and wrested it over roots and stones. James Ngolo Vonjoe sat passenger, manned the wing gun, and Kamadugu sat folded in a jump seat in the rear at Hussar's feet. He was a living totem resting there in woven clothes and hat and his adornment of prayers and protections closed in fabric squares and sewn into his raiment like spangles. He was anthropological, thought Hussar—an exhibition from the British Museum culled from its diorama and its time and set to a red-eyed ecstatic sulking at his feet, with an automatic rifle and a bandolier and company of the M2's ammo boxes for contrivance of affect. The Rover leapt and gamboled and they each jerked against it in pendular opposition, and the radios were still, and neither had they spoken some time. There was just the curse of the drive-gear and the tires' rumble and cork, and the munitions tapping all the time like coins in the ashtray, and the slap of fuel canisters, and Hussar's music, which reached out toward the horizon and played the setting sun.

They were six Rovers coming down the log-road northeastern pass toward Baomahun, and another cohort of Rovers approaching from the southern plain, and a pair of armored BMP-2s to deny the southern passage to flight, and the transports to drop the Kamajors south of the village, and once it had begun—the gunships to call. Nevertheless, it was not a plan to love, and the yawning chasm to the next Rover back on the pass and the remainder of the caravan bottled there, and perhaps even Kamadugu's despondent, great watery-eyed sobriety, were each sign and product of all that was unloved in it.

They'd descended the peak to a village on the steppe—six hundred meters crest, down four to the small stand of thatch and steel huts where the orange sky had pushed the canopy back from the road—a thing like termite works, leaf-cutters encolonized; low-rise man-mounds gathered from the dark and composed scattershot in mineral-fetters and brown tree-whisk: a log-camp fed bush meats and raw timbers, and for all the surveillance planes had said—deserted. It opened out satin daylight before them, and they had stopped, and had stopped the convoy out of play behind: the wisdom of aerial sampling would now need inspection by hand. And for this there were James Ngolo Vonjoe and Kamadugu.

Kamadugu listened in Mende as James Ngolo Vonjoe spoke. He said they would circle the village in the bush, would meet on the far side, and would search the huts in turn till they returned, and Kamadugu listened, and he listened again. Van Der Boor and Hussar greased up and readied their kit and Van Der Boor said, "He understand it then?"

"Many times I think that I am here from Kono alone to speak with this one," said James Ngolo Vonjoe, with a gesture to the other Kamajor.

"You're here for work in Kono," said Van Der Boor. "Good work there, and good work here."

"I was in Kono because I know Kono. I am not in my home because what was in Kono went well—but I am here for speaking with this," he said, and searched the shaded road for spirit of the convoy which could not be seen.

"What does he say?"

"He says nothing."

The three of them looked at Kamadugu, who watched them speak, peered intently into their faces, and then turned from them to study the village ahead. When he turned back, he spoke to James Ngolo Vonjoe.

"What does he say?"

"He is Kuranko and his Mende is pidgin—we are the French and the Scots at work in English. Let me ask him again." And he did.

"We'll lose our light still on the road," said Hussar.

"What does he say?" repeated Van Der Boor.

"He says the village smells clear, the village sounds clear—the village is clear; we should pass."

"Tell him there'll be checks the same, ja. Tell him, lead or follow, hey?—but go," said Van Der Boor. "Tell him—spare the rifles—something's there, prefer the knives, or send it down the road, right—send it here," said Van Der Boor, with a finger to the spot.

James Ngolo Vonjoe told him, and Kamadugu shook his head and blinked red eyes at them, and the two set their rifles nevertheless, and entered the bush of the village-side, at intervals.

Hussar watched them enter. He watched Kamadugu shed his lethargy and stride feline and angular into the cover—something fluid and off-tempo, a slippery halting steam train rod-and-wheel locomotion—until after a few paces there was not so much as an exhale to mark his passage. Hussar fit the lid on his rifle—feathered the suppressor to the mouth of the MSG90A1—and moved off the road. He worried of missing anything that might come from the village at speed: two or three chances and he'd be firing back toward the convoy; and he waved Van Der Boor back as a catch-net. Van Der Boor fell back behind the Rover, and from these posts they listened down their sights.

It was forty minutes before they first saw them again, in the village, skulking cross the road. Hussar sighted them from time to time, when he might—when they were in view—pointed muffled 7.62 downrange toward them like providence, waiting to catch, arrest. Soon Kamadugu emerged middle of the road, and watched, hands on his hips as James Ngolo Vonjoe finished the huts. The other Kamajor called to him in curses. But Kamadugu remained in the road till he had finished, and the pair of them strode from the village to the Rover.

"What does he say?" asked Van Der Boor, when they returned. Kamadugu had rounded the Rover where Van Der Boor lit skyf and pulled it to satisfaction against his beard, and Kamadugu spoke to him and climbed into the truck. "Vonjoe—what does he say?"

James Ngolo Vonjoe was irritable, and he said, "He is masterless, who will not be afraid."

"He says that?"

"No, I say that. He says: doubt is bird-stool in the eye of knowing. And I also say—I hope that he is quiet now: I am tired with him."

All the next kilometer was slow and Kamadugu was still, as were they all, but it gave James Ngolo Vonjoe no pleasure just the same. They'd summoned the convoy on the radio when they'd cleared the village of the log-road pass, and the road had opened out into descending terraces of low scrub and bush and copse of trees which snaked thick and thin and rose and fell in shambling tapers back to shrub and grass and earth. "They are like hedgerows," said Hussar to Van Der Boor, from the belly of the Rover noise. "The earth keeps to its own here, or she's picked at like gulls on carcass—cultivation's not for this place, nè?—scavengers have only mouths: not hands, ja; and no wholesome thing will grow where God looks away," said Van Der Boor over his shoulder. Far behind, the Rovers of the convoy broke from the road, north and south toward breaks in the woodline, and after a time, out of view. Soon they were alone as ever in their plan and their silence and the road.

"There's the donnerse," said Van Der Boor, when they'd eventually made the crest of the streambed. "When it's time, we cross 'n sit cozy far-side. That's where it happens." He stood out over the wheel and indicated with an arm the place he meant on the opposite bank, and he set his beret, and he sat back down to study his watch face. "Walk me down," he said.

"Why must it be there?" said James Ngolo Vonjoe. "Would it not better to be here?—the stream between us: it is not natural."

"Donkie is 'n wonderlike ding, Vonjoe. Best bait has an easy look. Walk me down," said Van Der Boor, and they all climbed from the Rover to spot it through the crossing.

They were a kilometer from Baomahun—a band of trees either side the stream raised on rainwater torrents, and a mud, stone-sharp and wet channel between. They eased the Rover down and then charged up the other side and ducked the spray in slurry and rock-shard—it was close and fungal, and the insects sung each to each in chains of song, up and down its twilight corridor, and they settled just beyond the opposite bank, in full sweat and tree-shade and a low turn of hillock for the benefit of cover to the engine and the tires, and for two hundred meters Kangari fell in one gesture to the plain of the village of Baomahun.

An arm of Kangari reached down and braced Baomahun to the rear, and the sun rest in low molten fury against its shoulder, and cast its sparks upon Freetown, and would soon slip beneath the hills and soon would touch the sea, and Hussar imagined—soon would climb beneath the earth mantle and comprehension and belief—soon would leave them with their unmoored trusting in the choices and hungry intuitions of men, and would return to the very core of the earth in its slumber—and there would not give light, but the blood-heat of all things which spills in the cool night of its absence. It was a private imagining, and he did not share it, nor speak to it in his features.

They each checked their action, and cycled clear breaches, and squared their first magazines neatly. They noted their supplies, their number and placement, their handedness and attitude. Except for Kamadugu, who did not: his prayers performed, he watched Hussar slide the heavy ammo cases for the M2s from stowage to where they were in reach and readiness, and watched Van Der Boor bend the terrain against the end of his field glasses.

"What do you see?" asked Hussar.

"Mine company estate—old Director's estate, I expect—some six hundred meters down the slope."

"Sentry?"

"Guardhouse, ja."

"Do they see us?"

"Nah, mên," said Van Der Boor, and handed the glasses to Hussar. "Fokkol. Drink an' maybe dagga, too—toying a little stekkie on a dirt-line. High-sentry guard; boys at play in a yard: they see fokkol, nè?"

Hussar looked and saw the small compound. There were ten . . . eleven . . . twelve: small figures—young boys—children, idling on the grounds tread-worn to roots and clay, riding a pair of tricycles along the hard-pack drive, with loping axles and slung rifles—auditioning wardrobe novelties of the estate one to the next, in spontaneous and theatric displays. There was a young girl on a stake-rope. When they thought of her it was with hurled trash and bottles and shouted slanders he could hear by gesture. And she sat slack against the post. And she sat fixed in the unmoving earth. And, after a few moments, they forgot to remember once more.

Hussar handed back the glasses and was glad to be free of them, and wiped the sight from his hands against his pant-legs. "What if they don't see us?" he said. "Unseen bait is an unbaited trap."

Van Der Boor did not reply at once, but looked through the glasses at the estate, and the children and their weapons, and the girl. "Imagine dat cost," said Van Der Boor. "Hung out by a gang a dronkie aap children? Little drols? Imagine dat."

"I am without affection for this the starting plan, from before. A bait sounds still unwise. Soon it will be dark, and soon, very bad for all the sorts of bait. Cannot traps be just what is unexpected?" said James Ngolo Vonjoe.

Van Der Boor raised his hand. "What does he say?" Kamadugu spoke beneath this and Van Der Boor asked Vonjoe to know it.

"He says they are not children."

"What?"

"He says: you say that they are children, and they are not. He says, they are not children: they are shades."

"He says the children are . . . *shades*?"

"He says they are not children."

"They're ghosts, then?"

"Like spirits. *Dis . . . em . . . ?* The form of children, without the child. Shades."

"Aap *shades*, then."

"Let it be on this that we make a new—"

"What does he say?"

"What?"

"What does he say now?"

"He says: good ground and bad ground take bones like rain—but idleness chances good dying."

They looked at Kamadugu who blinked at his knees, and Van Der Boor returned to the glasses. "Imagine it. Coevorden and Van Lingen had that on their map?—a turn on little queered-up aap drollies, hey? Think they had dat one, mên?" He lowered the glasses and lay the question out to Hussar with a frustrated glance. "We've to be seen, right?" he said to them all. James Ngolo Vonjoe rubbed his head with the flat of his hand and Kamadugu blinked at his knees, and they all took nervous shallow breaths when the tone came over the radio to indicate the other forces were on their marks and in position.

"Ag, shit!" said Van Der Boor at the sound. "They must see you!" He looked anxiously between the Kamajors. "Take the sage with you, Vonjoe, and go be seen. They must see you before the dark and they see nothing, and it's all waste, right. Not too close—don't engage, just be seen, right. Just be seen and be seen coming back—they've to call it in—no use in having the little tiets take after you, right? Right? You have it? Go! Go!"

Hussar watched them leave the Rover, climb over the sills with their warriors' tools—bullets and barrels for hammer and nails—and he saw that James Ngolo Vonjoe had said nothing. Van Der Boor had not directed the instruction, and James Ngolo Vonjoe had not shared it: and certainly, there was no instruction for which he might find happiness other than to ford the streambed once again and wait there for filigree of the occasion. Van Der Boor had instructed only the action; the Kamajors had slipped their legs over the Rover-flanks like they might be dropping from a vessel into turgid surf—and he'd said not a word to Kamadugu; and now followed down-grade, hewing through the heavier scrub, in what was the rapidly failing halo, not of broadcast light, but that warm and parting glint caught in the lens-edge of the atmosphere—that light like a sound captured in a room, leaping against itself into soft decay.

Hussar watched them descend. He watched for Kamadugu when he could be seen: he watched him appear with his high-knee stride and his articulating haunches and the incongruous tassels of his knitted cap, and thought he did not look like a thing that meant to stop half-way, to be seen and flee; nor to cull with clever shots or contest for victory, but to rush the hapless throng and drag one away squealing between his teeth.

Van Der Boor watched this too, through the glasses in concentration. "It's to be the witless tell of unfortunate scouts?" said Hussar. "With this gang of cretins, I'd hardly care. But that's the sauce." "He's a thing to behold," said Hussar. "What? Kamadugu? There's Viggo De Bruyn's Grand Kaffer, mên. He's genius—he's mystic, says De Bruyn. He's lucky-charm, says I— but he's here, hey? Right? Where are you, Marek Hussar? Hey? Where you—*gunner?*—you in his trick or he in yours, bru?" Van Der Boor pulled at his beard with both hands and shook his head and returned to the glasses. "Fokkol, says I."

"He's from the North?"

"Kuranko, ja mên," said Van Der Boor.

"Vonjoe speaks no Kuranko, then?"

Van Der Boor laughed. "Kuranko?—Mande?—'cause I'd know, right?—I'd know it. My goddamn Mende is two-parts drinks an' a-part munitions—and I've luck for the grain of that! They get on, is what I know—he and Vonjoe."

"What's for De Bruyn?—what does he have for him?"

Van Der Boor looked to Hussar and indicated an answer on the falling slope.

"He's a sort of feral cunning."

"Fearless—is your word, mên. Unbounded. That's for De Bruyn: that's De Bruyn's magic. He's a chieftain. Early days, he raised Kamajors of three villages to meet the rebels. That was early days— the Tamaboros. He was high-chieftain . . . they were away in the bush months fighting. They pushed off the RUF—and when they returned there wasn't one of his village left to care. Not one. All gone."

"Dead?"

"As you like. His parents and children and wives—all of them. He'll be with us till he meets them—finds a way to them. Hearth key—that's what *De Bruyn* has for him."

Hussar could no longer see them. His gaze cast over the rough
and down toward the mine-estate—an unlikely Western-style home
with a garage and a cleared grounds—and off beyond another fold in
the landscape toward Baomahun. His eyes moved, sampled features
from the terrain, and they did not see, but thought. They thought
downhill and through bush and into swift rush of nightfall—*thought*
the Rover dash and the seatback and the edge of Van Der Boor, arms
up and canted into the eyepieces, his concentration projected upon
distant meters as though it might be pressed up against terrarium
glass—and Hussar wrung old dew from his hair and *thought* the
damp groove of his palm, and *thought* the handles of the M2s polished
in the web of his grip, and history, and he *thought* the brass-woven
belts in their chutes, like ten thousand canisters fed to the mouth of
a machine for unmaking.

"Hey," said Van Der Boor. "Hey." He put his hand out to the side.
It was a call to attention, but read to Hussar as entirely more—crossing guard; traffic cop. "Hey . . . here they come," he said. There was a
single distant tap of Kalashnikov: "Contact," said Van Der Boor, and
passed the glasses to Hussar.

Hussar reached round the guns to receive them and felt a long
time in sighting them now. First there was James Ngolo Vonjoe
faintly, glistening, sprinting. Behind and along a diverging line was
Kamadugu: an even placid jog with sudden, off-tempo jigs. And
further—down at the yard-edge of the house, there were two boys
bickering. They were a smaller, and a larger—and the larger seemed
to be re-training a bead on the fleeing Kamajors, while the smaller
knocked up the barrel, snatched it away, and beat the larger in the
neck with the butt till he had been knocked to the ground. He stood
over him and shouted and pulled up the larger by the short of his hair
until he had climbed once more to his feet, and pointed the larger
in firm, illustrative gestures to the top of the hill—not toward the
Kamajors, but the Rover. Hussar saw him send the larger off, running

back toward Baomahun, with a kick on the ass and parting heave of the rifle after him. He saw him peering up toward the Rover with his own enormous surplus-Soviet-glasses; and he saw him skulking irritably round the yard with a pistol, till the remaining figures were scarcely to be seen.

Hussar handed back the glasses. Van Der Boor checked the progress of the Kamajors and studied downrange intently.

"Can you see?" said Hussar.

"Just," said Van Der Boor. And when there was the distant pop of small arms, he closed his eyes and shook his head; stroked his beard, and put them away.

4.

It was three hours dark since they had sent their readiness tone by radio. Van Der Boor played nervously with the pocket fastener for his second clip, and Hussar knew they all meant to stop it, but did not. James Ngolo Vonjoe sat again at the front seat wing gun. Kamadugu took a cigarette from him and tore off the butt and Van Der Boor glared when he struck a match to it. "We seek to be seen, and then hide from the sight?" said James Ngolo Vonjoe. Kamadugu spoke to Van Der Boor also. "He says: God may forbid it, and dead-men do it poorly. Best to have it now."

"What if you go to the devil?" said Van Der Boor.

"He says: Hell is the company of memory: if he goes to the devil, he should not lack for smoke," said James Ngolo Vonjoe.

Hussar observed the cameo-flare of Kamadugu smoking. His rifle lay cross his knees—a sort of throw against antagonisms, whose straps Hussar could hear with Kamadugu's shifting feet. His hand and his face rose and dissolved from the night to the brief punctuation of tobacco-coal. He held the cigarette by the last knuckle of his hand, and between two straight and senseless fingers—an unnatural and tenuous grasp that Africans were wonted to; and released great cumulus exhalations of cloud—as Africans were wonted to: and Hussar thought were they not so brief surely they would precipitate. Hussar admired Kamadugu's effortless but considerable inhalations, and like Van Der Boor he imagined, had thoughts for tobacco himself—but from here forward wanted nothing for his hands but grip and trigger: tactile fixations of an entirely more extroverted sort.

Within the Rover they made their own light. It was the amber and blue-black sightedness of the known: sound and touch and the measure of reach glowed with affirming familiarity, rather than the reflected and visible—and now to this was the addition of Kamadugu's face, swelling to momentary existence from a singular blushing point.

Beyond this living room, however, was the back and circling shoulder of Kangari, there, beside, and out beyond the plain of Baomahun. At the first full-dark there had been short, swift lights in the compound and down in the valley where the village lay. But these tonight had quickly been extinguished. Somewhere on high, starlight quavered untold perforated multitudes—here, this night trimmed a skim-coat grey and brown, something earth-blown and ruminant; and it was very, very dark.

It did not register at first Kamadugu was listening. Hussar envisioned his ropey neck twisted and his features vacated to the labor of senses. His chin lifted and panning. It was the tobacco that gave it away. His face had not risen into being for far too many measures—the coal hung dim and visible there, unmoved. No gesture, no swell, no breath of exhaust—no absent tap of ash. Just the point of low dim star, and veined knuckles, and a turn of knee.

"What is the call, when it comes?" said James Ngolo Vonjoe. Van Der Boor began to answer but Kamadugu had reached out to still the hand playing with the fastener. Hussar could not see this but felt the gesture in the Rover-springs and Van Der Boor's pause. Van Der Boor began again, quietly, but again Kamadugu tapped him on the leg: "Sss," he said.

Hussar felt him turning, leaning, peering out over the cusp of the Rover. He snuffed the cigarette under his heel, and then there was only his shuffling and truck-shiver. Kamadugu spoke. "He says: do you hear them?—whatever signal, it comes soon or is wasted."

"I hear nothing," said Van Der Boor.

James Ngolo Vonjoe shook his head.

Hussar did not speak.

"It's three tones. But we'd hear the gunships on the air first. De Bruyn's got the night scopes, mên. They can see," said Van Der Boor.

"He says: there is nothing on the air, but their smell. He can smell them. He says: you must shelter now behind the truck."

"We've time," said Van Der Boor.

"He says: damn your time and damn your tone, also—there are far too many—we must shelter, now."

Kamadugu and Van Der Boor climbed out of the Rover and took up positions behind. James Ngolo Vonjoe was silent. Hussar checked that the M2s moved free in their mount. And when Van Der Boor's radio toned, and he called "Fire," Hussar touched the M2s, and their first flame opened over the field as thunder-light, and shown glittering the four hundred eyes that were upon it.

2008

II.

Your letter only reached me a few days ago. I want to thank you for its great and kind confidence. I can hardly do more. I cannot go into the nature of your verses; for all critical intention is too far from me. With nothing can one approach a work of art so little as with critical words: they always come down to more or less happy misunderstandings. Things are not all so comprehensible and expressible as one would mostly have us believe; most events are inexpressible, taking place in a realm which no word has ever entered, and more inexpressible than all else are works of art, mysterious existences, the life of which, while ours passes away, endures.

Hussar read this and broke off. He turned back. The opposite page opened: 'Rilke was born in Prague in 1875, the son of a conventional army-officer and a religious-fanatical mother, who first sent him, most unsuitably, to military school. After that, largely autodidact, he studied philosophy, history, literature, art, in Prague, Munich, Berlin.' And ended: 'He died at Valmont near Glion on December 29, 1926, and is buried beside the little church of Raron overlooking the Rhone Valley.' An inscription: 'I think you'll find that Rilke is a kindred spirit. Happy New Year '95.'

Hussar closed the book and touched the objects of the table which were gently askew. He touched them in their turn—the broad fabric napkin, neither perfectly folded nor straight. The fork and knife, coffee and creamer, the salt and pepper—black or blue or green iridescent: he touched and turned them; corrected them—the cup, and saucer, and sweet: the little Vergani Gianduiotto. Mothers, he thought. Mothers. He thought it when he touched it—foiled chocolates: condiments of maternity. A man in distraction would forget there had been such a thing. A ration in cocktail dress. A man will suffice with meat and bread and never know he lacked it. Man wants woman but woman wants sweets. She wants more. Man wants perhaps, another woman, but woman—*another* woman—wants a third party still. Yet another actor. Forever some further agency, out of reach . . . of the man: a God, or a police, or justice for injustice, or an injustice for what justice her man can reach—she wants a man beyond her man. *Service à la russe*—and foiled chocolate. The wandering eye of a species. A father one leaves off in the drool of some final and cruel stupidity. But a mother . . . one seeks eternally to please, to enjoin—to ply with foiled sweets. Why? A revenge? An incitement? A final boom-drop of proof she'd loved the wrong man? A pacification? Honeyed offerings to ward off the hosting of incurable maladies—an aspirin against disease of the heart?

'Sent him . . . most unsuitably . . .' Hussar smoothed the napkin and pointed the silver, and returned to the book. It was a thing, fine and delicate—an intimate antiquity, with a stiff brittle cover and fragile high-acid pages. It was trade-paper antiquarian. And so too seemed Heddon Street, somewhere beneath its new finishes, black-lacquer paints and grey-putty washes, architectural lighting and good, new tuck-point—somewhere in its ancestral deep.

Heddon Street was a mostly pedestrian Mayfair back-way of paving tiles and window-glass, down which occasionally swiveled delivery scooters. Close brick façades leaned over the street, and down upon the black awning unfurled against the inscrutable English sky, and the restaurant patio rimmed of tidy green hedge-plantings, and a corner table for al fresco dining—where waited Marek Hussar.

Argos Argyros was twenty-eight. He might have been twenty-five or thirty-two, but was, it seemed, twenty-eight. He was young and slim and tall, he bore long dark Mediterranean lashes over large blue eyes; full brows; his hair was waved and black, and he greatly impressed the maître d' and a duet of junior matrons when he entered. His blazer was correct, his shirt uncollared, and Hussar regarded him with a smirking contempt as he approached: a thing casual and easy, and whose gratuitous beauties have delivered from adulthood; in satiety and abundance and free from the niggardly commerce of mortal cares.

Hussar bade him sit with a gesture. "Do you see this sentence, here? With the underline," said Hussar. He'd returned to the chapbook and turned it for Argyros to see.

"You are Mr. Lanze, then?" said Argyros.

"You asked the maître d'?"

"He said that you were."

"Then it must be so. Do you see this sentence with the underline?"

"It's a pleasure to meet you, Mr. Lanze."

"Don't be foolish. Do you see this sentence? Is it remarkable in any way?"

"It is underlined . . . as you say."

"Is there anything special about the underline? About the mark?"

"Is it colored?"

"It is. Ink or pencil?"

"Is it pencil?"

"It is. 'A work of art is good if it has sprung from necessity,' it says. Someone read this, and they did not mark it in pen, nor pencil—but they were so struck that they marked it—*in the book*—with the first and nearest thing to hand. Green pencil. It could not wait for ink. It would not endure separation for proper marking in good clean pencil-lead. It must be now. It must be now—and so it was marked-under by this first thing to hand. No one chooses green pencil for their mark-making," said Hussar, and glanced up at Argyros. "It was an emergency. Can you imagine such an emergency of recognition that you must mar the beauty you find with an ugliness, just to set it out?"

Argyros said nothing, and leant back into his chair. Hussar raised a finger to proceed. "'A work of art is good if it has sprung from necessity. In this nature of its origin lies the judgment of it: there is no other. Therefore, my dear sir, I know no advice for you save this: to go into yourself and test the deeps in which your life takes rise; at its source you will find the answer to the question whether you *must* create. Accept it, just as it sounds, without inquiring into it. Perhaps it will turn out that you are called to be an artist. Then take that destiny upon yourself and bear it, its burden and its greatness. . . .'" Hussar rest the book. He squared it upon the napkin and rapped his knuckle against the table. "What sort of thing is that? Argos Argyros? Do you know—what is an artist? Can you imagine what that might be?" Hussar asked this and watched the gestural Braille of his reply: Argyros leant in, and then adjusted his chair, and then straightened, and then slouched. His eyes flicked among his catalogue of answers; his hands twitched with restraint. Hussar could see his responses were too numerous and too strong to be moderated, to be chosen. He could not choose an answer that did not include him, that did not advance him—thought Hussar; altogether too fine for this politic and discernment, and Hussar was no romantic subject for pandering conquest. And so, Argyros answered in the null: in his respectful forward lean and his clasped hands, and the three-note phrase of his watch-bracelet tread against the table. "You imagine you *are* one!—Argos Argyros—do you not?" said Hussar, and smirked to watch Argyros struggle for the sensible levers of humility once more.

Argyros cleared his throat and turned in his chair: "I've my head-shot for you," he said.

"I have your headshot, Argyros. Here it is. Right here," said Hussar, and lay his hand upon the folder to his side. "I received it, thank you so very much. So. You are an artist, then?"

Argyros worked the tips of his thumbs in concentration, and cleared his throat: "Yes," he said. "Yes. I am very passionate for my work—it must be that I am."

"So you say it," said Hussar, "so must it be. But it is interesting, the frequency with which we take it that things which must be—by needs be, are. Do you not find the condition of need is of dubious affect upon the state of the needed thing?"

"Mr. Lanze—I am an artist. It must be so. And you also. So must you be."

Hussar clasped a pen between his hands and looked at Argyros; until Argyros had turned himself almost entirely sideways, away from the looking. "*Must* . . . you say. Argyros, you are a man for whom every urgency is a proof. Must. *Must* I, then? What is it you assume an artist is, that I too must be one?" Hussar gestured to the maître d', who summoned the waiter: "Argyros, I must feed you—employed actors die of food and drink: unemployed actors die of drink without food. Look for something in the menu."

Argyros seized the waiter when he came, with his full, florid brows, and took up the menu placard with a reluctant full-body flour-ish: "I have an appetite for clouded liquor—I do not see it among the entrées," said Argyros.

"What do artists drink?" said Hussar to the waiter, smoothing his apron and twitching with reflexive haste.

"How much does your artist have?" said the waiter.

"Indeed. What do they typically have when they dine here?"

"They do not typically dine here, as they cannot typically afford to, sir—least of all the ones I know."

"You can see, Argyros, your kind is unwelcome here. You've all the wrong currency."

"Something cool and cloudy," said Argyros. "It should be cool and cloudy."

"As the English, sir: which Ouzo will you have?"

"I'm sure he's never seen them in the bottle: whatever is your finest will do," said Hussar.

"By taste or price?" said the waiter.

"I have no concern for the ecology of Ouzo: whatever you set out for the queen mother when she shuffles by."

"The Queen Mother is dead, sir."

"Well, which one is this?"

"Elizabeth the Second, sir. Daughter of the Queen Mother."

"And the King? What is the dowager queen to a living prince?"

"And will you have one as well, sir?"

"The vodka of Athens?—no. Woodford and three cloves of ice. Thank you."

The waiter moved off in all his cosmopolitan black sobriety, and when he did Argyros clapped his hand against the table: "It must be passion! What is an artist if not passion?"

"You've proclaimed this position. What then is an unskilled passion? What is that art that only passion makes? This is passion wanting form in its wanting."

"Skill then, too. Of course."

"And what if he has only skill? Can that passion that must be lie elsewhere—in receipt perhaps, alone in that sense of the audience?"

"And no passion?—this is an engineer."

"An artisan."

"Yes, an artisan."

"And what then if he may *be* passionate *and* skilled, and yet, his work is not art—is somehow compelled; is not free; expressive perhaps, but is not generous; it is not expansive—is not . . . magnanimous."

"But how can this be—to be skilled and passionate brings its own virtue: it must then be art! He must then be an artist!"

"Virtue is readymade then in the skilled and the impassioned?—what good fortune. How lucky. But what if the product is not art—if the made thing can under no circumstances be *artful*? If it is not edifying, if it is not contributive: if it is deductive?"

"I don't know how this can be."

"But if it is. What is *he* then, that is passionate, and skilled—and perhaps even, expressive?"

"Is *he* an artisan?"

"And if *he* can be passionate *and* skilled and not yield art—perhaps one may be passionate and skillful and not be an *artist*. In which case, . . . can it be that skill and passion *make* the artist?"

"Perhaps . . . he is an artisan."

"Perhaps . . . less than that."

When the drinks came, Hussar watched Argyros stare into his glass.

"You've done the reading?" said Hussar.

"I have."

"How are your languages?"

"I have English—as you see—and French."

"And Greek."

"And Greek!—yes, of course—from birth I have that," said Argyros.

"There've been some changes and additions to the script," said Hussar, and provided a copy from the envelope. "You brought the original?"

Argyros provided Hussar the original.

"And you've made no copies."

"No copies."

"Study this one. This is still in process—very sensitive. No copies here either. Study this in the meantime," he said. "How much television have you done?"

"Your ad, I know, wanted some. I have done mostly the stage in Greece, but I have some commercials since I've come to London."

"Any drama? Documentaries?"

"No, but I'm quite sure I am prepared."

"Of course you are. This is docudrama—there'll be professionals, such as yourself, and the untrained: this could be a considerable opportunity for you. You've a good look, Argyros. I'll let you know what I decide."

2.

"One of two—merely two 'Bubbledecks' Don Aronow ever made—do you know Don Aronow?—you know of him, of course. 1980. Forty feet, by the papers. Pernicious rumor has a third was made: but it's balls. I have it sterling it's damnable false. She was Popeye's and the Halter, Fayva Racing, and the Bounty Hunter boat. Dart Tall Deck blocks; Holley Tunnel Rams and Quick Fuel Marine Carbs; Deep Pan Oil Sumps; Racing Trim Tabs; Callies Crankshaft; Mahle rods and valves; heads—fully ported and blueprinted: new drive shafts. One thousand five hundred horsepowers, or more, depending on her mood you know; and well over eighty miles per hour in right props and trim, understand. She's been a labour of love. A continuous . . . and laborious, love. Kevlar 'Deep Vee'—it was tight as a drum even when we got her, you see. One of the finest—or she will be—one of the finest historic offshore race boats there is."

Mo Skarrett cleared his pipe against the instep of his boot. "Ah, but she goes apiece in drips and drabs: this rate she'll be another twenty-four to thirty-six months a'for she's all together again—a'for she speaks her angry truth to the waters. Ah, what truth it is. I do love her."

"What of Mrs. Skarrett?" asked Hussar, with a provocative smile.

"What of her, young man—what of her?"

"She is handsome."

"You can't mean Mrs. Skarrett."

"I didn't have her in mind."

"That's a good thing—cause then I would know you for a liar, and then what business could we hope to do?"

Mo Skarrett packed his bowl from a leather pouch that lay in the breast of his coat. "We both know she's handsome as the sheepdog—but, by God's grace, loyal as her too. Isn't that right, my Pippa?" said Skarrett, and stooped to stroke the dog on its head. "Beauty's an emergent thing—isn't it, Pippa?—that's right, say it's true." He rose and put a match to his pipe, shaded over with practiced care, and nursed on the stem with a series of swift pulls until the bowl had taken light, and he drew in long, slow, and fragrant meditation. "She is beautiful," he said.

"I'm partial to downdraft Webers, but anything with a collective of four-barrel carburetion is an object of my implicit sympathy," said Hussar.

"As it should, my boy. As it should."

Mo Skarrett had similarly stoked the barrel of his pipe in the hearth-room of the cottage of his Hampshire estate. He loaded the bowl with a sightless reflex, from the leather pouch—pressed tobacco into the breach and cleared it with the swipe of his long-nailed thumb, and placed and clenched the stem in a worn bevel of his teeth, and replaced the pouch into the thick chest of his tweed, and carefully produced a matchstick from a monogrammed tin and lay flame on the shag with a loan-motion of patriarchal eternity, tugged the stem to smacking production—and all the while his eyes never left Hussar in the wingchair opposite.

Mrs. Skarrett shuffled in the half-light of the thatched cottage, with an apron and a stoop of cautious and choreographed deference, and laid cups and saucers beside Skarrett and beside Hussar. She set out a porcelain tea pot and a bowl of teas and a plate of cube sugars and a dish of cream between them on the table; Skarrett filled the room with a white-thick and turning smoke from the tea service to the hewn beams of ceiling; and all the time he seemed, not to be scrutinizing, but speaking silence, to Hussar.

Mo Skarrett seemed thus for some while: only loosing his pipe-stem to fix his tea and measure of cream, and to tip himself forward toward the point at which it tipped back toward himself—a union of mystical dimension Hussar observed repeatedly over the half-hour, and upon the identical geospatial location—and meantime loosed all the raw, unrespired articulation of his language into the potted signal fire, its stuttering blooms and yawning radial curls and its palpable diffusion, until he'd exhausted the depths of his telegraphic syllabary, and chased Mrs. Skarrett with it into some concealed eddy of the house, and leaned forward once more to the detent fixture of his tipping-point and said over the clenched stem: "Well then, shall we see the girls?"

Out on the field he wore heavy boots, loose and unfastened, and with them he thoughtlessly kicked the occasional stand of sheep-berries they might happen upon. The sheep bayed and roamed the rolling, spare, and mudded pasture between unseen fences. From these rises one did not behold the water, but the mood of it upon all the land-form, and the place which could: the back of him who can—thought Hussar. There were outbuildings and livestock huts, and an industrial pole barn shed toward which they moved. The herd dog flew from Skarrett to sheep-strays and round the building and back: she would circle and pivot and halt, and look, fond and glistening for Skarrett's affirmation in sight, and circle and hunt and gather, until she would land again in the shuffling blank-verse of his narrow gait.

"Such fine simple things," he said and stooped to touch her darting brow. "She's a shine to you: she's posing for you: performing. You fancy the hounds?" he said. It was less question, and more baited assertion in the dress of common cause.

"Is it necessary?" said Hussar.

Within the pole barn shed were tractors and tillers and mower-deck attachments; there were Norton motorcycles leant one against another, a pair of Aston coupes under silted varnish, and a Jaguar XKSS roadster beneath a tarpaulin slip—long-slumbering concubine, tousled and nude: an errant straw bale returning to earth, paint cans, lost tools, and supplies; Pippa, two great open-water powerboats on trailers with their tires troughed and sullen, and Mo Skarrett and Hussar.

Skarrett had cleared the bowl and repacked it, and woke it with a touch of match-light, and admired the vintage race boat. "This one," he said, and turned to the second of the boats, "is the Marauder 50'—The Grey Lady. Among the first of the mould, mind. A trio of Mercury Racing supercharged twelve hundreds: thirty-six hundred horsepowers in chorus; stepped hull; reinforced layment; extra tanks; navigation is best in the kitty; foredeck seating, sleeping, toilet, cooler—I'd her prepped for Cowes-Torquay, and for range at speed, and for being long on the water: she's bloody well best you'll find. I've helmets to match her matte silver, but you'll need your own for size—those I keep; and you'll need your sponsorship and numbers, of course. But you've time for that."

"Why will I want those?" said Hussar.

"For Cowes-Torquay, lad: you'd want those for what you'd want her for. You've to end of August for readiness."

"I want it for Cowes-Torquay?"

"By Christ you do! You want helmets and sponsorships and a throttle-man too! By Christ you want her!—she's best you'll find in all Britain, now to then. Don't be daft." Skarrett worked his pipe and the stem clicked like organ stops against his teeth as he peered sternly at Hussar in the high, lighted quiet of the shed.

"Perhaps you're right."

"And bloodywell so. You only make her more costly with pretence—an' I've no taste for it. Already she'll be quite dear, being such nearness to the race."

"You don't race her, because . . . ?"

"Because, I'd a rumor the race was off, and now I've committed elsewhere."

"Will the race be on?"

"I'm led now to think it. Surely."

Hussar smiled. "Quite dear, then. Surely."

"Do not mock me, boy. The race will be."

"And why do you sell her?"

"You wish to lease her?"

"No."

"And so. I've a canopy turbine ordered next season, so she'll be a bit middle-wood o'the fag-pile. Better now than then. Nothin' in her belly but sea trials—she's still virgin, boy."

"I've no use for virgins, Mr. Skarrett."

III.

From some invisible distance, the sea wall, perhaps—the Thames Barrier, belly in the water—Canary Wharf would rise a clutch of dew-licked boxes, steely and translucent, a staggered trio of high towers—rental flats, thought Freddie Oslo, to the auspices of enterprise; or so thought he today. Freddie Oslo sat in the empty boardroom at a table like polished longboat with countless unhelmed oars, and looked from the peak of London, east, out over the bent and sea-born river, over the pale circus tent—the Millennium Dome; a thing like a blighted landfill demurred by cranes and canopy—off toward the horizon where buildings cut low to sparse and meandering stubble, and to where ocean-cloud wept out upon the freshwater earth, and to the very unseen breast-edge of Britain.

One Canada Square bowed west toward economic true north of London center, but as Freddie Oslo stare out over grey England and the plateau of board-table and through panoramic wall-glass and the atmospheric spittle collecting marine-breath of the isle against the panes, it occurred to him . . . that unlike a house—whose back, and embracing face and hands and portal of smiling lips, are form and fixture, are anticipated and known; no matter the claims made with an awning or a sheltered commons or a fountained green space or stroke of electrified signage or the pretense of boulevard feed-ways, the office block is forever inscrutable, duplicitous; with portals and arms and contrary overtures for each wind of the compass; for each view; for every viewer; and for the indivisible preoccupation of each tenant in witness. And through just such a front Freddie Oslo looked forward from the rear of England's highest building—not north but south—toward the east, and the imperceptible continent which lay there, and toward home.

Ian Bretting entered by reflected likeness from some lateral distance. He crept in, suited and rubber-soled over Oslo's shoulder and through the verge of blind periphery, and placed himself and his broad double Windsor and his satchel down near one of the sterns or bows of the unmarked hull of the table, upon one of the leather and aluminum oar-stations, and lay his hands on the table-skin with a parroted finality—and flashed Oslo a treacly smile: a glimmer of constipated grimace the very image of which set square and leaden in his digestion, and which he tried to swallow away. And then he spoke: "Simone will be in shortly," he said, and then he stare at his satchel as though to entrap something there with the sole binding of his concentrated gaze.

Bretting was a Skadden, Arps acquisition, who little more than a year prior had come up to General Counsel from those lower floors, and, thought Oslo, must now be ill-assured of that earlier and incontrovertible wisdom. He was quiet and damp-handed and rose-cheeked and dressed in tailoring which seemed always entirely too dear for his bearing—and lacked utterly that semblance of imagination of which barristers are congenitally free: where instead is found neither meaning nor principle, but the great volume of endnotes which accompany them. Oslo imagined it might be this he kept sealed in his satchel and that all the weight of his force was required to keep it entrained there—in banal servitude.

Simone Helena did eventually come, as Bretting had said. She was an executive partner, and when she came she slipped in, and then again out, with the ease and inscrutable sheen of her position. She was continental and chestnut-maned, with a placeless diasporic accent of the continental peoples—a voice and features of nicotine and brown liquors—and altogether psychically disincarnate: silken; a thing without tooth or weft or warp, cuff or hem or cleft: of one glazed ingot, without angle or purchase. One did not grasp or apprehend her with the tines of mortal-handed apparatus—but perhaps, thought Oslo—bade her repose in the mold-form of some velveteen case: she was not one possessed, directed, comprehended—but merely, collected and deployed. She swung into the room with a phone to her ear and turned in a circle of her own arrested inertia, and paused to see Oslo seated at the belly of the table—"Yes. He's here,"—she said to the phone; and her gaze trailed through Bretting like a boot through dandelion clock, and she swept out through the door again, and closed it behind her, and paced, and spoke to the phone, visibly beyond it.

When Simone Helena had entered again she had stowed her phone. She was empty-handed and brought only her person and her close-cut nails and moved swiftly into the room, where she did not sit beside Bretting, but back to the windows on the world—face to the true-north star, center-table across from Oslo, where Bretting collected his things and moved and redeployed—the safety of a chair between them.

"Freddie," she said. "Good, dear Freddie. You will know— certainly you will—that hardly more than a month ago, Bear Stearns evaporated into the coin-purse of J. P. Morgan Chase. It presses on our minds—and now there's concern for Lehman: they don't look right. Unfit for the moment."

"I've heard that," said Oslo.

"I've also heard that," said Bretting. "Recently."

"Rothman is firm; this you also know. But she is not invincible. Neither is she invisible," she said, and cleared her throat with an emphasis that floated between exaggeration and punctuation.

"This is not tea leaves, but sea—and one whose troughs and swells are perfectly hard to read from this distance. Can you make them out?"

"I wouldn't claim it," said Oslo. They both glanced to Bretting, but he had grown circumspect, and said nothing.

"If it turns in earnest, we could be in it soon enough—and from that posture it should prove utterly illegible," she said, and drew gentle figures against the table with her middle finger. They were motions like collecting motes of dust, but languid and prolonged. Oslo imagined they said 'fucked.'

"Freddie. You were a trader, early doors, correct?" she said.

"I was."

"Bretting, will you give him the ill-tidings."

"And they are so plentiful—can you have them all in your case, Bretting?" said Oslo.

"It might do for today, Freddie. Shall I start with Libor?" Bretting asked of Helena. "The US has been quite concerned with stress-tests and asset ratios—they're pouring over everyone's paper just now. Fast as they can."

"Very well."

"Some conversations here have spilt over there . . . Their Attorney General for the Southern District—New York; has some interest in the matter—it pegs markets there too, and they consider it a crime on US soil."

"I know this, Bretting."

"So, they've opened a file. And they've been leaning on the Attorney General of England and Wales to belly-up: show it can do more than sit on its spectacles and take pints—and so now they've opened an inquiry as well—and now the Serious Fraud Office is skulking around trying to peek up skirts on Libor again; everyone's really, but principally ours."

"You're familiar with the workings of Libor, in principle . . . and practice?" said Helena.

"This is old hat, Simone."

"Bretting," said Helena, and Bretting stayed Oslo with one of his warm, moist paws.

"Yes. Quite familiar. But this is a seasonal affliction. Every few years someone, somewhere, thinks they've stripped the matter—thinks they've touched gold, and turns up a noise: and every few years someone discovers a Christmas pony in their cupboard, and they lose their train of thought. It's like gout, or allergies, or moral indignation: it's seasonal. You must be saving up Bretting, you didn't call me down to talk up the perils of Libor."

"You also did some work in the structured products unit, did you not?" said Helena.

"I did as much."

"The US A.G. is looking into our Mortgage Trading Unit, also. There is some concern there about our packaging of mortgage-backed securities," said Bretting.

"They may wish to speak with you, Freddie," said Helena.

"Oh yes. Certainly, Freddie. They will. They will want you deposed. But this is quite new—wet ink and all. But . . . should it proceed, Freddie, should they find anything of interest to them—here or there, among these different fronts, and should they issue charges . . . depending upon what you think you *may* know on these topics, or perhaps even, what you think you *may* have done, relative to these topics . . . : compelled to testify. You could be compelled to testify."

"Convicted even, Bretting," said Oslo.

"That's cavalier."

"Yes, but . . . compelled to testify, . . . Freddie," said Helena. "Bretting, do be a dear and see Freddie's assistant about some coffee: what is her name again, Freddie?"

"Cygnet."

"How lovely—quite right: Cygnet."

"Do be a dear and see Cygnet will you—Freddie looks positively ghastly without his caffeine. Is there some Gaulish way you take it: does Cygnet know how you like it?"

"Yes," said Oslo. "Not tea," he said, and he smiled at Helena and at Bretting, in their turn.

Bretting closed his binder and scrupulously threaded his pen-cap. He stood, and padded out on his rubber soles, and the pair of them watched him in a union of silence as he made the long, carpeted passage to the door. When he'd gone Helena continued to observe the portal—as though waiting to bar Bretting's sudden return—and then moved to address Oslo again.

"Libor, Freddie—"

"Can you be serious about this?"

". . . and structured products—"

"Simone."

". . . and vile annoyances—Freddie. They *are* annoyances. But that is hardly for Bretting, n'est-ce pas?"

"Aren't we friendly with the Americans—Rothman is an American firm in the end: we have people in the administration, do we not? And the Serious Fraud Office?—please—can Bretting be sober?—toss it in the bush and those hounds will be off the scent and back to napping. This is all but one holiday from amnesia. Some drink, some gifts—and resumption of the negotiated peace. Can there be a real concern here? Do we care if I am deposed—can it possibly get that far?"

"Freddie . . . Freddie. You misunderstand, I think. It is not that looking leads to questions and questions lead to answers. It is that looking leads to seeing; and that questions lead to more questions. What hides in plain sight survives all looking, but is greatly imperiled to be seen. Build a city in the sands—and all is well: to question once the foundations?—that is the earthquake. Libor—if indeed there were something there; and if indeed it were got to the bottom of:

structured products—should there prove anything distasteful to their handling or composition, Freddie—should it come to pass that they were ever core-sampled and decoded: were there the least, or the largest impropriety: I could not give the last and faintest goddamn. These are monies: these all are questions of monies. But Freddie . . . The Belgian Foal, Freddie. The Belgian Foal is not a thing that cannot be seen: The Belgian Foal is a thing which can't be thought. It cannot be imagined."

"Loans, Simone—those are but loans. Just loans. There's nothing to see, and they would never look."

"They are looking now, Freddie. There are questions. There are motions."

"They are asking after it now?"

"They are. Along with all the rest."

Oslo lay his hands on the table and chose a point out the window, above Helena, and far from here—unearthly—clouded and ephemeral: high above the channel; high over France: a vague grey mat for angelic rapture, for repose: a place to park an aeroplane, and hide.

"Simone. We have a heavy—very heavy—short position on the euro. When they see it, they are sure not to like it—but we are entitled to it. However gruesome, it is legal, and that is all."

Simone Helena looked at Freddie for a very long time. And just when he thought she must speak, she endured in her looking: "And what . . . if it weren't. Freddie. What if it weren't—all?"

Freddie Oslo shook his head. It was a mark of slippery and indolent non-comprehension, and filled the room like the prelude to an exhausted shrug. "Was that Manhattan, Simone? Who was that . . . on the phone? Was that Manhattan?"

"They are very concerned about The Belgian Foal, Freddie."

Oslo issued a gesture of frustrated indignation with the thrust of his raised and opened hand.

"Very concerned," said Helena, and again she studied him for a long and uncomfortable interval. "Go play, Freddie. Feed the ducks. Pack an overnight bag, and I'll send my car for you tomorrow, for dinner. I have a thought, and we'll talk more then," she said.

"Double espressos all around," said Bretting when he entered, with his cardboard tray and his flushed cheeks and his panting, shambling stride.

2.

She squeaked when her cervix bumped his erection. She had climbed on, and slipped down; to commemorate brunch, and twenty-five hundred thread-count linens, and light through filtrous curtain-veils: and to commemorate the morning persistence of broad Gallic phalluses. The peep was a sudden revelation of exuberant insatiety, of the belt-line of greed. Freddie Oslo's broad Gallic phallus, was, he thought, more sense organ than sex organ: it was not assertive and primal but tactile and curious, itching with exploratory urgency. It yearned to probe the feathery geographic bulb of vaginas the way the fingers of young boys pain for the moist gratification of nasal passages; the way the tongue prizes the nipple; the way the infant dreams of the bath. It was a sensitive and accomplished explorer, who one day would collect his works—compose the definitive taxonomy of these landscapes: perhaps Oslo would hold the pen.

Lovely Cygnet sat, and she sat, and she sat, a sort of perpetually reconsidered falling; with the inflective tug of a rotation of the pelvis just at the end. Every contour was unique, he thought; how generous the salivation; the strength of each kiss: but the vacancy was the same: not merely identical, but the darkness of the same void. He had never yet been with a woman who sensed this—who suspected this riddle of the vessel of generation: that this place was not named or degreed or even contained within the person, but was a fissure through which one might reach to cast from the depthless sea of creation. And at the least glistening provocation—the cup-bearer—she might be repur-posed—or purposed—to the tending of a chalice: to keeping the thing which keeps her; and for cherishing forces which are ambivalent to her—to not spilling foreign wine: wine which will eventually come aromatic of its cask, but will not be entirely of it. Cygnet persisted in her recursive fallings, her pale morning fallings, and Oslo smiled at his thinkings with his broad Gallic lips and breathed pleasurable affirmations through his broad Gallic nose, and to reward him in his cultivation of these joys she offered him a breast.

When their communion reached its final agitated precipitation, Cygnet lay on him. These were moments of saline and exhausted peace beneath the striations of a rare London strength of light, before she collected her hair and slipped off to the bath. Eventually she moved to the kitchen and prepared strongly gritted coffee in the nude, and returned with it to the bed, where they lay with it, on their naked bellies, and drank it from Italian ceramics and smoked Gauloises and shared a heavy decorative glass for their ash, and took turns with the sections of the *Financial Times*, which they read and folded and exhaled upon. The ink from the pages felt powdered and viscous, and its chemical perfume and the straw-bale smoke of the Gauloises and the way they clung to the skin of the lip, and the careless way she held hers, and the bite of the grounds at the bottom of his cup, ripe for their tasseomanic tellings, and the slow-drying sex about his genitals—gave him a feeling of exalted richness: he was emperor of satiated carnal expressions.

Spangles of light, narrow lozenges, fell against their forms, against the bed, into the bedroom, shimmered, dissolved, replaced. It grabbed at the smoke and made incense of it, made it sensuous offering. Cygnet was a fastidiously prepared blonde. It was the costume worn with such persistence and deliberation eventually it subsumes the wearer. Eventually the invisible man will see himself in the artifice of bandages. Her body was faultless and indulgent, and she was marked through with that charitable youth which forgives all futures yet to break rise above the horizon. Oslo admired it in her: that impulse in willful oblivion of the young for the unmade—that sense of weightless and suspended disbelief: that sense of unfettered inconsequence—that all costs must rise from lines already in the register, and that in any case, all costs are negotiable: that self-regard is the first and last payment for all things. It was the beautiful and readymade corruption of solipsism—the forever-unbroken dawn.

Her hair was heavy and full, and probably, thought Oslo—it had been dark. It was a secret he might speak to, but cared not to know—the bastard confabulation was worth its prize. She said to have loved his *parfum des français*—his brogue of the continent, of cheese and garlic, of a speech that never moved in the throat or leapt from the tongue, but emerged in strange harmony exclusively from the diaphragm and the sinus and the lips: all breath and wetness and cranial concavities. He had been in Britain so much and so often, this seemed greatly softened beside his countrymen; nevertheless. She was said to feature this in her attraction, and he might ask her. He might ask her if it was attraction to opportunity she most appreciated in his composition. Whether it was his sleek tended flat, or his tailored clothing, or his first winter-frosted grey—that first dusting in the fringe of sideburns. Whether it was his peculiar *savoir-faire* of the clinically unconcerned, or perhaps spontaneous and human affection, or the quiet urgings of that parasite-to-be—that larvae which grabs the host by the cleft of the brain and sends them off, nodding toward the Jerusalem of their bidding. Or might it be his affluence or his position—the attestation of men for one another; not among themselves, but as an ordering principle—that unacknowledgeable pheromone, powerful and secret, that administers women toward their appetites in men. He might ask her this. He might turn to her, just now, in her starlight and nakedness and beauty, and clarify her ambition for him with the entreaty of words—immediate and strange.

And she might smile at him and lie, and wink at her darkness. But regardless her hungers—her graceful scaling the bald face of status; her eager tinglings for the itch of her vacant womb: the tickling, not of his phallic touch, but of potentia to occupy her void, to reach through and bite him on the penis with serrated teeth—he would not. He would not ask her. He would not turn to her, just now. He would not entertain the black spasm of her comforting lie. The one to himself, or the one to her. The misdirection of biology's own designs. He would not entreat her with chords of question in hay-scented smoke. Because he did not care. He did not care. Not in the least.

They walked through Grosvenor Square in the afternoon. The lawns were in health and the trees wore their May plumage, and Cygnet collected their lost down from the paved walks. "Perhaps we'd rather visit Berkeley Square," she said when they'd paused on the main causeway before the Roosevelt statuary.

"You don't like Roosevelt?" he asked.

"If it were only him," she said.

"And Eisenhower and Reagan . . ."

"It is too many Americans in bronze for me."

"A more precious metal perhaps? The US mission is just there."

"In flesh, they are enough," she said.

"Had the sculptor only been Buddhist, they might be wood."

"Had he been an American they might be plaster."

"Had he been an American, they might be papier-mâché and nickel-leaf."

"With a torch."

"A torch? Only if the sculptor had been English—this sculptor was Scot."

"Or maybe French—then he'd have a torch."

"A French sculptor? No: then good Franklin would have a cigarette holder and braces instead of the cane—and slapped with clay till he looked like Balzac—"

"And glasses . . ."

"Yes, wherever they've gone: and a snifter—"

"And a pistol—"

"And a pistol: no, he must be Russian for a pistol. A pistol and a sheaf of wheat, and a peasant knelt before him to oppress with his gifts."

The monument was a pedestal upon a dais upon a dais upon a platform before a threshold. "Is it a bit Soviet?" she asked.

"It has that, doesn't it," he said.

"And Spanish . . . ?"

"It would have a halo."

"And Portuguese?"

"It would have a mandorla."

"And German?"

"A horse and sword."

"And Italian?"

"It would be good."

She smiled and tapped him for a fag. He removed one and gave it her, and the light. "If only I'd Franklin's cigarette holder, then wouldn't I be smart," she said, and they stepped away from the monument and its wide clearing, and into the shade-embrace of trees. "Or would it be some French affair, all Dali-esque and corkscrewed?"

"Melted."

"Ah, then keep it."

"I'm dining with Helena this evening," he said.

"Alright," she said. "Is there a problem?"

"It's fine."

"Didn't you meet with her and with Bretting?"

"There's no problem. She's sending her car."

"Bretting's purpose is the blessing of problems."

"It's fine."

"Shall I wait at your flat, then?"

"That should be fine. I'm asked to pack a bag."

"A bag? Are you travelling?"

"Didn't say."

"Are you going home?"

"No."

"A sleepover then," she said, and he smiled.

"It is certain to be. It's fine. Stay if you like."

"I don't think so."

"You're welcome. It should be brief."

"I don't think so."

3.

"It's a light shouldn't be out, marm," said Sean.

"I'll put the boys to it straight away, captain," said Simone Helena.

"It's a right-good job security is for me, marm—and making light is a matter all for you."

"Yes, captain. Surely," she said, and winked to Oslo from the kitchen. "Sean; captain, darling—it's the dinner hour now, why not go have some in your comfort?"

"Off premises, marm?"

"Yes, captain," she said, and slipped him a few folded notes. "It's a quiet evening—I'm quite sure I'll be safe with a houseman and my company for just a few hours."

"Ms. 'Elena."

"It's a certainty, captain—I shan't perish in your absence!"

"You will call me straight away to return, and deliver your guest: return Mr. Oslo."

"I shan't fail you, captain!" she said with a mock salute, and Sean passed grudgingly downstairs, and out.

The townhouses of Belgravia were one continuous butter-cream façade by the wake of the headlamps, and their chimney clays rose as pipe organ flutes from their ridges of narrow common-wall crown. Oslo leant into his own breath captured on the glass to see them, cast in ranks of silhouette against the light-haze of the empire's last and collective candle, and the ragged strakes of night-soft cloud. He imagined they played like the organ at Chartres, or Notre-Dame—a great monied unison of Bach perhaps, or some chord one never fully hears, but feels rattling in their shit chakra: twitching in his prostate.

Sean was wide and thick and the untouched pallor of Belgravian white. His black suit of clothes looked a bitter assemblage in fine cloth tubes—something more pipe-fit than tailored—and his tie was the improbable appendage for them: too short and too thin, and all vaudevillian. In cartoons, Seans hold the protagonist by his feet and empty his pockets with a few firm shakes. When Oslo stepped out, Sean was there to receive him. He'd put his computer and a compliment of cables and change of clothes in a bag, and Cygnet did not embrace him but leant heavily into a hip with folded arms and filed at her thumb with her teeth. She was angry or nervous, filled with a seatless feline malcontent that had her nipping at her claws—tuning geomagnetic forces with her whiskers. She stood in his foyer and said nothing, and watched him go out.

"Mr. Oslo then? Ms. 'Elena for you sir. I'm to collect you," he said and moved to release the rear compartment of the Bentley. "Sir," he said: it was a single word, half question and half instruction; a sentiment perfectly capable of persisting in the interval of blistering silence; patient and assertive and intractable—a word the manner of being led by the shoulders and folded beneath a palm against the top of the head—and being served a cordial. "My name is Sean, sir," he said as he closed the door.

Chester Square looked out onto a private colonnade forest of dark and heavy leaves; but they did not stop here. Instead, they entered at the rear along the private mews through a weathered portal the width of the wing mirrors, and here now was the Liverpool-end of Belgravian life: the cobbled alley of irregular coach houses and stables. In the supple leather-handbag perfume of the Bentley's

Connolly hides, Sean thread the big sedan down the dim way of parked-up saloons and overhead doors, and gave the impression of gaining exclusive entrance to a private club—but once, this narrow purchase was home to coachmen and brooms and those slim conceal-ments of gutters, the effluence of great animal keeping.

Sean drew up before an unlit pair of garages, let him out, and led him in through the rear. Inside they were received by a houseman who took them upstairs and bade Oslo to seating in a well-appointed lounge, and Sean to the kitchen where Oslo heard him with Helena, complaining on the state of the garage light and bickering over her instructions; and he contented himself to an inventory of the objet d'art: an Asian ink brush painting, and the totems of exotic statu-ary, and in the corner beneath its own lighting and upon its own acrylic stand, a greened Corinthian helmet and panoply: greaves and breastplate and shield. And this against a uniform and persistent satin grey. Behind, beneath, or upon—everything, it seemed: satin grey. The wallpaper under ornamental print, the suede nap of the sofa and chairs, the end tables, the rug, and each and every thing that was not chosen in some measure for its own, or for its clever and complimentary spite of it.

Helena herself wore a burgundy gown which fitted handsomely. It was long and slender and there wasn't the first purpose Oslo might conjure it for, unless she'd recently come, or they presently were going, to the opera. She drifted in, sipping Cabernet and watched as the houseman served Oslo a prepared cheese plate and a Cabernet from his own plunging vessel. She observed his service to Oslo, and then she watched him leave—and her gaze lingered on his absence the way it had lingered on Bretting, when he too had seemed well and gone. When he could be neither heard, nor scarcely imagined at last, she lay herself along the sofa with an aggressive leisure. "You will forgive my choosing, but one assumes a proper Frenchman wants only Cabernet, when the bottle is from Bordeaux."

"It's a happy choice—but had you only told me it was a black-tie brie tasting: as you see, I am painfully underdressed," he said.

"Dear Freddie—all occasions are special: one must simply dress as though they might discover it at any moment."

"Are they all formal?"

"There is no distinction. If you've an appetite, I can have something brought out, but I thought we might enjoy a piece of private conversation."

"And your houseman?"

"Oh, he's half-deaf and two floors down by now, and incurious: he minds his own affairs."

"And Sean?" said Oslo; and Helena offered him her Cabernet smile.

"Might I revisit our talk from yesterday, Freddie?"

"I will understand why I've packed a bag, then."

"Indeed so. I hate to proscribe the mood."

"Please. Proceed," said Oslo, and drank from his wine and sampled his cheese—manner of dress notwithstanding—and plucked crumbs from his lapels and replaced them thoughtfully upon the tray. But Helena did not proceed. She drank and stroked her neck and offered Oslo what he found to be an uncharacteristic and forlorn expression. "You'd had an epiphany: I believe we left off there. I'd asked about Manhattan; you'd expressed their concern—and then you'd had a brainwave to rescue us all in a single and elegant gesture: that's fairly close, is it not?" said Oslo, and brush the faint tactile food-ash from his hands.

"Oh, dear, sweet Freddie: are they all made as you—or is it just you with such a lovely and irascible flourish of pique?"

"We come thirty percent by decree: the rest they give to Spain."

"Of what use is indignation that is not foremost cosmetic."

"They teach it in the schools that bore me."

"Perhaps you should visit them."

"Ah, they've finished with me—"

"On holiday."

"Holiday. What is this now?"

"On holiday. Freddie."

"I've no holiday plan, Simone," said Oslo, after a pause.

"Perhaps you should. Perhaps you might."

"I've no time. And I have no plan—just now—for holiday."

"Perhaps you do. Freddie—no matter that he's wet crackers, our meeting with Bretting was no bit of humor. The serious fraud office; the American Attorney General—these are real actions, with real costs, and very very real risks; and they are now, and very much in motion. Freddie," she said, and took some wine and shook her head. "Freddie."

"Why would I—"

"Be still, Freddie. Listen. You are going on holiday. You are going on holiday, tonight: you came here tonight precisely to tell me this—and you intended to begin your leave this evening . . . when you depart, tonight."

"Is this yours, or Manhattan's grand design?"

"Freddie, you injure me: why can it not be mine alone? I told you I spoke with him—and I told you there was grave concern about depositions. And I told you there was grave concern about The Belgian Foal, Freddie. What can be handled with monies, can be: will be. What cannot be handled with monies, . . . cannot be handled with monies."

"This seems unnecessary. As I said, when they see, if they see, our short positions on the euro—they are sure not to like it; but we are entitled to it, Simone."

"Yes, Freddie—and I said to you; what if The Belgian Foal is not exclusively a matter of the short?"

"What does that mean, Simone? What could that be?"

"Let me not smother your imaginative faculties, Freddie. I'll leave it to time and silence; or leave it to darkness—but I've nothing more to say on it. Your holiday starts now; tonight. My man will accompany you to keep you from harm's way, and out of reach. Beyond reach."

"Sean?"

"He's waiting in the car for you. He will attend to you and keep you from reach."

"Simone."

"Don't, Freddie," she said, and Oslo drank thoughtfully from his wine. "Yes, let's do that, Freddie," she said, and rose from the sofa and fetched the bottle from the kitchen. "Yes, let's finish it," she said, and tipped up the bottle into their glasses and returned to the sofa. "A lad can't be deposed that can't be reached, Freddie. He can't be indicted that can't be found, and he can't compound his jeopardy that has no idea he's being sought. And Freddie—*they* cannot be perjured, who've no idea of his plans, or location."

"Where am I going, Simone?"

"Now, Freddie—I'm hopelessly uninformed in the matter. You came to me this evening, to visit. You said you were exhausted, and sought some time away. I approved it, and you left in good spirits. I couldn't possibly know where you went, as you did not say—and were under no obligation to tell me. I assumed you were in the city—but knew you've family on the continent. But, that of course is a matter for their asking, and not a moment before its time."

"Simone."

"Freddie. The Belgian Foal is not a trifle. Mind my man. He'll attend to you. Keep your head down. Travel. Enjoy yourself. When the matter's situated, I'll reach out, and back you'll come."

"How long might that be, Simone?"

"Few weeks . . . we think. That's our guess—could be a month. Just don't wave a flag: we should have the measure of this shortly—and when it's all blown to the lee, you'll rise up and return; and none but you will be the wiser for it. You do see?—my dear, sweet, Freddie."

"I see . . ." said Oslo, and he looked over the helm again, and the panoply, and with quiet diligence they both took to their wine.

Oslo lay his hand across his cuff. He was feeling the wine. He was feeling it back in his tonsils—a bit of chalk trapped in the organelles: he envisioned dusty mushroom caps, wine dribbling down their cheek as delivered from some high-forest canopy: he felt it in the roof of his nose, high, where the walnut cavities open cerebral tissue, grey and vascular—another type of blood-pumped sense organ; and he felt it in the prefrontal cortex—that glassy-eyed compression of thought-bag leant all against the anterior forehead; just like a bit of early flu taken in recreant pleasure. They did not speak. Helena looked toward him, observed him in a way that appeared not to see him so much as envelope him: it was an observation with the keen of appetite to it: seeing with unspecified hunger. The discontented hand—the hand against his cuff; drawing back jacket; cloying at the French fold of sleeve—had hunger too: the ungratified hunger for the wristwatch that was not there. He could see them now, a trio of leather-strapped complications tilting on winders—a fourth station vacant and unfulfilled: a parking space waiting for the terminal consummation of lust and discrimination: empty but for the perfect thing. For some reason he had the image of Cygnet standing in his dressing room, before them; watching them turn among the tended litter of dark-pressed suits and ties and affect of coordinating pocket squares; and all beneath that brittle light of rooms in which one must always see, but never live. The missing tie had been at first a performative regret, which now had begun waxing at some aimless form of body: a regret one pretends and then gains by the pretense. The watch, and the naked wrist he wore in its place, however, gave

him genuine and growing heart-fall. It was the uncommunicable
and immaterial disappointment of a private errant thing. A pin, a
charm, some object token, cherished in the concretizing certainty
of its presence. He did not know what the missing watch might give
him, beyond order—to be rescued by a detail, in a detail, in the structured gratification of feeling the breezed vacancy of a knowing, and
casting light in looking. Order. Ballast doesn't keep the boat dry, it
keeps the sails in the air.

Helena noticed his recognition, his sudden registration in disappointment, and she raised an eyebrow at it. His bowl of stemware
was nearly empty; Helena's trailed behind. "Don't wait for me," she
said, "I'm having another. To chasing wisdom with the bottle it came
from," she said, and raised the toast. He'd turned up his glass, and
she had not, and when he'd set it down the houseman stood in the
threshold. "Don't let me keep you, Freddie. Busy days. We'll talk
soon: he'll show you down. And Freddie . . ." she said as he stood to
go. "The door will latch behind you as you go out."

The houseman led him down to the lower floors, and to the
unlighted garage, and he moved through it to the man-door on the
far side. He looked back at the silhouette of the houseman at the feet
of a stair before going out; and the door latched. And there in the
broken-lighted dark of the cobbled mews sat the Bentley, lights-out
gurgling spittle of exhaust tendrils, like hot breath from gleaming
pipes, and released the door-hatch and slipped into the rear compartment, and once again the bracing aroma of sacred calves made supple
as infant bottoms, by planing blades and aniline dyes, and the colla-
gen fats of buttercreams and Hide Food.

There was difference about the profile, however. The line of
the ear and neck; the slightest hollow beneath the cheek—and in
the mirror: the brow and gaze there, were something tool-worked

with drowsing fury—coming heavy weather, or which just has past. "Monsieur Oslo—you have the look of chancing upon the wrong Bentley. I assure you—this is the only one for you."

"You are not Sean."

"Quite right, Monsieur Oslo: whomsoever that may be—I am Mr. Lanze; and I am to accompany you along my way."

IV.

The filter in the coffee machine bore a week's mud-crust of grounds and loess of ornamental mold. He replaced it and probed the collapsed and empty packet of cigarettes from his coat, and rummaged ashtrays for a serviceable butt, and drew a chair and raised the window to smoke it and listen to the close, emphatic-scented, gravity-fed slurp of brewing. At 10:30 Argos Argyros had lay in his clothes. He lay in the sofa bed of his Brixton studio flat, and when he realized he lay in his blazer as well, he swore. Argyros stood bar in the evening, and then sat returning his pay into the small hours, and lay in his clothes with his sleeve to his eyes—determined to stay there until they might remain open without weeping: sometime after eleven, he mistakenly thought he'd breached this verge, and rose to fold his bed.

Argyros washed a spoon to stir oatmeal, and ate it from the pot. When he'd finished he spied the cinnamon he'd sought for it stalking soiled cups; took his toilet with another length of soot-and-charcoal butt from the ashtray, and showered with his suit hung from the rail. Argyros let a flat in a row of semi-detached Victorians all turned to rooms. He had one hundred square feet of rippling carpets and white paint and open-plan convenience: a bicycle, a window onto a gangway, a toilet and shower with closing door, a kitchenette; and outdoors, buses and the six-laned sound of Streatham Place; and today, he had an appointment as well.

Argyros' script had lain in the chair when he smoked, when he ate porridge from the pot, when the lady of a recent evening followed home, when he tied his shoes. He'd read it repeatedly; tested the lines to the window gap in nicotined exhalations, to the undercarriage of dripping faucet, to the cupboards and corners in distraction—but now for several days; in that time it had lain cushion or cover, or text upon that desk of chair. Until now.

Colliers Wood was a three-quarters hour by the seat of bus and its interminable stop, hesitation, and departure: motions long enough to revile stoppage; stops long enough to lose the intuition for motion. It was a waiting like sitting in queue, but with the occasional bob of unexpected sleeping. It was a gentle-rocking-trance of action that sent him into shallow swells of Aegean childhood. He fished with boyhood rods, improvised and pliant; pocketfuls of dates, squint against blue-water sparks, from the harbor wall, kicking heels against the stones. His father lay on the sofa in sleeping. His mother pressed her uniform and readied him for school: he would look from his breakfast to the halo of day in the window sheets—dim and portentous; through the scaffolding of ironing board and shifting weight, to decode the television that played as an audible lighting for all her various states of chore. And then the jolt of curbside deposit, from which it was a quarter-hour walking through scenic industrial estate in fashionable and jarringly uncomfortable shoes. Argyros was mostly cured of shower-damp when he arrived—an unremarkable high brick fortification, and a pair of plain glass doors. The walk had put air in his clothes and moved some gloom of lingering excess from his core of faculties and into the tired and benumbed cadence of extremities; so that when he greeted the secretary at reception, corner of the bright foyer, he buttoned his jacket and smiled above the touch of unlaundered socks; and regained some prime for ignition of his full Mediterranean luster.

"I'm to audition for Mr. Lanze," said Argyros to reception.

The secretary paused to review her schedule book: "I don't see Mr. Lanze in my book: do you have the production name, or company?" she said.

"I don't know it," said Argyros. "Wait," he said, and fished the script from his pack and turned through it for these details: "No," he said. "I do not know it."

"Well, what is your name, sir?"

"I am Argos Argyros," he said. "For an audition."

"Oh, I have you here, Mr. Argyros: apologies. Studio 2 is ready for you, sir. I believe you may already have talent waiting. You're acquainted with our space, or can I show you in?"

"That will not be necessary: if you will just point the way."

"Through the double-doors, just there, Mr. Argyros—and you will follow the signs for Studio 2 from there—the spaces are clearly marked."

And so they were. Argyros found his way readily down the hall and to the heavy studio door, and through this and down a short stair; and alone among eight thousand square feet of thirty-foot ceilings—high and black and rigged-in-waiting for kit of light—sat Mr. Lanze. In the midst of a vast empty floor, he was sideways in a folding chair with an arm over the back. There were great black curtains hung round the walls—but out before a bare patch of brick and a simple length of mounted florescent tube was a common-looking camera on a stand, a common folding table, and for it, a chair.

"Let us begin with a piece of housekeeping, Argyros," came Lanze's gratuity in welcome. "Do attend to the door, please—we are recording for sound. Sit anywhere," he said. Argyros fixed the door and descended the short stair and surveyed his option for seating, and Lanze pointed to the table and its vacant chair—and he took it. "You've reviewed the script, of course?"

"I have," said Argyros.

"And you've brought your passport."

"I have," said Argyros.

Lanze rose and moved to the table: "And, may I review it please?" Argyros retrieved it from his pack, and Lanze returned with it to the chair, and the small monitor display behind it. Lanze turned through it coolly and played and sniffed at the cardstock and paper.

"I think they may have had me mixed for you, when I came," Argyros said into Lanze's deliberative silence.

"I noticed as much when I arrived: they seemed to have us turned round. Alas, whatever is to be done with the help. Are you free to travel, Argyros?"

"In general, or immediately?"

"Either. Both."

"I've shifts I would need covered—"

"That's hardly a concern. You've no other obligations—you are free to travel unfettered? You're not wanted for any crimes here or abroad? Interpol doesn't have your face on a collector card?"

"I've committed no crimes."

"If we're honest, Argyros, you strike us as a pickpocket; shoes and womens' handbags—the occasional errant Vespa, perhaps," said Lanze with a smile.

"I'm wanted for nothing. Anywhere," said Argyros, with a rising indignant flush.

Lanze swapped the passport for an envelope from atop the monitor to his side. He drew a sheet from it and considered it: "Your visa's in order?"

"Perhaps I have not attended so many auditions as you, Mr. Lanze—but this may be more like customs and immigration than any I have yet attended," said Argyros.

"You were a custodian for a time?"

"Yes. Shortly after I arrived."

"This says two years."

"Yes."

"Argyros, you can't have been a custodian for two years. I don't believe it."

"If I've it in print, it must be my best memory for the dates. I can check my records if there's any issue."

"A rounding error, perhaps."

"These are always possible," said Argyros, with a thin smile.

"Perhaps, two," said Lanze. "That was Canary Wharf?"

"Does it not say?—yes. Canada Square."

"Number One, Canada Square?"

"Yes, number One."

"You were social then as you are now, I trust—charismatically Latinate?"

"I am a social person, Mr. Lanze."

"Your constancy is my favorite trait, Argyros." Lanze reached into a satchel at the foot of his chair and retrieved two small cassettes. "You've brought your script?"

"I have."

"Let us have you read then, and cease our dithering—I'd hate to become reputationally bounded to customs and immigration," said Lanze, and inserted the cassette and armed the camera. "We're recording. Begin in your own time."

"Shall I have some more lighting?" said Argyros.

"I'm sure you are quite beautiful. From the top of page one, please. Begin in your own time."

And so in his own time did Argyros begin. He read two scenes, one-half the dialogue fed to camera while Lanze stood to scrutinize the monitor with full material force, and paced away, and back, and leafed along with Argyros through pages and breaks, and all the intermediating lines paid like rope into silence.

"It is quite awkward, Mr. Lanze: the reading only for the one part," said Argyros when he'd finished. "Are you sure you wouldn't like me to go again—and you read the other parts?"

"I would not," said Lanze. "You were quite fine. Let us do the first scene once more, but from your . . . best memory. Begin in your own time," he said, and removed Argyros' script from the table, and temptation. And so Argyros began again—from the best of his memory—in generally fluid lines, and halting corners; but complained uniformly of his performance, as was his duty, in the end.

It was true, Argyros had auditioned many many times; only not so many as he'd encouraged Mr. Lanze to believe. He'd auditioned in conference rooms at table-ends; before color screens in pop-up production facilities; in small offices with a gathered panel of corporate discernment: here and there and in-between, but never yet had he auditioned—screen-tested, whatever you like, in the replete monochrome and vastness of a true-to-life, outsize and actual, film production studio, and with so inscrutable a crew—a director . . . a man, in leather-coat and blue jeans . . . who waded out in his measured steps and distraction, into the colorless depths of the great, dark, naked space, with nothing but his monitor and Argyros and the bare fluorescent tube, for light.

Lanze stayed for a time in this distance. He looked back at Argyros through this, but the heavy cloak of space played on his vision, and gave Lanze a spontaneously shifting focal plane of character: he was relaxed and thoughtful; he was in tense deliberation; he looked at some point beside Argyros in meaningless parallax; he looked at Argyros; he considered Argyros in looking; he grasped and contained him in his look; consumed him; he looked into the shapeless cavities of Argyros: he looked entirely through him. "I have something for you," said Lanze, and moved back toward Argyros—who imagined the accumulated dun turned like cloud with the motion. It seemed to Argyros a uniform and industrial gloom—something refined and sorted and rated by grade—and Lanze's sharp movement disturbed it, made it thick, and briefly discernible.

"Do you smoke, Argyros?" said Lanze. "Well, naturally you do— it is your second cologne," he said, and fetched a small box and a round carton and a pair of small tempered glasses from his satchel, and delivered them to the table, where he set them before Argyros.

"I do," said Argyros.

"Yes," said Lanze. He drew a bottle from the carton and wiped the glasses with the cloth on which they'd nested, and he filled them to the waist with whisky.

"You'll forgive the stemware—it's what was to hand," he said, and opened the small brown shoulder box of Shermans, and carefully lifted the tissue, and offered one of the Maduro-wrap cigarettes to Argyros. He selected one for himself. And from a substantial lighter he lit them both.

"Are we permitted to smoke here?" said Argyros.

"You imagine it will spoil the pictures—or shall we regard the mere question as a prohibition?" said Lanze, and slipped a glass before Argyros. "Are you acquainted with Oban?"

V.

What does it mean?—thought Freddie Oslo. His elbow rest in the window-well: a point of leverage against which his fingers were cantilevered upon his face. His fingertips velveteen snares; treaded calipers. Beside the lubricated swathe of Bentley-hides: the unshod cloven hooves of man.

But what did it mean? What might it mean? The wine was working on him, in that space between the run-up to inebriation and the retreat into headache, and it was a sound that leapt live and sudden from the slippery preoccupation of his memory—an article of recollection raised from slumber as it were a djinn-vase knocked from a table in the violent stumblings of a night-dark room: It was the sound of a heavy book, let to fall closed. It makes a most distant noise, this thing: it makes a noise one expects, but also, a noise one does not—it is full and sudden, empty and long: one hears it and one feels it, and one senses in it the impressions issue contradictory assertions about one-another: conflicting stories.

A dictionary, or a grand Bible: Tolstoy—large and heavy, and let to fall closed. It was not quite right, he granted—too deep, too slow—but it resonated with the same bracket of unplaceable overtones and undertones: a tactile triad, the experience of the experience of which seemed necessary to contain all the ingredients of the instant of connection: a point of ignition whose blast radius required full survey in order to reconstitute the flash. It was not quite right. But it was imprinted this way. And this was its sound.

It was before London. It was London beginning—seed-germ moment of the fact in forming. Jean-Pierre was four then. Lila was from somewhere California—the sunburn slopes of San Diego, where menace of the San Andreas seemed perpetually suspended, and the sea, by agreement never rose upon the surf-side bungalows, and rains never washed the city more than lightly down its own ravines, and Mexico kept mindfully behind its check-fence, and the sun made all things green and beautiful, and brought always smiles to the visages of the peoples of Eden. One tasted this in her vagina. Her righteous bearing. Lila's vagina tasted of oysters. All vaginas taste more or less of mollusks and shellfish—freshly caught or left to time and sun: this, thought Oslo, was to prove they were not affairs for the tongue; lips sanding against the slivering burrs of such ill-tended beards. But Lila—hers was of cool oysters, suitably fresh, and with the affect of being served from a copper spoon: somewhere we all taste of copper coinage and saltwater: 1-cent euros and half-shell hors d' oeuvres. He thought it must be for her health and temper—because she was American and virtuous. An Eve out of Eden. Mirthless penitential Scandinavians sped to the pacific verge to drop their gravid birth in the sands and mail virginal offerings air-post thirty years into the future of the Indus River Valley of San Diego conurbation. Her parents had come thus from the cold interior of the continent to bask in this easy perfection, and in its spirit had birthed her and given her a name after the atman, or channeled spirits or sacral tinctures or astral colors, or some such—and all her youth she had lived this de-wintered, neutered, untrammeled solar enlightenment of living. She was gorgeous and brunette. Lightly speckled by the sun in that gentle, ruddy, American way. She had been a model until she'd filled out in womanhood. She'd gone to school in France, and they had met there. She was clever and studious—and for an American, she was found to be lovely. And she had resolved her loveliness and her cleverness to France; and her peculiar American certainty in virtue—and in fullness, had taken up instruction in dance. Jean-Pierre was four then.

It had been a cold, wet and snowed winter day in the hind-lawn of Chartres. The house stood on a small plot and cloister of trees. It was a work of the 1600s, made slick and new by discreet additions and white and black paint and the smooth applications of hand-glazed tiles where the floors had once been rough and uneven. They were an hour train from Paris there—and so this is where Lila had been—and where, but for time-off, he would typically have been as well. It was Monday in slippers. The Spanish au pair had taken Jean-Pierre to his nursery school that morning, all bundled in his weathery things: his dangling vestigial join-ment of gloves, and his great swallowing of hat and his clumsy child boots which move everywhere as false limbs—and then she'd gone for a day shopping in the market. She'd stowed him at school and then slipped away from children and laundry and the special penetrating furtive leering of Frenchmen—and Lila would be overnight in Paris, for a performance and a pedagogy and a cocktail prologue to return—and Oslo would have himself for company till then.

In Paris, he worked for a firm trading esoteric derivative constructs. But he'd taken some small piece of holiday, and was at home. Months earlier he'd attended a reception at the Grand Palais and he'd met a vexing singularity of woman in formal dress, Simone Helena, of the London unit of Rothman. Lately she had reached out and summoned him there for talks and prospective wooings, and introduction to a New York counterpart—some feature of high-entablature, some Seraphim of Celestial Hierarchy. There were meetings, there were introductions, there was an attendant who moved him about London—moved with him, instructing and instructed, from the lofted corporate to the tufted incorporate: the formal to the programmatically informal, to the structurally uncertain, to the systemically concealed: a mobile concierge—directing him to the parties and party favors and sexual favors which were Rothman's New York inheritance: the encanonized, unsanctioned negotiating terms: the blank back-pages.

He'd gone, he'd dressed, he'd spoken, he'd listened, and now was at home in Chartres to drink-over the weekend upon it. And so, with great success he had. He'd cleared the house of his preferred store of Pinot, and last night two more bottles beside. It was Monday then. His morning of a fogged afternoon. Or perhaps closer to lunch. His teeth were blue of wine and his lips bore black crust of tannins: lipstick of the goblet's kiss; and all his hinges ground with sulfites, and his head was swelled with the thumping pulse of erection. Through the windows fell snow-light: that flat and bitter, dim and squinted illumination, which reflects ceaselessly between earth and sky—trapped—until it is no longer light, but paint—hard and blue. Until it is that shade in Van Gough—Monet: a thing so burned by interfracting percolation that linseed, zinc, and the meddling brush-works of man, become somehow more faithful than the thing in its own rendering: a Robert Ryman-ic damnation of the senses. The snow was uneven mat in the yard; it lay decoratively in the trees and loaded slender branches with lazy draw-weight. It capped the low stone wall and lay in the road with two long slender ruts. It rounded the rooflines and clung in gutters, and beneath its dresses Chartres was medieval once again and always. It was the least inflection of cosmic ambivalence—the least sneezing reflex of season, which refutes progress and refutes time; shrugged at his electric candle-light, and his dappled Range Rover in the drive—as just so much dandified oxcart for the rutted, cobbled ways. And it was in this light into the kitchen, through the windows and patio doors which looked over thinly drifted yard furnishings, his bare feet on the steel rungs and his creaking elbows rested on the polished counter and his eyes blinking mortal retreat—that the call came through.

He'd rest in the armchair in the furnished common-hall outside the rooms. There were old untuned pianos and wall-mounted handicrafts and toys and books and things for the entertainment of children. Snow-veiled skylights let down the color of ice-blue shade—so that even here beneath Persols his brow furrowed against the cool shame of place; and there were the odd bohemian confabulation of furnishings, the group of unmatched chairs and a low-cart made coffee table. Oslo nested in the chair in sunglasses and cashmere topcoat, and evaded the connective gaze of children who stare at him through picture windows onto the hall—or was it counter-wise?—and searched for a place to rest his eyes in natural self-concentration. And he waited for the director. He'd ridden his dandified oxcart down the narrow snow-rails of pavements and cobbles and tramlined and buffeted; and hung over the wheel, pulling and re-pulling focus; and now waited in over-warm coats and whorey shroud of solar diffusion. And all the while he bore an agony of suspense at any moment he thought may tip into illness.

The director was a slender Nigerian. When she came she was graceful and slow, with close-cropped hair and modest, well-tended clothes, and her French was perfect. She approached from some unseen course and slipped gently into the opposite chair. She crossed her leg and fixed her cuff, and smiled that warm, broad, African smile, which inverse to Caucasians—one accepts immediately, and only later questions. "Are you comfortable, Monsieur Oslo?"

He felt himself smile: an autonomic reply. He'd shifted his glasses with his finger: a gesture reassuring composure. He thought of his teeth—were they medicinal iodine blue, still?—and his lips: did they bear still the thin black brush-marks of Salvador Dali mustache?—the little whimsy strokes of wine-stain in the mouth corners one discovers like a cartoon revenge. He swiped at his lips with his thumb. And he was cautious not to smile again.

She thanked him for coming. Her eyes were large and glistening. They were large, round maternal headmasters' eyes, and they glistened with wisdom and with knowing—and with kind and treacherous patience: they knew the boy Oslo had punched in primary school, that he'd once stolen a toy and then destroyed it in the moment of capture, about his masturbatorial habits; the curses and slanders issued in the home—the special colors of profanity which are distinct to each household as a kitchen smell—but that Jean-Pierre could not be dared to repeat; and sat there as he was, that he bore a high residual drunk—the sort that passes most occasions for strong casual plaster. All these things she could have no means of knowing; nevertheless, she must. It was certainty: he could see the perfect intuition in the temperate severity of her gaze.

"Can I get you anything, Monsieur Oslo?" she'd said.

"I am quite well," he'd said. He thought he'd said. He heard himself say. She'd cleared lint from her slacks with a moistened fingertip. It is good of you to be here, she'd said—good of you to come. We are grateful for your family—for your attendance here, Monsieur Oslo, she'd said. We are grateful for Jean-Pierre: he's a lovely little boy—bold and curious: reflective, she'd said—introspective. Lovely. Monsieur Oslo, she'd said: "Jean-Pierre bit another little boy today. I have called you here for this."

Jean-Pierre sat as he sat now: couched into the shoulder-embrace of doorsill and puddle of misted window glass. He was not shamefaced or pained in conscientious bondage—no. Merely slumped. As small children are on long journeys where the destination is forgotten and dim. There were no signs of constricting slipknots:

the cord-marks of heated self-consideration. He was merely bored, and still. The Range Rover slithered and chattered back down the same grooves upon which it came. Oslo blinked and strained out his sunglasses at the greasy white pinch of glare, and the details which lay upon it like pencil scratch. He steered his little black oxcart and batted at the petals of self-reproach enfolding him—what is a rose in reverse?—a lily? A secular sinfulness: a guilt of malpractice. It was a mean and ill-made contrition; a fore-tide sign in mortifying foment—and he fought at it. But these were muddled and confabulated waters: his and Jean-Pierre's . . . and his. He turned strenuously from these emotional mottlings—nowhere through yesterday's wine could he feel sharply which belonged to when. And when they arrived home . . . they did not speak. There was no reprimand. No corrective. Oslo did not serve him chiseled words and then careful sandwich wedges or chilled fruits. Jean-Pierre was not ensconced and fortified among toys and playful things. Oslo poured a heavy glass of antidote in the kitchen, and with wine, took to his office, and left Jean-Pierre in the kitchen in his boots and dangling mittens, standing. Left him there with himself, and the gelid unturned broth of Oslo's collective contempt.

Oslo had sat sightlessly before four monitor screens buzzing imperceptible static. They flickered refresh and populated and repopulated tables and stuttering graphs; real-time fields and cells with numerals dancing across decimals the way a perturbed spirit level claws for center. And he'd sat and watched—and today, thought of London, and pedagogical-dancing-Lila in Paris, and the terrible fixity of the nursery director, and sought only to balm his mind pressing it gently back beneath the waterline. And when he'd gone for replenishment, there had been the pop of bottle-glass. Jean-Pierre had stood there in his boots, still. By some means he'd swept the bottle from the counter to the floor. And what filled Freddie Oslo then, was not worry or dismay or paternal resolve, but rage. Instantaneous and complete.

And he rushed the boy where he stood and struck him against the cheek. He'd flung against the ground, and his head bounded from the tile. And though it was not right, not quite—its sound: that sound that had played for him in that moment, and now again, against the door of the Bentley, was the sound of some great tome being let fall closed: something grand and well-bound and unabridged with slick-weighted pages and tooled leather covers—that rang deep and bright and sharp and wet, and played with sustain; and with a recoiling echo.

VI.

"England is photographed in all disproportion to her beauty," said Lanze. They'd pulled off in a carpark and stopped, and Mr. Lanze had turned to speak over his shoulder. "There are very many cameras in England—do you know how many sites are free of them, by deliberation, omission, or failure?"

"Where is this?" said Oslo. "Where have we stopped?"

"Precious few," said Lanze. "Lee-on-the-Solent, Monsieur Oslo. The fastidiously kept and presently vacant Elmore Car Park of Lee-on-the-Solent. Famous for absolutely nothing, one imagines, but its celebrated public slipway," Lanze gestured toward a dark bit of roadway that tipped toward the sea: "and its nearness to the perimeter of Browndown Battery—also, and perhaps not coincidentally, vacant.

"Also, Monsieur Oslo—"

"Mr. Lanze."

"I must tell you that I despise complications. However . . . upon our itinerary a complication has arisen . . . for which there are no practical and also timely alternatives."

"What is it?"

"I regret it, but I will show you. First—you must wear this, please," said Lanze, and handed back to Oslo a dark heavy coat, knit hat and gloves. "There may be alternatives later, but I am afraid this will be necessary for now." Oslo unfolded the coat and twisted himself and his suit jacket into it. "You will pardon the trespass against your tailoring, won't you?—the hat and gloves too, if you please . . . Now, Monsieur Oslo, when we leave the vehicle we will move calmly and swiftly toward the water's edge and then left down a path—"

"Mr. Lanze."

"Yes."

"Is it at all possible to stop at my flat?"

"To ask at the coast of England?—did Belgravia not seem more fitting?"

"Would that—?"

"Not at all. —We will move calmly and swiftly. We will speak in quiet voices. And you will do as I instruct, precisely. Once we have left the vehicle there will be no further negotiations. D'accord?"

"I don't like the sound of any of this."

"And so you are wise not to. —D'accord?"

"Je l'ai."

Belgravia by the A3 to Gosport would be a two-hours labor. But they did not go this way. Instead Lanze had hewed in this general direction, but along two-lane byways which sawed toward and away from their intended route. And so their work was longer. The city had been the languid smear of marker lights and slippery high-glass paint striping; the flickering checkerboard luminescence of human niches, in resplendent collective isolation—high and remote. The asphalt and stoneworks glistened with abiding memory of rain. And this in time gave over to the high-crown county lanes where hedges and dry stone fences leapt at them from verges of the night. Oslo was quiet and despondently preoccupied, and leant into the bolster and the window glass. And Lanze's gaze upon him was revealed in the sweeps and flashes of mirror light.

Lanze had asked for the phone and the computer. He had searched the bag for electronics, powered them down and slipped them into a pouch all their own; and from then he was matte stillness. Still as dusk on boyhood paths; green mossed and copper gabled; the lick and murmur of Prussian waters coursing underfoot: quiet as the handrail. The Bentley, too, was still. It purred feline from distant engine rooms. Somewhere tires trod softly on road pavements, felted and apologetic. Knurled dials and perfected lever weights pleased the touch, and Lanze wore the whole of the enterprise like fine woolen topcoat, with Freddie Oslo carried against some deep interior of pocket seam.

"Je l'ai," Oslo had said, and they had exited the car and moved to the trunk.

"You will carry this, please," Lanze had said, and laid a small boat motor in his arms.

"It is quite heavy," said Oslo.

"It is," said Lanze. "Anything less could not be relied on."

"Are we fishing?" said Oslo, as a rod and tackle box were removed and Lanze sealed the trunk.

"I shall carry these," he said, and they moved for the water. They turned left beneath the restless coils of high grass dune, above a shingle beach moist with night.

"It is hurting my arms," said Oslo, as he struggled with his grip.

"Yes," Lanze had said. "It would."

An onshore breeze whistled crisply at his ears and neck and batted a low white chop against the beach gravel. And when the fence first rose from the dark, a green panic deployed in him. It did not radiate, but released in him as an aerosol: each chamber of him, everywhere at once. It snatched at his testicles and strummed at the cables of his knees, and made his grip weak and numb where he struggled with the motor. When they were upon it, it read not so much tall as stern, and ran from sea to headland and off toward imagination. It was chain link strung between dire concrete pillars, and wreathed an angle of barbwire crown. Wind upon the metal ties and cement stakes played some note in his hair and fingernails, and he spoke over it and the onshore fluting in his ears: "What is happening? Mr. Lanze, tell me what is happening—I don't like any look of this." Lanze rest the rod and tackle beside the fence and took the motor from Oslo and put it on the ground. "I would have my phone, Mr. Lanze."

"And who would you call, Monsieur Oslo?—your friend of Chester Square?"

"Simone . . . Simone Helena."

"Yes, Simone Helena of Chester Square—and what shall we imagine she'd say? Where did she leave you in parting?"

"She said that I should take leave, Mr. Lanze—take holiday."

"And so you are."

"—Not skulk about the dunes of a beach of a night . . . and disused battlements, beside."

"It is a singular complication, and I have already apologized for it. Christ, Monsieur Oslo, carried his own timbers and complained less I think. I have explained our terms, and we shall keep to them. Now come help me fetch something," said Lanze, and led them in clambering up the soft footing. Oslo followed. And at thirty or forty meters Lanze stopped beside a pillar, moved directly away from it to reach into a swaying brake of grasses, and from it tugged a small, weather-beaten dinghy.

2.

'Straight into The Solent till you can make out nothing but
the lights'—he'd said. 'Hold there an hour. Don't drift
into the sea-lane. Air temperature will soon be barely six
degrees Celsius—water temperature only slightly better: pray, do
not fall in.'

They'd carried the boat to the shore and fitted the motor. Oslo had
asked again about the gear: "I know nothing of fishing," he'd said.

"If you are waiting, you are fishing: the look and the act are the
same."

He'd put him in the water and turned back for the car. And now
Oslo sat in the breathing Solent: the shore reduced to the prescrip-
tive glint of fixtures, and the waters tapping at the floor of the boat
like rain against a paper cup. Shipping was quiet and far away. The
horizon tipped and tilted. Lights of earth and sea blinked and moved.
And the strait lifted and fell in great sighs of rippling black fabric.
Fizzing and incalculable—and impossibly stupid, he thought. An
article once described the boil of the bottom of the universe—and
in this place concealed in nakedness upon a whim of probabilistic
surface tension; unseen water rising up his shoe leather and making
his toes damp and painful: he felt it; thought he must be riding it—an
imperceptible thing, impossibly finite, in an over-small boat.

He thought of grasping the throttle handle of the motor and
turning for shore: continuously he thought of it. And his mind
throbbed with misgiving every instant between. He cared nothing

for boats one way or another: the civilized and grown traveled by air; creatures of the sea rendered themselves to ice chests or the regard of fishmongers. These were pontoons for the exertion of the state, battle platforms or playthings—but in this polished ambivalence there was nothing for respite or recreation in the Solent—in the dark—in so small and thin a boat as this. Every motion perturbed it. He clasped tightly at the slender plank of bench. He did not violate the boundary edges putting his hands atop the hull, and he'd taken to holding his breath at the motion of each cant and turn as an act of quieting stillness. Repeatedly he checked time from the bare wrist under dual coat sleeves: a reflex in the measure of conscious forgetting—and with each memory-return his throb of misgiving had grown, and his dimension of waiting had unfurled in some new yard of cloth.

The sound which overturned this waiting resembled propeller aircraft. It came from the east—he thought it was east—still. It severed his misgiving first as distraction: a sound like vintage warplane on low approach. And when the sound grew but did not arrive—did not overfly in some strafing pass—that misgiving born distraction bore concern. By the time his eyes had registered a sight, the throttles had been halved into a snapping off-tempo cackle, and the object of the sound appeared as little more than a knife-tip snugged against the water. Eventually it was a ship: it sliced into view a silvery powerboat—long and slender—and it was upon him: the engines thrummed and cracked and the helm slipped overhead.

"You look a pitiable sight," came Lanze's voice. "Whatever is the matter, Monsieur Oslo?—sharks eat your Marlin?"

"I am ready to be out, Mr. Lanze."

"Too long in the tub—have you got a bit crinkled?"

"I am ready to be out now—Mr. Lanze."

"Would you be so kind as to open the ball valves then, Monsieur Oslo?"

He toss Oslo a line and drew him against the stern.

"What are these?" said Oslo.

"The blue handles—one at the bow; one at the stern: front and rear: lift them if you please. You'll wish to hop up swiftly when you do."

VII.

They were a slender sweating African in spare lint-and-bristle beard, and a suit made to shining from constant starch and iron—and Van Der Boor said this was Joseph Adisa, Counselor to the General. And a man in heavy fatigues and epaulette bands and a beret worn full-crown like a bottle cork: and Van Der Boor said this was Solomon Koma, the General. And a man in black boots and necktie and linen field suit, small round sunglasses and a broad smile—and of him Van Der Boor said nothing.

Kamadugu heard it first. He paused in his rocking and from his stick-and-earth conjurations and he peered westward. Marek Hussar ate meat-parts from red sauce broth and clung with his gin hand to a lighted Dunhill. He and Van Der Boor and James Ngolo Vonjoe had fetched their mess and smoke ration and drink and returned to the shade where they'd begun. Van Der Boor sat cross-legged in the dirt where he'd worried a cradle for his soft-cupped provision. He daubed sweated fingers repeatedly against his thighs so he might grasp it, and flicked his ash over his knee. And when Kamadugu stare off into the bright silence and issued furtive mumblings from beneath their cover onto the brilliant horizon, Van Der Boor asked James Ngolo Vonjoe to have it.

"He says: Mind the coat," said James Ngolo Vonjoe. He had quit the lift-gate for the shade, and he too sat in the building lee among them, all in a line.

"What's the coat, mên? He's talkin' kak, sure."

"I think he talks to himself," said James Ngolo Vonjoe—"Who else to talk to?" But Hussar smoked over his drink, and drank over his chewing, and considered the lawn chairs Coevorden and Van Lingen had left at the clearing-edge, and David Koning's suit jacket which lay with them.

"Tell chommie: go dite! His mopin' gives me headache."

James Ngolo Vonjoe told him, and he replied. "He says he is not hungry."

"What's this?"

"He says: 'Bread bakes tomorrow; water flows yesterday: only today is fruit.' He says: 'Today, supper in wine and tobacco.'" James Ngolo Vonjoe said this, and then they all paused to hear the sound. It was a faint bass mode that leapt like a tick over the western Kangari ridgetop and fell down the near face to the plain.

"The other Hind," said Van Der Boor. "That'll be De Bruyn back from errands." The gunship rushed over the canopy, grew a deep percussive rending as it creased the low plain toward them and its shriek of turbines came to bloom. Heavy copters ride their rotor-tips mostly—paddle about to the sound of smacking oars, thought Hussar—but the Hind always sounded on the rotor-stubs to him, and little blade whip: sounded of tearing and turbofans. It climbed and slipped the five hundred meter stepped western ridge and skimmed the four-and-a-half klicks of tree-and-grass plain, and was upon the plateau in an instant. It heaved overhead to bleed momentum and turned on the rotor shaft and descended over the clearing to an ever-sharpening pitch of whine Hussar imagined to have its own ballistic properties: it entered at the brainstem and severed all reason till it abated. Personnel hurried to cover the open mess. They trained their cigarettes in their palms and might have covered their ears, but covered their drink instead; and Van Der Boor said something like: 'Russ call it 'crocodile'—but 'dragonflies-a-fuck' . . .' This is what Hussar thought he'd made out, but couldn't know if there was more to hear or if the belligerent whine had simply rendered Van Der Boor's words into speech of tongues—struck him senseless.

The lawn chairs drug and cartwheeled. The tan jacket of David Koning was cast violently to heaven and never seen again, and motes of dust lashed their faces like shards of sand.

When the wash had lifted and the engines cut and all their anger leeched off in heat-luster and the sound of free-wheeling machine parts and the rotors looping their defeated last turns: first then was Viggo De Bruyn. The troop door came up and out he stepped in shorts and high-socks and his comb of brown mustache. There were a pair of mirthless National Provisional Ruling Council soldiers came as well. And there were the man Van Der Boor had called Adisa, and that he had called the General, and that he had not called.

Van Der Boor saw them and emptied his cup in one bitter turn and rose to standing. "Up," he said. "Up mên! You'd have that cup or lose it, ja—Boy King has sent his man."

"It's full," said Hussar.

"Drink or piss it—it's Strasser's man, right—up!"

These men—four Africans and De Bruyn—dismounted and stooped reflexively beneath the swinging rotors, where they were presented hearty greetings in handshakes, and for the General and the man in high-boots and tie, a kind of head-tipping bow—a sort of curtsey of the chin—and Van Der Boor had tugged at Hussar's collar until he too had come to standing. He took what he could from his cup and passed to Kamadugu—who remained as he was. And James Ngolo Vonjoe rose too, and asked why.

2.

"What's the trouble with your crouching nigger?" had said the African in high-boots and tie. He said it and dried the bridge and temples of his glasses in the hems of his jacket and replaced them. He no longer smiled and had broken from congregation: "This one. Here."

The group of them had moved in listless reception from the Hind and tumbling brown air, toward the canopied mess and near the lee-shade to which Hussar and the others had attached. And now the retinue paused as he fetched and lighted a cigarette in a series of weary, inscrutable gestures: "This one," he said.

From the way his cigarette wagged and gyrated, turned and pointed, Hussar understood that it was not a chemical appliance, but a fixture or appendage: a burning sixth digit. He bore a shadow of mustache like a rumor. And where the General was round and full and seemed vaguely older than Hussar, he was a lean and fluid blackness, and vaguely the younger.

"Introduce us to the men, would you, Viggo?" said David Koning to De Bruyn, and the retinue approached to inspect them.

"That will be Jan Bekker in the village—General—with the Kamajors. Those are Smithson the Aussie, and Lange the Swede, who watch him from the gun-mount, there. Felix Graff, to our rear there—do you see him? Coevorden and Van Lingen are quite familiar to you here," said De Bruyn, and the General laughed. "And this here is another goodie veteran: a brace of Werner Van Der Boor—"

"There is more than one of him?" said the General.

"There would be an army of him, but Mandela kept those: we were issued three," said Van Lingen dryly from the rear.

"And your crouching nigger . . . Does he have extras?" said the man in high-boots and tie, and the General laughed again: his jolly fat man's laugh in his merely rounded frame.

"The younger Koma," laughed the General. "Jugun Gebungeta Koma—back from University in England: and my brother," said the General, and pat the man on the shoulder.

"Among a litter of thirty, one shall always be junior to something," said Koma, and his cigarette turned and flicked and wagged, and Hussar thought of irritable shuffling feet.

"Kamadugu, Mr. Koma" said De Bruyn. "This is Kamadugu. Fiercest chieftain of the Northern Province, and greatest tracker in Sierra Leone."

"Why not West Africa then?" said Koma.

"So be it: West Africa," said De Bruyn.

"Kuranko?" said the General.

"Kuranko," said De Bruyn.

"Chieftain and no tribe?" said the General.

"He is with us now," said De Bruyn.

"Broken-legged and all," said Koma. "What a find, that he cannot even stand for the General."

"He is Kuranko, and difficult, General," said James Ngolo Vonjoe.

"And this is Vonjoe: guide and translator—he was great help in Kono," said De Bruyn. "Kamadugu keeps to his own ways and counsel, General. He is great use and important to us: I hope you will forgive him."

The General laughed. "What do you say?—shall I forgive the Kuranko, Minister Koma?" he said, and swatted his brother on the back.

"Mr. Koma has arrived with a land grant from the President," said Joseph Adisa.

"Yes, just as you," said the General to the Afrikaners and Koning. "He too has his land grant. He is friends of De Haas—as am I, as are you—David Koning—and they have sent him to collect it. Secure it. I have called him back from the university Birmingham, of the UK: De Haas and I, we think he should be Minister! What do you say?!" said the General, and again swatted Koma on the back.

"Hussar is a university boy as well—right? Ja? That right?" said De Bruyn.

"Correct, sir," said Hussar.

"Hussar's a swimmer like you, Koning," said De Bruyn.

"That so? Mines?" said Koning.

"Combat swimmer," said Hussar.

"Ah, the hard stuff: who for?" said Koning.

"Kampfschwimmer," said De Bruyn.

"Ach, wir habben ein Deutscher mit uns: you have become so international, Coevorden. A Fin, a French and you'd have half the tribes of Europe," said Koning, and laughed. "And what university, my boy?"

"Perhaps it would not interest the General, sir," said Hussar.

"Nonsense, we're breathless with expectation," said Koning.

"Cambridge, sir," said Hussar, and immediately felt the stumbling pause of conversation, and regretted it.

"A very Oxbridge gentleman among us!" said Koning.

"Naa—come on!" said Van Der Boor. "You did not!"

Koma flicked his lighted butt into the earth between them, and lighted another.

"You didn't," said Van Der Boor.

"Is it true?—clergy among the heathens?" said Koning.

"Two years, sir. Yes, sir," said Hussar.

Koning laughed and clapped his hands. "Most excellent!"

"Is that better than your university Birmingham of the UK?" said the General and swatted Koma upon his tender silence. "It seems they give away your precious milk from the other teat, Minister Koma," he said, and loosed a roar of laughter.

An RPG took flight then. The Afrikaners—Coevorden and Van Lingen—smirked dryly from the rear, and Koning smiled his reluctant but true, mirthful smile: he was amused; and the General's beret bobbed up and down on his ebullient tide, his round jaw and his thick neck and shoulders shook, and he laughed his fat man's laugh; and Koma smoothed his black tie and looked at Hussar and issued a painful grimace and smoked and flecks of ash tumbled about him as the flurries of a personal weather; and from the stage of tree line where scrub-grass stepped to canopy foliage, from the corner of his vision Hussar saw the white cough of launch among the trees and the faint ochre belch of motor-start, and it overflew Felix Graff and the Kamajors in the hillside and airburst at the rim of the plateau, and at the clap they all flinched in unison—a tip of neck and dip of knees and flexing tension of shoulder and elbow—and they all peered from their ducking stoops to see.

Felix Graff and the Kamajors had opened rifles on the position: they trod northward through the sharp stalks of grass along the hillside toward it, and from the camp mortars were trained and walked on target; and now they spoke as into a collective deafness over the chorale of rifles, consonant and insistent—and the mortars which played percussion in their chests: "That'll be for the gunships," said Van Der Boor.

Coevorden had smiled and shouted into the deafness: "They'll have to be closer than that."

"How far?" said Adisa. He gestured from his ears to where the hilltop smoke once had been, and where now leaves and trunks were blazed and punctured, and where earth-clods and tree were lifted by mortars in cloudy flotsam.

"One thousand fifty meters," said Hussar. "As you stand."

"Will there be many?" said Adisa.

"Who can say," said Van Lingen, with a shrugging grin. "Fuse trips at nine hundred twenty meters—'less they've craft to disable it—however many, they'll want to be closer than that." Van Lingen said this toward Adisa, and adjusted his spectacles to mark he was unimpressed.

"It's comforting . . . I say, it's quite comforting, Mr. Van Lingen," said Adisa. "The General . . . Sir . . . The General—I say, the General has a matter before you. And . . . And Mr. Koma, too," he said, and indicated the Minister-in-waiting with a long outstretched arm. "Perhaps . . . Privacy," he said. "Privacy," he repeated, with the entreaty of his naked palms. "Perhaps, before our transport is made to pieces."

Adisa had said this and been taken beneath the flat white hands of the Afrikaners and Koning—he and the General both. They had been turned and guided by the shoulder toward command—and Hussar thought it was the gesture of preemptive consolation: it was the touch foreshadowing 'no'—parents lead their defeated children home from contest with this touch. The NPRC soldiers had followed as well, looking all the time uneasily into the noise of the hillside. It was only Jugun Gebungeta Koma who remained. He stood and smoked and blinked through his whirl of ash at Hussar. At Hussar, and upon Kamadugu, who did not return his gaze but drank and crouched comfortably in shade, and looked off toward the gunfire-song—and he put another half-smoked butt between them into the earth with his facile nervous hands, and he too turned away. And Hussar noticed the way only the soles of his boots shown red soil upon them, where every other facet was clean of it. The way new shoes do.

"Jugungubungity," had said Van Der Boor. "If only he'd a crop an' a pith helmet."

3.

Hussar thought of snowfall. The way it catches in streetlight like dancing swarm. Moths communing in full night-throng. He thought of the first step one takes from the front stoop—the sheltered stair which is clean, and the next which is not: the strange tonal inversion, its negative sound: stepping into crisp, brittle velvet. "I'm trying to give you some advice, you understand: I think it would go easier for you if you would try less hard."

The fall of evening had made the guns quiet. The placements on the hill were still, and nothing fell beneath the shattered boughs of trees but gloom. The same ordinary gloom which falls in all places at this time, and makes even the intimate and the common exotic and peculiar. And so it fell here. At first making the Kangari Hills rich and then rough, and then smooth in their uniform foreboding. The Hind had lifted before the guns had stilled. The Kamajors had all returned, but they did not sit at the fires or sing. And when Van Der Boor had fetched him, Hussar had taken his place at command.

"I think it would go easier for you if you would try less hard," had said Koning. He fixed his hair vehemently with both hands, as though he were knocking dirt from it, as though he had been hit with rotor wash but a moment ago—as though he'd just thought of it. "Does anyone believe that?—that's a long fall, there to here, boy. Or perhaps we're matter for your thesis?"

Koning, Coevorden, and Van Lingen sat at the back of the tent in the sling of chairs. They had been drinking, and Koning smoked a cigar whose ash he released wherever he pleased. Hussar stood middle of the room beside a map table, and said nothing.

"Hmm?" said Koning.

"David," said Van Lingen.

"Ah, bollocks!" said Koning, and they all left him a berth of silence.

The walls of the tent shifted in motionless air. Some gasp of high pressure in Libya tickled them, perhaps—some unfelt sigh of the continent, but they were untouched in Sierra Leone by anything such as motion, anything but night bird call and the bark of distant primates. The space was all pole-stays and closed vent-windows and 10oz canvas cloth, but had a spirit of mahogany panels and baize club chairs.

"Have a seat," said Coevorden. "We'll have a moment with you."

"Shall we wait for De Bruyn, sir?"

"We've spoken. This is for us—have a seat."

"Koning would like to offer some rum. Take a cup from the sideboard," said Van Lingen.

"I would not," said Koning. "Do you even like rum, boy?"

"Every soldier likes there to be rum. None, I think, like what is offered," said Hussar.

Van Lingen smiled.

"Van Der Boor was just here, and he praised it," said Koning.

"Van Der Boor would drink hot motor oil if it provided the right effect: I do not think he is particular," said Hussar.

"Damn you, boy," said Koning, and Coevorden and Van Lingen laughed. "Take your cup! We must drink it from porcelain so that none may know its fineness. Promise not to enjoy it and you may have your fill," said Koning, and waved Hussar to the sideboard until he had taken his cup, and a seat with them.

Koning poured rum for Hussar, and he noticed they all drank from the same chipped and random mugs as coffee service. The window flaps were down and closed for the same reason no fires burned in the camp and there was no song among the Kamajors— they were sealed against their light. They were sealed also against the least hope of clear air, and they sat in yellow-green cloud which moved as ink through liquid, issued new and refreshed by the moment; they were wet wherever their clothes touched them—at the collar and waist and fold of sleeve, and their faces gleamed with heat and drink.

"Tomorrow we deploy: northwest over the hills against the RUF camp. It should rout them in Kangari," said Coevorden. He leaned forward in his low sling chair. He was thin and elfin, with fine features and a thoughtless mop of hair, and he played his concentration against Hussar. His was not an ever-present attention, thought Hussar. You did not feel him at your back or sense him from across the way. His was not always on—he moved about in his bare knees and his flop of hair: but to catch the full beam of his attention, direct and unmitigated, blinded the eyes.

"Yes sir," said Hussar, "and I am prepared for that action, sir."

"Naturally you are," said Coevorden.

"There's been another development," said Van Lingen.

"Ja so," said Coevorden, "and there will be a matter for you to attend."

"As happens, somewhat important," said Van Lingen.

"Ja so, and means you will not join us in the action over Kangari. You will have another task."

Hussar leaned heavily into his chair and quietly sighed the coarse air, and he drank from his rum.

"Do you know our primary sponsor, Mr. Hussar?—here in Sierra Leone," said Koning.

"The National Provisional Ruling Council government," said Hussar.

"It is not," said Koning. "Not properly."

"Know where you're going, Koning," said Van Lingen.

"To bed after a few more nips, and to London in the morning," said Koning. "You may care where I'm going, what I'm onto—contractual decorum or some such: but I bloody well do not. Not properly—" he said returning to Hussar. "No. Do you know De Haas?"

"The diamond cartel?"

"The one. It would be more accurate to say they are our primary sponsor. Do you imagine how this sponsorship might work?"

Hussar nodded.

"After a fashion you do. Payment of course. Payment. But alas—some forms are unseemly and overdirect. Unpalatable to the general taste, you would say, perhaps," said Koning, and paused for ruminations as he dipped the wet shoulder of his cigar into his mug of rum, and then thoughtfully puffed it back to life.

"You enjoyed spoils from London earlier—today—good tobacco and such?" said Koning.

"I did," said Hussar.

"These were some treats in commemoration of a land grant—for which we are all quite pleased," said Koning, and looked to the Afrikaners for their confirmation in pleasure. They nodded with a vague brevity, and he continued: "This has the imprimatur of the state, and the ink of Strasser's pen, naturally—but this, it may be said, is the work of our sponsor."

"De Haas," said Hussar.

"Indeed. Drink, drink! Lord knows when after tonight you might have another," said Koning.

And Hussar drank.

"This is payment after one form. The grant, its mineral rights, et cetera. But there are also funds, which must come, time to time, from the state. How so ever that state may come to have them, you see."

"I see."

"And that jolly little villain you met at the helicopters—Solomon Koma, the General: you remember?"

"I do."

"He is the right-hand to Strasser—his heavy and deputy, and sometimes ad-hoc secretary of state: and so—rather disagreeably—he finds that his is the dispensary and administration of these funds, you understand."

Hussar nodded.

"How so ever the state may come to possess them . . ." said Koning.

"These are private things," said Van Lingen to Hussar, and adjusted his spectacles.

"You will see to it you keep them so," said Coevorden.

"You'd send him off with half the thing in his imagining and the other half to fate. I don't trust fate; I dislike imagination. I tell him only what needs knowing to do the thing. He's a swimmer—a swimmer understands—don't you boy?" said Koning.

"I do, sir."

"Indeed so. Good boy. Well that General is one of a brood of pups, and that brother—Jugun Koma—is one got off to university in the UK, and the General, he reckons him for bright," said Koning.

"The General wants him for Minster of Mineral Rights, and has taken steps," said Coevorden.

"He sees consolidation," said Van Lingen.

"He said this?" said Hussar.

"No. No more sometime advisor sometime secretary of state: he sees his thumb on the scale of the ministry—with this: and every yes and no and do and don't of it," said Van Lingen.

"De Haas must think he's got some air of the continent in his britches—a bit of English up 'im," said Koning.

"Jugun Koma is hedge against the provisional government, from where De Haas sit—and that it works for the General, works for them," said Coevorden.

"They've issued him a land grant," said Van Lingen.

"A security against his honor, you know. Signed for. They've issued him a land grant . . . and now he wants it," said Koning.

"Let him have it, then," said Hussar.

"Indeed so," said Koning.

"With respect—what should this have to do with me, sir? Why should this keep me from deploying?" said Hussar.

"RUF in the hills like termite in mounds," said Van Lingen.

"The General has asked for escort," said Coevorden.

"Where to?" said Hussar. "Where is his grant?"

"Pujehun," said Coevorden.

"In Kangari? Northwest," said Hussar.

"Yes," said Coevorden.

"We shall give him a lift then—it is just him?" said Hussar.

"We shall not," said Coevorden. "It is along our way, but not in our path—and it is entirely beside our schedule."

Hussar studied Koning, who merely moistened his cigar once more in his rum and worked it to new life, and filled all the tent with the acrid coiling new life of it—and returned this examination with a distant reserve.

"We are not going that way," said Coevorden.

"The General wants escort, clearing, and security contingent . . . until the Minster-to-be can put his own people in place," said Van Lingen.

"Does he have people?" said Hussar.

They were silent.

"That's unfortunate," said Hussar.

"He asked for you," said Coevorden.

"He asked for me, sir?"

"It seems you made an impression," said Koning.

Hussar finished his rum, and Koning reached forward to refill it.

"Who shall go?" said Hussar.

"Van Der Boor, James Vonjoe, Kamadugu, and yourself," said Coevorden. "But there is a complication."

Hussar set his feet and clasped his mug for the complication.

"There will be only one Rover," said Coevorden.

"Why so?"

"Because one is what can be spared," said Van Lingen.

"Mr. Hussar, Koma is being furnished with one of the General's own NPRC guard—there will be no space for you all: and beside, the Rover's instructed to run ahead to draw any fire and secure the position for your arrival. Mr. Hussar, you will escort the Minister and his detail on foot," said Coevorden.

". . . On foot," said Hussar.

"On foot, sir," said Coevorden, "—you will escort the Minister and his detail: once arrived at the Minister's village in Pujehun, you will rejoin your fireteam there—you will coordinate clearing of the village, and secure it."

"Three and a half klicks," said Coevorden. "Without interruption, transit shouldn't take more than a few hours: your truck will be in place when you arrive."

"You will secure the village . . . and you will secure the alluvial mines there . . . and you will provide for the security of the Minister at all times," said Van Lingen.

"You will," said Koning.

4.

They were two crayons. Red and blue. Their paper was clean and tidy, still neat against the wax. One—the blue—bore planes and bevels: all the signs of a modest use. An evening?—some evening? What evening, where? The butt bore the only signs of its hiding—chips and light gouges and the tumbling work of the march. The other. Was broken. The red: two-thirds and the missing end at a clean paper tear. The bottom had been used instead—the stray proper tip, the short nub worked and rounded: how humble necessity is. He did not imagine music. He did not imagine snow. But held them thoughtfully, doubtfully: as the limbs of an apparition.

Somewhere Van Der Boor was laughing, and Hussar looked up to see him laughing. "Pack those, did ya?" said Van Der Boor.

"Ja? No? *I'll* have one then," said Van Der Boor.

Hussar shook his head.

"Left mine in me other boot, mên," said Van Der Boor, and laughed again: the hearty, trailing laugh of his gait to the truck.

Hussar shook his head.

Hussar had risen to Van Der Boor. He'd pushed back the flap: "They've sent the Hind down-path," he'd said, and Hussar was left to his cot and his disorienting wakeful instant—to Van der Boor's meaning which hung in a sound, and at first, would not come out.

He'd risen to check his boots and clothes and to the penetrating silence of the company gone. There were no motors or conversation: it is impossible to sleep through the Hinds, he'd thought. There were only Kamajors—a small contingent left to mind the camp, guard the fuel and munitions, and under any circumstances to keep the landing site secure. They dithered in a quiet nervous waiting: already they missed the noise and self-righteous surety of white men, and the proliferation of heavy arms; already they had night in their minds.

A half-morning fire burned in a pit, and beside it sat the Minister-to-be: sat the younger Koma. He took coffee while his guard was at comfort. His clothes were unchanged but for an addition of creases, and it was only his errant skew of tie that properly marked the scene change. A jump cut, thought Hussar—a continuity flaw. The sky was a granular orange, and to the east it piled in climbing dry-brush turns—high sweeping curves resting one upon the next, not of cloud, but the wet paint motion of atmosphere itself. Kamadugu leaned against a tire of the Rover and examined this sky, and James Ngolo Vonjoe loitered near the certainty of the fire, and he peered time to time toward Kamadugu expecting he would speak—but he did not.

Hussar had sat near the low fire. He took coffee from one of the cups in service of rum the night before. Koma studied him across the fire through his small, round sunglasses. They were the sort worn by cinema beggars in black-and-white—a crumpled hat and an infirmity, and a tapping cane. Here they were dignified and new—something fine, if also before their hour of day. Himmler would have enjoyed a pair. And Hussar readied his pack, and fit spare magazines and checked the compartments and pockets and there had been the two crayons which had brought him to stillness. He'd held there and tried to conjure the setting of their incipient stowage—where had they been?—where was the pack?—were they home?

Van Der Boor loaded the truck in silence, but for his laughter at Hussar: "It's Lord's third mystery, mên: First creation, next is woman—next is, how by Christ I'd 've marbles in my cooking tins, right? . . . I've 'ad jacks in spare socks, mên! —Hind's flown down-path," he said again, as he swept casings from the Rover bed with the edge of his hand, swept them from edges and corners and drain-grooves that boots and brooms had not already reached—burrs are like this, up the pant-legs of pants already cleared; today's gravel in tomorrow's pockets; the inevitable water of a manifestly dry boat— and they fell to earth in a close chain of powdery thumps; a sound distinct and visceral, and portentous in any other where and any other when, a sound utterly submerged beneath the scale and malig-nant ferocity of their collective undertaking, but here now uncom-monly, strangely, noticed; and Van Der Boor paused to see them and Kamadugu glanced after their noise against the spoilt ground, and Hussar stood from the fittings of his pack to see them across the way, and he held the crayon parts in his two hands, and Jugun Gebungeta Koma stare into the peri-visible dancing tongues of flame of the weak morning fire. He did not see them.

Van Der Boor loaded ammo boxes and fuel canisters into the Rover and closed the drop-gate, and it was a felled gavel over their recess. James Ngolo Vonjoe collected his things and kicked earth, and moved reluctantly toward the Rover. Van Der Boor saddled-in and stirred the truck to an irritable knocking bray. James Ngolo Vonjoe mounted too, and when he called to Kamadugu, he moved from his resting into the rear, where he vanished into a space behind the hull-sides. And when they set off Koma leapt from his seat at the fire: "Stop them!" he called to Hussar. "Stop them! Where are they going?!"

"They break the trail," said Hussar. "We're on foot."

Koma was rigid, tipped forward in exasperation, on the toes of his feet as though captured at the moment of falling. The NPRC detail came rushing up from some private verge then. He was loose-cuffed and breathless and tucking his shirt when he arrived: "Stop them! What do they do? Where do they go? Make them stop," he said.

"We walk," said Hussar.

5.

The road from the mine camp plateau of Baomahun ran north as a broad red boulevard with shambling edges and snatch-grass curbs. It began at two trucks' width, and narrowed to four walking abreast, and then three; at each juncture and crossway it seemed, without order or intuition, to calve and dissolve, until it had grown to a single-width axle track and the loose hump of soil between. One breathed and tasted the late morning over their teeth. It tasted of high-iron dirt and the underside of leaves: fogged and gritted and greened. It tasted of opened earth and perspiring spittle. And some thin sour note of sea. The road lay out upon the thigh of the seated hills, and often the wood was shy and spare. Often they were exposed. It was a flat and dusty bowl of unhelpful scrub and Hussar could see them in its basin from the peak of any imagined elevation, or, as the road narrowed vegetation might rush in thickly—pinching tightly at the sliver of clay. From setting out he thought of ambush, from above and then beside—always one and then the other—until this attention wearied to vigilant resignation: peering into the hills and undergrowth, he put the march to a needlessly stupid necessity of present.

Hussar thought the air was tidal, and he drank it for breath, and wondered what it should mean to exhale one's last native respiration? What follows when a man trades his last original air—his final congenital oxygen—for the new? Might he be changed?—he wondered—to take only this foreign new air down into the deeps and darknesses of self—and to feed on it alone. Like as to power from electricity of unknown voltage; to consume foods of unknown matter. To bathe in lights of foreign stars. Is it different to be unmade, than to be made so changed as to be unknowable to oneself?—he wondered, and his mind wove among these thoughts and his gaze flicked into near and far distances and he listened to the westward cant of road, and the muted hollow tread of their collective step, until Koma spoke.

"Why two years?" He had advanced a few strides out of their walking rhythm and now was in Hussar's ear. Close.

"Pardon?"

"Two years. Why only two years, Oxbridge?" said Koma. "Who is it goes to Cambridge . . . ?" he said, and trailed off in lighting a cigarette. It was an action almost upon Hussar's shoulder: any closer he thought—and he'd be smoking it from his own eustachian tube.

". . . throws-in at two years. Says: 'Right!—that was good, but I've got the itch.'"

His English was fluid and Britished: jocular and flavored with milked-tea and bitters—but still there were the large West African over-round vowels, and the occasion of a hard consonant landing. Hussar glanced at him and his satin black face, his glistening rivulets, and the middle finger of his smoking hand which pushed endlessly at the slipping bridge of his glasses.

"I wouldn't do that," said Hussar.

"What is that?—press your credentials?" said Koma.

"Smoke," said Hussar.

"You are worried for my health?—that is kind. Or, perhaps you imagine the RUF sitting in the brush listening for lighter strikes? They'll see my smoke across Kangari and mistake it for call to arms?"

"No," said Hussar. "The smell. We now have an enemy in yet a third sense. Now our safe passage is called to question even where we have been."

Koma smiled back at his NPRC guard: "Am I calling to question your safe passage?"

"No, sir," said the guard.

"Does my smoking make enemy of a third sense?" said Koma.

"Sir?"

"You see—I may smoke," said Koma to Hussar. "He does not share your view. Besides—did not your Van Der Boor say your gunship had already flown our route this morning? And the truck—which must have been pleasant to ride in—'broke trail'—all to the end of our 'safe passage?' You said as much; *you* said this." Hussar looked at him, and Koma grinned back with a corrupted glee. "Two years!" said Koma, now with a vigorous animation: "Two years? It boggles . . . *boggles*?—it is boggles?—yes, boggles; it boggles the mind: two years. I've never heard of it at Birmingham—but Cambridge? Or, perhaps you left to go to Oxford?—did you leave to go to Oxford?"

Hussar looked at him.

"But you did not leave to go to Oxford. What sort of university did you go to from Cambridge—what middling thing would do?"

"Life intervenes," said Hussar.

"And providence, also. But you wanted brass on your collars, right? You wanted long guns and some equatorial hair pulling, right? Some piece of native-going, right?—you left there to come here. Right? Or, perhaps Cambridge was just hard. Was it hard? Cambridge?"

Hussar smiled.

"Is it not true?—you left for this: hiking through rainforest of oil palms and bathwater air?"

"It is not."

"To go wear pins and armbands, then—to be a soldier?"

"No."

"You did not leave to become a soldier?"

"You are persistent. It would be better that we were quiet," said Hussar.

"Where are you from then that you go to Cambridge so blithely?"

"I am not the General's brother," said Hussar.

"Indeed you are not. Where from?"

"I think it concerns you more than it does me, Mr. Koma."

"You may call me, Minister," said Koma. "Where from?"

Hussar watched the ground beneath their step. "You have already been told."

"I want you to tell me. Where from?" "Where from?" "H, u, s, a, r?"

"Two 'S's."

"What is one 'S'?"

"Further east."

"H, u, s, s, a, r?—like the cavalry soldier? This is your surname?"

"Yes."

"At birth?"

"Yes."

"The Christian name is—what? What goes with 'Hussar'?"

"You may call me Marek."

"Marek Hussar? Where is he from: Marek Hussar? Where are your people from—that send you so easily to Cambridge?"

Hussar looked at Koma.

"Your grandfather, then. Your grandfather: where was he from? Where was he born?"

"Danzig," said Hussar.

"Tihun," said Koma, "of Bonthe District—that is where my people are from. My grandfather was Paramount Chief." Koma stepped back from Hussar and straightened his shoulders. "My father, too—he is also Paramount Chief. What is your father?"

Hussar looked at Koma.

"There are thirty of us: of his nine wives," said Koma, and grinned proudly.

"A Koma is a many-mothered thing," said Hussar.

"Nine wives is a love bed of many appetites, and nursery of many hands."

"That is an old Birmingham wisdom?"

"He despises what he needs; she despises what she must ask for. Better then to have all things in abundance," said Koma.

"Clearly, the cure of all droughts is deluge."

"And why not?—and why should they not eat cake?"

Hussar cleared his brow with his knuckle and dried his fingers with a flick against the earth. "Those that have it," he said.

"And why should they not want it, that don't?"

"Perhaps it lacks nutrition."

"You should not be so simple: we all are fed on our aspirations, or we starve on them. —I will show you, Oxbridge," said Koma. "Have some cake," he said. He edged closely in to Hussar's side and dropped a stone into his sweated palm. Hussar clutched it between his fingers and held it out to see: a rough clear yellow stone the size of his fingertip: a yellow diamond.

"What is this?" said Hussar.

"What a company you are: a Kuranko chieftain so broken he cannot stand to salute, and a Prussian gunman too blind to see what he holds in his own hand. You know what it is," said Koma.

Hussar held it closely once more: a chunk of amber, but more pale—an ingot of honey, lightly tumbled. "It is quite beautiful," said Hussar, and reached to hand it back to Koma.

"You keep it," said Koma.

"I cannot."

"You must," said Koma, "because I will not take it back. I don't want it—I have them like pocket lint."

"And you give them like jellybeans," said Hussar.

"I do not. Does he have one?" said Koma, and gestured toward the soldier with his chin. "Does Koning have one?—your Coevorden?

No, they do not. It is for you, Oxbridge. You don't want it, throw it in the dirt," said Koma. He adjusted his slipping glasses, and toss his cigarette against the ground. And Hussar stopped to fetch it. He rubbed it out and collected it, and he scoured the ground where it had been with his boot.

"You're compulsive. Do we not leave tracks?—why do you bother?" said Koma.

"We do," said Hussar, returning to the march. "But they at least, are more difficult to read for time."

Koma immediately lighted another cigarette, and rubbed at his shade of mustache: "If only I'd some poppy seeds," said Koma, and paused. And then broke into a spitting guffaw that grew twice before it faded. Hussar watched it roll up the hillsides and along their road: a weather front turning, coarse and rounded.

They walked in silence some time after this.

The buckles of gun straps tapped against rifle butts, or knocked spare magazines. The forefoot of boots clapped softly against the road. Belt leather creaked with gear-weight and motion. Packs slipped and shifted and were called ceaselessly to the ground. Canteens slapped with fluid irregular rhythms. Canvas touched and whispered. They sighed when they cleared their brow in the palm of their hand. The jungle whistled and clicked. It struck against wood in calls of patterns, and fell through heavy frond boughs. It sang with the work-song of species. And each pulse of air rumbled in sinuses between breath-clouded ears.

But for Koma. He carried no gear, or supplies of water. His linen cloth brushed far beneath his footfalls. He sounded only of the draw, and soft exhale of smoke.

"Give us a bit of space, could you," said Koma, to the soldier after a time. "A bit of space, would you," said Koma, with a show of his hand, until the guard had slowed to a position some distance behind. "The General will make a good president, don't you think?"

He had once more closed on Hussar, and walked confidentially at his shoulder.

"I didn't know you were lacking one," said Hussar.

"Oh, we are not," said Koma. His glasses had once again slipped to the middle of his nose, and he looked over them at Hussar. "But these things change. —How long do you think you will be in Sierra Leone?" he said, after a lapse. "Have you been to our beaches?—you should see our beaches, they are quite lovely."

Hussar looked at the ground, and the swinging toe of his boots where they punched into frame.

"It is good to have friends," said Koma. "It is good to have friends where one is. Don't you think? Able, useful friends . . . The General would be a useful friend. I might be a useful friend," said Koma—"A very able, friend," said Koma, and followed it with a long and portentous silence. "I have many friends," he said. "I find it very useful to have friends of many types, and places. What do you think?—Oxbridge."

Hussar lifted a brow at Koma, and turned to check the NPRC detail straggling behind: who raised his beret to clear his brow with his sleeve and changed his rifle from one shoulder to the next, and watched them closely from his distance.

"Strasser is a friend," said Koma, "and Koning, too, of course."

"And De Haas," said Hussar.

"They are very good friends. It is lovely to have such good friends. I know many people, Oxbridge. I have many friends. Charles Taylor: I know him. He is a friend."

Now Hussar looked hard at Koma, and for a long time. "Is he friends with the General, too?"

"Some cannot be friends of every occasion," said Koma.

"The poison of Sierra Leone—"

"Yes," said Koma, and smiled. "He is a friend."

"And the goblin prince, Foday Sankoh—I suppose you are chums as well."

Koma flicked his spent cigarette to the roadside then, and lighted another. And Hussar made no move to fetch it. "I mean to have my cake," said Koma.

And again he fell quiet.

Koma removed his glasses and cleared his brow and the bridge of his nose in his sleeve. He wrung the top of his head with his palms and wiped them in the breast of his coat. He tightened and adjusted his tie before stealing a glance at the guard. And he moved close to Hussar once more.

"What do you like, Oxbridge?" said Koma.

Hussar looked at the road.

"Pussy is tired, don't you think," said Koma.

Hussar looked up and to a near distance where all the botany of Kangari, handsome and rude, swept up upon the roadside.

"I say it is tired," said Koma. "Pussy is overrated, wouldn't you say?"

"It is an expensive habit," said Hussar, "but I'd never thought to complain about the high."

"Context is everything, Oxbridge. Maybe a difference would make it better," said Koma.

6.

Koma was plumb from the hips to the crown of his head; exaggeratedly upright, mostly. It was the biological bombast of thin young black men—geometric virility; the aggression-state of penguin fluff. In Africa it was now a familiar curiosity to Hussar: because in white men it is not so—it is no resting shape, no nature pose; it is always conscious, it is never meaningless; it is always a confrontation. One rises to it or one leaves it, but one does not converse with it. But now the cake talk was out of him, and the draftsman's line as well, and his shoulders had rolled slowly into the angles that drew the distance to his smoking hand. Koma had not spoken for some time. And Hussar took relief in it. When last he had, Hussar had looked at him. He'd had no intention for the look but spontaneous expression. He'd not wished it to be flanged or sharp, but he'd felt something stony in it nonetheless; something taut and immobile. And now they walked in merciful and reticent quiet. Hussar heard their sound of walking and of Koma's knuckle tapping from time to time on his cigarette; and Hussar wondered what Koma heard. Did he hear footfalls or clothes, their canteens or the nervous strain of the guard relegated to the backseat of their transit; the tapping of his own finger against the paper of his own tobacco? Hussar glanced at him walking a few paces abreast, and thought not. The sound of Koma's world was one of his own grinding machinery, thought Hussar. The sensory stirrings of his landscape were produced from within.

The layered high cloud of morning was pressing over Kangari now. It had thickened and colored, and was no longer made of sky, but ash. It was not yet directly overtop, but strained upward, rasp-tendriled and sparking thunderless lightning. And Hussar thought they should hurry. He wanted to draw in the guard and to tell Koma they must pick up their pace—that it would rain. But he was loath to break the silence, and so Koma spoke instead.

"H, u, s, s, a, r?" said Koma. "Is that right? Do I spell that correctly? And you are from Danzig?"

"I am not from Danzig," said Hussar.

"Of course you are—you are from Danzig. You said that you were from Danzig.

"Your people . . . from Danzig.

"I am from Bonthe: you are from Danzig.

"Your name is spelled with the two 'S's—yes?—the two 'S's; and you are from Danzig. Yes, Danzig. You will call it what you like, but in London we have these—oh, yes. Oh, yes, we do—they come for work: we have them. They sit at jobsites on lunchpails, or make deliveries—*if they can read*—or they clear tables at restaurants they cannot serve: or they hide in dark pubs like roaches after spilt beer. Yes, yes, yes. I know you, Hussar with two 'S's. Call it what you will: call it Danzig. It is Poland—your Danzig. Poland. The Hungarian has one 'S'—right Hussar?—right?—this is right. One 'S': you have two 'S's—two: this is the Polish. *You* are a fucking Polack—with your Polack name, from your Polack town—did you think I wouldn't know: come to Sierra Leone as you do in London—just as you do in London—to take of the deserving and darken the streets. Yes. Yes, I know you Polack: like a Freetown vagrant. Yes. See. See there . . ." said Koma, and pointed as they approached a corpse in the low roadside scruff. It wore bright and festive orange floral print, and jerked with the tugs of two vultures presently at work upon it. "Yes. See there, Polack?" said Koma, and waved to the guard many paces behind. "Hurry, you!

Come, mule!" said Koma to the guard. "Your rifle," said Koma to the soldier when he arrived a-trot: "Your rifle!" And the soldier gave it him. Koma stare at the trigger assembly until the guard reached to show him the safety: "Back, mule!" said Koma. He removed the safety and did not seat the rifle in his shoulder, and squeezed, and it bucked loosely and spat three rounds at the birds; and one leapt heavily onto the air and took flight, while the other worked its great wings to beat the ground and tripped and skittered against the corpse; and Koma fired again and the rifle jumped in his hands and fed out five rounds in a burst, and the bird became still. "You see, Polack. I will show you," said Koma. "Hold this," he said to the guard, and handed back the rifle. "Give me your blade," he said. And the soldier drew the machete from his pack and gave it him. "You will see, Polack," said Koma, and moved swiftly to the bird, and took a wing from the shoulder in a few ragged strokes. "You will see." And then he dropped the blade several times to take the other. At their roots where he clasped them, they were mudded and glistening black, and their feathers flayed by the knife, and they drug the ground behind him.

"What is this?" said Hussar.

"These are your wings, Polack. A Polish Hussar must have his Polack wings—it is their difference." His eyes were bare and wild, and his glasses lay in the dirt beside the wet knife.

"What would you do with these?" said Hussar.

"You shall wear them: wearing is their purpose. The Polish Hussar must have his wings."

"I will not wear these," said Hussar.

"Oh you will though! Oh, you will," said Koma, and snatched back the rifle from the guard. "It is my promise. Polack. On my honor you will. Let it be your final act of Sierra Leone if you wish—but you shall. –Fix them in his pack," said Koma to the guard who stood motionless. "Move," said Koma. "In the sides of his pack. Do it!"

The soldier fitted the wings in the straps and buckles of the sides of Hussar's pack, and the soldier tightened them against the weight, and looked at Koma—who said nothing, but lighted a cigarette and swung the rifle idly across them. So he fitted them more deeply and more tightly still. And turned once more to Koma. But now Hussar resumed their march. And Koma collected his glasses. And the soldier collected his knife, and followed behind.

7.

When it rained, it rained with impossible violence. They had walked a duration Hussar no longer measured—himself, and Koma in some armed middle distance, and the NPRC detail drifting at the hinges of perception, and it had opened upon them. It rained with malice. The road dissolved beneath two inches standing spray. The objects of the world bent beneath a glazing rebound. Became distant. Indiscernible. And were taken whole by noise. And from within this noise Hussar took measured, cautious steps along the slippery laterite road. He canted his head so that his mouth was clear and the waters parted over his brow and coursed from the tip of his nose, and so with his eyes cast at the earth just so, he might briefly see. It occurred to him then, he did not want to be in Africa. Breathing through his mouth so he didn't drown on rain, blinking and squinting into a halo of sight: a half-meter of road raised in a moment of strobe light, a rolling stalagmite boil frozen in glass—and Hussar thought, he didn't want to be in Africa. Didn't need to be. Punched the card. Odd pebbles of rain struck at him, tapped heavily at his back where he thought Koma's bullet might enter, above the kidneys or between shoulder blades, where the muscle fixed in stony knots. They burned, like their own preemptive wound. He didn't want to be in Africa: it rose in him suddenly, with a smile so broad it nearly turned to laughter—little stifled drowning snorts of laughter—little choking winged sobs of laughter. It was hilariously funny, just now, waiting to feel a shot he may never hear, treading along the greasy floor of a porous deep, stroking moist angles of sidearm, fingering the slick curve of trigger—listening, for the shot he might return.

The mind pairs down in simple wordless ways. Not to mortars and munitions per se, but the direct antipathy of arms. The body breathes small, vanishing, full-body breaths. Arteries flare like nostrils. The heart drums out low formless rollings of mallet and toms; rings sympathetic faint perturbations of snare. The *corpus animus* hovers at an odd suspension; stands an inch off the floor; jags between the chemistries of certainty and the chemistries of doubt; claws at the pulse of the mind of the firearm. One can acclimate to these signs and seize them, like the closing blackness of asphyxiation or the faltering swoon of blood loss—one can know them and grasp them by their coils, but they wait just the same. Even the practiced hand may slip.

He thought again of snow. A book he'd read opened with ice, and this opening came to mind. He saw snow collecting in the green gutters of night-quiet eves, and like this ice of the book, it was foreign to the present as speculative nature—a fiction spoken in fray tenders to a cloven page of a once mythological time. He thought this. And then he came upon Kamadugu in the road.

Kamadugu was close when he saw him—when he was revealed to Hussar. He emerged from the rain and was close enough to touch. Arms crossed, waiting in the road. Carried his woven shoes. His unbowed sun-toughed face. He did not blink or squint. He did not gasp through his mouth. He was something of bark and shadow-wet stone. And Hussar thought he looked grown from the spot—locked knees and folded arms: thought the idea spoke some furtive truth. He looked at Hussar's face. He looked past him into the rain. He turned and walked before him. And Hussar followed to the side. Kamadugu could see in this rain, he imagined, could make fire here.

He could make fire here.

Hussar followed him, sometimes in form, sometimes in contour, often as the weight-shade beyond a frosted pane. Sometimes he came upon him stopped and looking; back across their path and him: couldn't he make fire here?

As they approached Pujehun they had not seen Koma or his detail for some time. But Kamadugu had seemed to sense them in his backward looking, and Hussar believed this sense. It was the truck, however—its stationary haunches lunging at him from the rain—and the voice of James Ngolo Vonjoe, and nothing of Kamadugu, that marked their arrival in Pujehun.

"What has happened upon the road?" came his voice. "What is this matter of your pack?" said James Ngolo Vonjoe, and then he too appeared beside the truck. He emerged from within the heavy white-grey noise of rain and he shouted over the noise of rain, and beside him in the rain, stood a small boy, and he held the boy by his hand.

"What has happened to your pack, Marek Hussar?" said James Ngolo Vonjoe, and Kamadugu stepped close and spoke to him, and Hussar heard they were speaking by the gestures of Kamadugu, and James Ngolo Vonjoe, by his eyes.

"Van Der Boor cursed him when he left to fetch you," said James Ngolo Vonjoe. He stepped forward so as to be heard, and Hussar watched the boy stare against the ground.

"He was not sent?" said Hussar.

"No," said James Ngolo Vonjoe, "he left in the rain, and Van Der Boor cursed him. He waits at the mission for you. Kamadugu will take you there to see him. I will await the minister here."

Hussar followed along a footpath stream away from the road and to the form of a building which rose in blue and white pastels, from the plot of rainfall where it stood alone. Van Der Boor crouched upon a small step of porch—Hussar thought it was industrial pallet—and beneath a roof in steel sheet, and when he saw them he stood to receive them. "Mouse bring da cat," said Van Der Boor. "Christ, mên! What is this shit?" said Van Der Boor.

The steel eves rang loudly, but for a moment Hussar was not swimming, he was not gasping or diving, the rain was not striking against his ears or head or shoulders. He had stepped from the tank. And just where the water rushed from the roof into the earth beside the porch, Hussar saw a cache of weapons piled in the rinse.

"Who's the boy?" said Hussar.

"We didn't finish the village," said Van Der Boor. "Straight-away been pinched up here," he said, and motioned with his rifle toward the door. "Inside, a priest, a man, and what might have been woman, right. Decapitated—that priest; you'll see."

"What are the weapons?"

"Twelve boys. Yeah, mên, they're inside sleeping it off, mên— lousy with drug and wine. Heroin? Opium? I didn't ask, right. They're sleeping it off. Ja? We took der shit, mên," said Van Der Boor, and gestured to the weapons standing in the runoff.

"Who's the boy?" said Hussar.

"Was on the porch when we come up. Sittin' right here," said Van Der Boor, and pointed to where the rain crashed over the step-edge. "Right 'ere, mên. Says to Vonjoe—he says, 'the boys were here when he came back,' he says. Tells Vonjoe this, and not a word since."

Inside it is dark. It is stained and it is disheveled. He cannot see all the features of the room, but he can see where the back wall is treated with new and foreign paint. He cannot see all twelve of the boys, but he can see the modest furnishings overturned, and these bodies he can see—he can see in their repose: four or six or eight. And the one: distinctly small and near the door. He can see his eyes open, and he can see them see him, standing in the light of the doorway. And he can see them see the wings Koma gave him.

VIII.

November 1969, Teo Macero rests in a control room lighted to a temperate of nicotine stain. The console reaches before him, illuminated dials speaking volume units, backlit swiveling eyelash needles. He wears a pair of glasses for a crown and a striped tie under an unbuttoned broadcloth collar. He plays a desk of graduated rotary knobs and lays his chin heavily against his palm and stares out the window into Studio B—it's a control room, like NASA, like a nuclear power station, he thinks; they have military-grade pots and buses: they have windows and monitors and gauges, too—but they chase what they make; while he catches it—an eavesdropping Lord-as-editor, he thinks. A potent Lord. A present Lord. He thinks—that Lord of the Ark could be like this: that Lord with his radio chair. He presses the intercom.

"Ok. Is this going to be part two?" he says.

"It's gonna be part nine! What difference does it make, mother-fucka," comes the growl-and-gravel undertaker's whisper—comes Miles Davis, like hiss in the line.

"Alright, alright. Here we go—standby. This is part something..."

And then. Slowly. Sitar shimmers like dancing chimes, . . . like bead curtain. Tabla lights candles in cupped hands, lays dishes, sets places. Bass and electric piano announce the theme: it is a fugue-waltz in three minor chords. Billy Cobham rolls a carnival snare into a vicious onslaught—kicks open the deadbolt door. And there,

Miles enters with his Gabriel horn, his folded shoulders and prayer-bent elbows, and issues a bi-form mournful cry: he is a Pied Piper of mayhem and vengeance, and they move dutifully in the heat of his step. Bennie Maupin lurks here, on bass clarinet, behind, beneath, between him, in warm foot-falls and unlighted corners: in black silk and brass knuckles, and crouches, touches the ceiling with the draw of every breath.

Open water is a house where the floor and ceiling move—sometimes toward each other, sometimes away. Marek Hussar noticed Freddie Oslo notice this over the music. And as they crossed the last wake-traces of ferries and as the lights of container ships cooled and tightened upon the water, and as the rolling of The Solent deepened by octaves, as they crossed into the channel mouth. Hussar observed this in him, where Oslo finally forgave the darkness behind and the sad little tide-swallowed boat, for the uncertain present. For the darkness to hand. It was "Corrado" played over boat speakers. It played above the stage of Hussar's imagining, and over the angry lope of unused horsepowers, and over Freddie Oslo in wet shoes and pant-cuffs turned back and lamenting.

The waters were a condensate of night for Hussar. Deep night, made dense and thick to a surface mere dark licked and worried as the touch of wind. And this is what the boat rode—the immiscible weight-planes of night. The gauges glow like the dials of Macero's console: speaking of knots and prop trims and fuel rates and oil pressures—they moved in concert with the throttles, and the engines spoke their truth to the waters. Rose. They rose. They sang it. And Miles played to this and the growing rush of air, until they were on plane and the boat hopped from crest to crest, skipped and lifted and landed. The sea-cloud was dim pearls on velvet. As though radiating some inner light: depleting some daylight charge of sun. Beneath them the boat cleaved and crashed, and they were snapped and buffeted by a terrific velocity of air, and the engines raged high-throttle abandon between the sea and night sky. The noise clapped over their ears, Oslo bore into his seat, quiet and cold. Hussar checked navigation and readied night vision goggles at the helm. He pointed the wheel little at a time north toward the Strait of Dover, and with each nudge of throttle, into thundering ecstatic expression. And for these hours Freddie Oslo was a shivering silence.

2.

"What shall I do for clothes?" said Freddie Oslo.

They had entered the harbor port of Zeebrugge after 0100 in the morning. They'd trolled the Grey Lady among the concrete fortifications and container ships and the great blue loading cranes the look of feeding sauropods in yellow lamplight. In the marina the powerboat had been moored. And the tram had been thirty minutes to their hotel in Blankenberge.

"I'll provide whatever you require," said Hussar.

Hussar checked them in to a presidential suite of rooms which looked from the tenth floor to the sea, and he'd slept gratefully into the private, listening stillness of late morning. There were breakfasts ordered in, with orange juice and coffee.

"Ours is a three bedroom suite?" said Oslo.

Fresh napkins and enameled trays. A living room, dining room, and kitchen. Wide sun terrace behind a sliding glass door. In the afternoon they walked the long, deep strand of Blankenberge: a soft beach plane patterned along by foot of man and wind, and the insistent licking of the North Sea.

"The presidential suite comes as two or three bedrooms," said Hussar.

"Are you expecting someone, Mr. Lanze?" said Oslo.

There were winds: fourteen knots, ten degrees Celsius off the water. Apartment blocks strung the beach as a seawall in day-rate rooms. They lined the visible coast, in a slow, straight crescent and a sky in grey cotton wool. Hussar thought it was a resort town from the black sea clapped at the Belgian coast—a turn of fresh-painted Sovio-Croat merry-making: with its flying saucer, fin de siècle, Russo-futurist pier—run like a bit of Stalinist memorial into the foaming break-tide—and the tight, straight scowl of buildings crowded one to the next in a glowering unison over aspirational bathing huts, and be-coated wanderers, and all the frigid respite of a breath-stealing surf. Landward Blankenberge was row houses, Frankish and charmed. But here, from the sea, it was a cold, pale, overcast and drizzling Rio de Janeiro.

"I am not," said Hussar.

"We are two. What purpose then for the third room?"

"It adjoins the suite, monsieur."

They walked the pier and looked into the surf. And once Freddie Oslo's chill of the night before threatened return, they took a table at the window of the bistro over the water.

"Wherever I go it is the same: always spittle on the glass," said Oslo, and rest his elbows on the table. "Why have you brought me to Belgium, Mr. Lanze?"

"Because you are on holiday, Monsieur Oslo."

"And why then are we in Blankenberge?"

"Blankenberge is a *holiday* town."

"Is it a bit between seasons?"

"To the contrary, it is their third-busiest of the year."

"Is it?" said Oslo.

"It is. Also, there is something to collect in Zeebrugge."

"When is that?"

"In a few days."

"Shall that be my holiday, then: an errand and a waiting?"

"It shall."

"You presented papers at the hotel, Mr. Lanze."

"I did."

"Were they in my name?"

"They were not," said Hussar, and slipped a business card from his coat, and across the table to Oslo. "This is your card, monsieur. As you will see your name is clearly marked. I suggest you keep it for your memory."

"This is my card?"

"Indeed it is."

"And this is my name?"

"For now, it seems so."

"And you are?"

"I am your trusted valet, monsieur," said Hussar.

"Met but a few short hours ago, and already a trusted valet?"

"Indeed so."

"I think you are not my valet."

"Of course, I think you are right."

"I am tired, Mr. Lanze: tired and quite sore."

"But you have slept in."

"All the same."

"Well, it is with all due apology, then, that you are checked into the presidential rooms of the Beach Palace Hotel of Blankenberge, Belgium, monsieur. Perhaps that will mollify your aching bottom," said Hussar.

Oslo turned from the windows to him and squinted tightly. "You are an unusual valet who talks this way."

"I am," said Hussar.

Their drinks had just come, and were yet to be touched. Oslo wore his handsome and tieless suit, now coarse with wrinkles. His manicured stubble was neglected and in need of keeping. The exterior wall was a round of plate glass, and they sat at a table beside it with their coats upon their chairs, and Oslo leant strongly into his place setting and the knots of his palms. They sat and watched the sea and cloud join and part, begin to threaten darkly, and then shift: lovers in their dance of interest, the sea and sky—thought Hussar. He'd wanted to put Oslo on the beach. A Blankenberge landing. He'd always wanted to put him on the beach—drop him in the night surf to wait in a bathing hut for his return, he'd even brought a wet suit for the purpose. But he'd have had to put him in the water at his own height, and he saw that he would drown. He'd go into the water up to his hair product and it would snatch the air from his lungs in a single smothering blow and his heart would draw that sharp, stunned, protracted thought-blinding pause, and his scrotum would wad up in his neck, and he'd be a dead mammal in neoprene knocking about under the boat. Any closer in the dark, and surely he'd launch the fifty-foot Marauder in the sand: the introduction of a second complication for the tooth-chattering Gaul in his knitted cap and borrowed coat blinking at Belgium in the throes of moving night, seemed a complication too far.

"Are you an enthusiast for music?" said Hussar.

"I'm sorry? I don't know," said Oslo, and shook his head distractedly.

"Because it occurred to me last night that you were not an enthusiast for music. Do you enjoy music, Monsieur Oslo?"

"Is this important, Mr. Lanze?"

"Is it not?"

"I don't know. Yes."

"A Frenchman ambivalent to music?—is this possible? This is an Italian ambivalent to Ferragamo loafers and Scaglietti coachwork—this is fantasy."

"I suppose," said Oslo, and took wine to forestall the question.

"It is jazz-fusion that you do not like?"

"I don't know, Mr. Lanze."

"What do you enjoy, then?"

"Baroque, I suppose. Pre-classical. Mostly. Liturgical music," said Oslo.

"There you are, monsieur! Baroque indeed. That is no learned taste, monsieur: that comes of its own or it comes not at all. You have a private center in the end." Hussar toasted him and they drank, though Oslo, with cool reluctance.

"Something is not right, Mr. Lanze."

"That I am not your valet?—we shan't tell anyone, Monsieur Oslo."

"That you are not a driver, Mr. Lanze. That you are not an ordinary security man—surely you cannot be."

"Not even for your friend; for your Simone Helena?"

"Not even for Simone Helena, I don't think. Not unless I wholly misunderstand what they do and how they are made."

Hussar smiled.

"I don't think you are an ordinary security man."

"Anyone may do security, Monsieur Oslo. It is only a matter of dimension of the occasion, and of fee."

"I think that is not correct. I think that you are not the common type, and I think this seems an extra-ordinary effort for the holiday-making of an expatriated Frenchman in structured products."

"Perhaps you are in some measure of legal jeopardy, Monsieur Oslo. Could that be?"

Oslo turned again to the window and the turbid sea snapping at the pilings beneath him.

"It strikes me your welfare is a matter of grave concern. An extra-ordinary concern, perhaps."

"Could that be?" said Oslo.

"The facts, as you observe them, support it."

"I will need some clothes," said Oslo, and hunched upon the table and played at the stem of his glass. "Mr. Lanze," said Oslo after a pause. "You imagine that I am a fool, and a coward."

They looked at one another then. And Hussar noticed the relative quiet of the bistro. It was sparsely filled at that chilled and damp constitution of day. It was not waxing with boisterous conversation or scraping forks or searing skillets or whistling tappets. The touch of the rain against the glass was audible between them. And even Oslo handling his stemware. The short squeaks of his cold dry thumb.

"Surely, I do not," said Hussar. "But is it true?"

IX.

The Royal Portals mark the western face of the cathedral of Chartres. It is the grand façade of the cathedral and it is marked by the rose window and two grand spires. But however grand it may be, the façade of Chartres is asymmetrical, and it was a fact that Freddie Oslo had always struggled to understand: the two grand spires are not the same. They are not the same height. They are not the same shape. And they are not the same style. Indeed, the architecture beneath them is not the same either, but this is pure misdemeanor beside the disparity between the spires— the so-called 'Flamboyant' and higher northern gothic spire, and the 'Plain' southern spire, so-called for its relatively lower, simpler, pyramidal architectural form. And yet, nevertheless, they are the two disparate pieces of one body. They are the contra-comparative organs of one compositional whole. Later he would come to know that the cathedral had burned and burned and burned, and burned. Over and again, and over, it had burned. So that the spires had grown like oddly-kept toenails; like termite heaps born out of sequence; stalagmite pillars under the pap of separate calcium drips. There they stood, at once in time and yet they were from distinct chronological locations. Staggered and staggering elevatory stair-steps of construction and ruin; until at last in 1506—it is said—the northern was destroyed by strike of lightning. A decisive transfiguration, which by the ceaseless touch of man-hands clawing and shaping and moving—in 1513 arrived in its present condition: that condition of an ambitious excess—that of a compensatory rejoinder in labor, to the loss, and the body it must join. Freddie Oslo experienced this wonder when he went to Chartres. These two themes of the sonata rising from resolution in tension. And he experienced it on the bright winter vacant mid-day he'd passed through the Royal Portals in damp and squeaking shoes, and found himself drawn unthinking, to the path of the entrance to the labyrinth of Chartres.

His shoes had been tight that morning. Wet in the night, and shrunk in the repair of their drying. And now . . . tight. Too tight, perhaps. Another day would tell it. The shrunken shoe. Its shrunken virtue . . . Horseshoes are watertight . . . Is the horseshoe parcel to the horse?—wondered Oslo . . . Removed? . . . And the unshod horse then?—a replenished whole, or a sum reduced? . . . Without foot-gear he may be free, but not labored. The beastly mark: shoes. He cannot be a beast who is unburdened, and he cannot bear a burden who is unshod . . . The nobility of work: a diminishment in service. Paradox . . . And the callus? . . . What is the callus, if not to the labor but to the shoe?—a dissent, a revenge, an objection? . . . And if to the labor?—that callus might be paradox itself: rubbery accretion of the very forces in contradiction . . . And if not the callus, but a boil?— refutation? . . . Fault? . . . A split in the masonry. Yielding. His shoes before the sliding doors. Laid in what passed for sun. Flat and shad-owless. Pouring into the luxury of space and kissing balm upon him and his shoes and their now ever-so-lightly upturned toes. A healing by Apollo; to a conditioning of discomfort, he would discover. Better the naked foot, before the shoe?—with the shoe?—with the addition of shoe made worse in drying? A body part by marriage, made worse for the body: the body now the worse for the marriage. The condi-tions of the body are impossible. He'd said it—'The conditions of the body are impossible,'—out loud then, to cloud-lit shoes and to Lanze reading cross-legged in the lounge, who did not look up. And Oslo did not yet know in that moment the discomfort of his shoes: it was psychic prefiguration in the style of memory.

They'd sat-in the morning—that afternoon, as it was—Lanze at reading and Oslo at the table. With a tenth-floor vantage onto ocean, tumbling white on the lip of beach and of his shoes in the light of the terrace door. In Chartres he had doors like these, but they looked into garden lawn . . . and a hedge for railing. Like the railing there. Just there. From which, if he might fly one thousand feet, he might stand to leap to freedom. And water. Neither horse nor man—but bird or squirrel maybe. Gliding to his doom. Oslo saw the absurd image of the outstretched animal gliding at speed into the North Sea like a golf drive into frothing hazard, and he'd laughed. Loud and surprised, and then with his head into his hands. Lanze had watched him when he'd stopped to breathe—but he'd said nothing. Fool and coward. 'But is it true?' Lanze had said. Later. When the shoes were tight.

They had roared and bounded. Across the Channel. Lanze had blasted a music. As they'd moved among The Solent. Was it The Solent?—he was not at all sure. It was some moody angular dirge, and for all its exotic instrumentation, felt medieval to Oslo. An acid-tinged bugle cry for the onslaught of ghosts and boats. Furious boats. When the music had finished, it was just the fury. Long and frigid. When they approached the harbor in Zeebrugge, Lanze had put him below decks. There the chill would finally ebb, but there, too, he would feel for the first time sincerely ill.

2.

"It's Simone's decision in the end. I just tell her what to do." His eyes made Oslo think of reptiles from documentary film. In motion rather than aspect. He could see the close-up: something rangy and nervous hanging from strange tree barks. The shot zooms to the pupil, which pivots with mechanical precision, here and here and here: moves in endless quick-sharp gestures to take in every visible material thing. And then somewhere somehow, pauses upon the invisible—on the unseen—because this too it sees, or feels, or knows is unseen . . . Or sees is un-seeable. It stares vividly off into a vacancy one knows is not vacant. An occupied vacancy. One senses this among the powers of the reptile, and it frightens some fold of brainstem—some low part which adheres to the blood with electrodes, and can see un-seeable things and speak deep wordless thoughts. It was Oslo's first meeting with Manhattan when Manhattan had said this, in his simple wonderful suit. Oslo coveted it. It was clean and simple, and wonderful. Beautiful cloth, he'd thought: dark as ash. Blue silk lining that peeked at Oslo when he'd lifted his arms. Folded his hands. Adjusted. Close grey hair that had leaned all one way. Collar bar and tie. And glasses slung round his neck on a leash. It was not too expensive to be a banker's suit, but it was too fine, and the dumpy bit of cord for the glasses was not adequately superficial. If he was a banker now, had thought Oslo, that is not as he began. He did not have a banker's bearing or taste. He lacked a banker's pageant and ostentation—a banker after all is an exclusively soft-handed protagonist. He was sturdy and vaguely handsome—in that symmetrical, low-relief American way. And he brought to Oslo's thinking more the image of a work-a-day aristo-crat: an old-money American diplomat of forgotten and uncounted holdings, and a reflexive distain for all things right of the decimal.

Freddie Oslo stood at the back of the lobby when Lanze had checked them in. As instructed. The night manger had collected the passports: "Mademoiselle, qui suis-je, en effet? J'ai réservé la suite. Je suis le valet du monsieur. I booked the suite. I am the valet," said Lanze, with an illustrative compound gesture to Oslo, and their baggage heaped at Lanze's feet. "Et assurez-vous que ce sont let trios chambers, s'il vous plaît." Oslo moved in exhausted reverie when they'd made the tenth floor and shuffled with Lanze into the presi-dential rooms. They were rattan and bent wood and dated soft-luxury trappings—the windows issued the one indigo of pre-dawn becom-ing: but it did not move up and down or to the side or skip or leap or land—whatever its particulars, they were stationary, and for this Oslo was moved in gratitude.

Lanze turned through the rooms, the curtains and cushions and cupboards and drawers: the unused third bedroom, which he checked and re-locked again. Oslo waited in an armchair metrically nodding until he had been directed to bed. "I would like my phone—may I have it?—my electronics?" he'd said, as Lanze closed the door. Oslo had sat at the dining table in the thin light of their morning of after-noon that followed. He'd wiggled his toes in his turned and shrunken shoes at the brasserie of the Blankenberge Pier. Where they both stare at the pensive gloom of sea in weary silence. Until Oslo had excused himself from the table.

Lanze watched from a deep low chair as Oslo stood in rigid raw fabric patterns upon a dais. It was Knokke-Heist next day, north by train. An affluent leisure town and bustling High Street they might have shopped, but Lanze brought them here instead, to a shaded haberdasher in the ground floor of a bright building upon a sunlit apartment square opened to the sea. "We might have stayed here," said Oslo. "Why could we not have stayed here? It is quite pleasant."

"It is the post-aspirational concession you like. Waffle breads. New cloth. Unsoaped dyes; shopping bags of fresh-cut stock. This is what you like."

"And if I do?"

"Mind your claws don't show."

"You are a most peculiar valet."

"We will need three of this cut," said Lanze to the tailor. "Black, white, and grey, I think."

"And blue," said Oslo.

"We shall need four. —And blue," said Lanze.

The tailor measured and marked in silence. He was young, tall and thin—wore a somber black suit and vest: the pencil mustache and oiled hair of a boy raised among aged tastes. He chalked the lapels and the shoulders. —Cuffed pants? No? The lay? Here? Here? Sleeve above the knuckle? Above the thumb? French cuffs, then. Yes? Yes.

"Delivered," said Lanze.

"Of course, monsieur. And when would you have it?"

"Week's end."

"Week's end?—no, no. That cannot be possible."

"Is there a rush fee?"

"If there is nothing before it, of course, monsieur."

"I will double the rush fee, but it must be delivered by week's end. Shirts and ties, socks, et cetera. —And a second pair of the shoes."

"It is per suit—the rush fee, monsieur."

"Yes. Double. Week's end."

The tailor lay the measure over his shoulders and went to the back. "He looks like a mortician," said Oslo.

"He is a mortician," said Lanze, and they both laughed so heartily the tailor was pensive and watchful when he returned.

The new cap toe Oxfords worked with angular sharp-heeled formality. The sky was clear to the corners of the earth, and the brick pavers of the plaza were warm of it. Gulls kited and turned and the ribbon sea rose as a bend of grey-green tarmac joined at the cobbles of their road. Oslo wore a rack-suit of clothes and tie, and socks and sundries, and all his old suit in a paper tote, and he and Lanze moved through the brief, bright valley of apartment glass to the sea.

". . . Post-aspirational? This is what you said? Not, aspirational?"

"Oui."

"And this is what you meant? You meant to say it?"

"Oui."

Oslo was expectant, and he walked beside him toward the snapping flagstands and bathing huts pure white as canvas, and he looked at Lanze expectantly.

"The aspirational want the bag for its contents," said Lanze, indicating the tote with a shoulder. "The post-aspirational want the bag. They have the contents—it's the packaging they want: new crisp packaging. The mood of it . . . Dr. Jekyll—yes? He aspires to the power of Hyde. Mr. Hyde, despite his power, is insatiable. Rapacious as the dragon. Yes? But he is a monster. His means are beyond the pale. Power deforms him. He cannot be clean. Therefore he wants truly, the only thing he cannot have. He wants the condition of Dr.

Jekyll. The naïve beginning. To have his deeds, and yet to be clean of them. To feel once more the sated hunger, that the satiation may finally appease."

"The packaging?"

"Children share this. Uncorrupted by the reason of a thing."

"They are pre-aspirational, then?"

"They are."

"This is your philosophy? Philosophy of him who is not the driver," said Oslo. "Méditations du valet de chambre? And what is power?"

Lanze shuffled his feet and weighed his pockets with his hands.

"There are three," said Lanze. "The power of the politician is that of the reception of trust: he is executor of deferred power. The power of the general is anointment of the deified state: his is to invoke sacrifice and the call to harm. The power of the man—the ungifted power of the one—is the will to do anything."

3.

Nine narrow floors like an apartment house. A kind of beige-grey stone and squinty windows with faux rail molding, Oslo supposed was to convey the airy sense of balconies. Nothing at all to mark it out from the commonest beige-grey buildings of the Mediterranean, but a sterile forecourt of carriageway. Somewhere, a tan and windowless meeting room within, Oslo sat perfunctorily with Yanis and Milos, the deputy ministers of finance. The pair of them wore identical grey and ideologically non-committal suits, and ties that differed merely by pattern. They wore similar month-old haircuts and a common residual placating impatience. Milos wore glasses. But for this they might be the same. The tan walls were hanged with the plaqued and framed likenesses of all the contemporary and historical persons of the Greek Ministry of Finance. They sat in tan chairs at an oak table in disagreeable white-wash, and beneath a low drop ceiling. It was for Oslo, the variety of space that calls to mind an aircraft cabin as refined and unrestricting. Oslo checked his watch. "Shall we wait on the Minister?" Milos and Yanis did not refer to their watches, but appraised Oslo. "I'm happy to describe the structure of the arrangement."

"The re-arrangement," said Yanis.

"The re-structure," said Milos.

"As you put it—you are both, naturally, correct." Oslo brought three folders from his attaché. "The master signatures reside in my file—we will sign these ... These, naturally, are for the two of you, and

for your records. Any residual signatures will, or have been, provided
by the Minister or his office. You are duly endorsed and empowered
to sign in his place here, and on behalf of Greece?"

The pair looked at each other. "We are," said Milos.

"Shall we wait then, or shall I describe the mechanisms of the
instrument to you?"

"You have described these mechanisms thoroughly to the
Minister?" said Yanis.

"Directly," said Oslo.

"He assented to the products and instruments you described?"
said Milos.

"Directly."

"And to Ms. Helena?" said Milos.

"Yes."

"If it is to the Minister's satisfaction, then it is to mine," said
Yanis.

"Mine as well," said Milos. "I for one may forego the sleepy
particulars."

They all smiled at this, and Oslo moved their respective folders before them. He offered them pens and removed and ordered
the papers from his file for signature. Yanis leafed idly through his
papers. Milos watched Oslo place the first section before him.

"What is this?" said Yanis. He'd reached the end of his file and
extracted a magnetic stripe card. He held it before the three of them
and looked curiously at it.

"I don't know. Does it say?" said Oslo.

Milos looked irritably at Yanis. He snatched the card from his
hand and tucked it back into the sleeve of Yanis' folder. And then
Milos returned to Oslo and the papers. "This is the signature line
here, correct?"

. . . Jean-Pierre was four then.

"I don't think that's what the story is about," said Oslo. The halyard knots and snaps played the flagstands in a blank verse of rhythms. Lanze fetched sunglasses from his breast pocket.

"Isn't it?" he'd said.

They'd walked the short distance to the café of the Knokke-Strand, where waiters opened parasols, and where they sat with their shoes and chair legs in the sand, beneath the brown shade of white parasol and drank Belgian wit and the shopping bag folded and chaffed in the wind, and Oslo kept it like noisy hatchling between his feet, and thought of ice cream and they stare off at the same low hill of naked-grey and watery horizon.

"When would I have my electronics again, Mr. Lanze?"

Oslo had thought of Lila by train to Blankenberge, when they returned. They'd stare to sea through the jostling train car, and bright beach of Knokke-Heist, and the day before from the doom-view of the brasserie of the Blankenberge Pier. A picture window onto a living Turner. –Was it Turner? He wasn't at all sure. The sea neared and withdrew: the scalloped and tapered edge of the manifest. Beside him Lanze gazed into his folded hands, and he looked out and saw himself walking alone upon the beach—through this break of dunes—and this—and along this plane here: beneath the blazing sun of a cool day in May, where everything is blind-hot . . . but the air and the grain of land, and the cold touch of surf, and every other thing beyond the veil of senses. He clutched the bag between his feet and it shivered with the quaking train, and wherever he did not see himself on the

beach . . . searching . . . wandering lost and ignorant of what is lost—
of being lost; he saw Lila, and he saw Jean-Pierre. They were behind
this rise, and this, and this—this dune, here. They walked out to the
water. With a pail and a shovel. To wet their feet. To parch the earth
to moisture, in work of play. Just where he could not see—behind
that bathing hut, and those parasols—these impenetrable grasses.
And they smiled to each other the smile of unspoken omission. They
smiled to each other the smile of an expectation, but not a hope. Of
the missing thing—of the missing thing; of being the missing thing
which one cannot forestand to name—for by the word it is given
truths. Truths like volatiles which cannot be put back into solution.
And everywhere at every moment . . . he was passing them . . . and
passing them. And leaving them behind.

"But is it true?" Lanze had said. They had sat there turned to
weather displayed in sweeping glass-faceted panorama. The rain
tapped along the length of it, and played this consonant touch in
semi-audible room-tone. Oslo's thumb squeaked against the stem of
his glass. He rose from the table—"Excuse me," he said. Round the
bar, near the entrance, Oslo circled to the host stand where the doors
stood oddly ajar; opened onto the boardwalk length of the pier. The
host stood near them and looked out through them and received
the treble of cool and turbulent airs. He polished stemware from a
cart. Oslo thought he used a napkin reborn in service. He asked for
directions to the facilities, and when he received them, he asked for
a house phone: "Excusez-moi, mais y a-t-il aussi un téléphone fixe
que je pourrais utiliser?"

"You do not have phones, monsieur?"

"At the hotel—so stupid—and my companion, has no charge: we
are the blind leading the blind," said Oslo.

"It must be within Belgium, monsieur."

"I'm afraid it is not. I would reverse the charges, but I must make the call." Oslo followed the host with his glass and his cloth and his doubtful look to a service near the kitchen. "Merci," said Oslo. "Merci."

4.

Oslo's tailoring had arrived from Knokke-Heist. The following day Lanze received a call on his phone late morning, and by afternoon he'd collected their passports and checked them from their hotel, and they'd passed once more by train to Zeebrugge, and stood with their bags and all their things on a paint-striped pavement unbounded but for the cleft of portside. Distant gantries loomed above the water. Before them, whole kilometers of automobiles lined in regimental file. And between, a great blue vessel like an office block toppled and windowless—and berthed harbor-side under stays. 'A vaguely watertight carpark with a rudder and a weathervane'—'A roll-on, roll-off,' Lanze had said.

A silver BMW sedan had been pulled aside, and they waited beside the car with their things in this clearing. A man in hardhat and reflective poncho stooped over the car. Oslo wondered what might fall on him from here. He marked a clipboard with the model and VIN plate numbers and mileage. Oslo supposed he was from clearance. And when he'd finished Lanze had removed his jacket and lain it carefully folded on his bag, and made him wait as he'd scrutinized the fenders and doors and engine bay and wheel arches and peered under every corner of the car and tested the rebound of each spring with a thoughtful shove. When Lanze freed him he'd paced off muttering and shaking his head. "What is this?" asked Oslo, when he'd gone.

"It is my car," said Lanze.

Dean Denton was an early late-middle-age youth. He wore heavy black-frame glasses with smoked blue lenses and a perfectly knotted bowtie. He was always shaven clean to an oval alabaster palette. He featured dark, heavy clothes, and a three-quarter-length topcoat he seemed always to possess. And were he not English, it would be an incongruous detail that however he might have preferred his hair, nevertheless, he wore it always vaguely unwashed and with that look of recent sleeping. Denton had received him from Heathrow in precisely this condition, and during Oslo's exploratory London stay, he would serve as minder and persistent companion. The occasion he was to be first introduced to Manhattan, Denton fetched him from his suite at The Lanesborough. They walked Knightsbridge with Helena to The Rosebery at the Mandarin Oriental, for the meeting. Denton loitered behind in company of Helena, and bore a kind of stooped and surreptitious deference. The Rosebery was high and bright. The Mandarin itself struck Oslo as crisp and unfussy, and he'd mentioned it to Helena—'I might have stayed here,' he'd said. 'What's the trouble with The Lanesborough?' she'd said. 'It's wonderful, if also somewhat stuffy.' 'And here I'd thought it was a perfect match,' she'd said, and cast a glance at Denton, at the next table. 'Freddie Oslo—somewhat unstuffy for the Mandarin from here on,' she'd said. They'd smiled over his gracelessness and had a tea of cordials and cocktail infusions into which Manhattan never appeared.

There was some stroll about the zoo as well—the trio, Denton shuffling in shadow of their shadows. There were rugby tunics, and oversize fizzy drinks and baby trolleys—drinks carriers of baby trolleys—and all the passersby had looked at them, and Helena in her irrepressible evening wear, as though their hired car had spent its fuel of perfume, and they'd been trapped with concession Chardonnay until it had been topped-up. Principally, Oslo had thought about the tiger enclosure—its paths and ramparts like the shabby plank-hewn trenches of the Great War; and that it had been bright for London— and that was his chief memory of the occasion. But he didn't recall if Manhattan had been promised or implied in this, and so it went uncounted.

Second then?—the occasion of the cigar lounge of his hotel—The Lanesborough. A named and heated covered terrace affair, whose name escaped him now. Helena ordered them cognacs and something of the family Montecristo. She had lighted over the Bunsen flame with her hair lifted away like this, and smoked in her long and sincere formal gowned pleasure—and these images overwrote Oslo's every other particular of the evening. To this, Manhattan had also been foretold, but Oslo had not lingered on the omission.

It was later, a cocktail vignette. Another day he could hardly square. There had been early meetings, handshakes and conference room glass. Scrutineering worn as breezy conversation. Up/down votes staged as hallway intercepts: smiling banal introductions, frameless peer visits, seated office chats. Multiple floors—always seemingly up. A brunch. A lunch. Another site. The cocktail hour was instructed—Helena had instructed it. An instructed unstructured formality. Such conceits did not touch Oslo, not really. He was unbothered. But the thread of deceit amused him. He marveled at the structure: which cocktail was required, which was elective— which aperitif; whose. He felt wheeled there as in Denton's pram—or perhaps a furniture dolly, more like. A luxury high-rise. A concierge. An elevator in high-polish panels: he thought of a shark cage; not a chute where one is eaten in a villain's pool, but the frame of aluminum bars through which one pretends to witness in safety. Naked feeding. Below the waterline. High-pile carpets. A corridor of objet d'art. A doorman. A server installing stemware for door prizes—it was newly full wherever one looked away. The venue was glittering and smooth: white marble and electro-plated metals. Denton had drawn his especially non-ironical bowtie for the occasion. He looked proper—comfortable, even. And the thought of Dean Denton at his ease gave Oslo disquiet. Always just there: teetering above his shoulder and beyond the peripheral arc.

There were balcony views. There were accumulated business cards in his pockets; a purposeless trio of euro note coins he played with fingers the way one plays an idle ring of keys; there was a loose thread in his pocket-floor with a proud knotted crown he cloyed between the nails of forefinger and thumb; there were the touches and reaches and handshakes he collected and stored in these pockets, to trade and dispense them later. There was his stemware companion—Denton—the long leaning tulip, and that duly issued stemware: lead crystal or merely fine glass? Denton performed his wilting lean to deliver names and positions into the orbit of his ear: intro– and extro-ductions. Helena moved from some unseen threshold: it was an unlikely feature of her physicality given her perpetual conspicuousness. She approached with words and greetings; she said things into the unused ear, the one unoccupied by Denton; by Denton's words. He smiled appreciatively; he nodded knowingly; he shook his head to invoke repetition. He spoke words which fell promptly into the common darkness. He was clever; his words were clever, whatever they might be: he knew because they won Helena's smiles and won her laughter—they were clever, clever words and she touched his shoulder. One of her words which she gave him was 'Manhattan,'—'Manhattan is here,'—'Manhattan is here,' she said—'Manhattan is there,' she said.

And there he was—or so there was a man to receive the psychic likeness of him. Half the room away, and a clearing between them: someone speaking into the ear of him like as the way Denton and Helena poured into his own: a semi-short grey lean of hair, a pair of reading glasses on a leash, a suit which was not black but void as empty cosmos—he listened like Oslo, but weighted against a hip and folded arms, and he peered across this clearing. He listened and he looked, with that listening furrow, and he watched. He watched Oslo, and Helena spoke into his buffering attentions: 'Manhattan,' she said—'there he is now—perhaps he will meet you,' she said, and Oslo looked at her—to see the lips and eyes and face that went with these words. And when he looked back . . . what was purportedly Manhattan had gone. In a moment, so too had Helena. And in some unmarked interval that followed, when the faces and handshake introductions began again, but sparingly, and fewer, more reserved or more eager, more loudly, followed upon by more disparate talk—it was then that Denton stewarded him along some far hall, into some far room . . . where waited a most handsome woman. She was very happy to see him.

Lanze fueled and then in a stall before the compressor hose, carefully checked and set and rechecked the tire pressures. He did this with a gauge with a dial face, and Oslo imagined he was taking their pulse. Crouched thoughtfully, listening to their heart, reviewing the reading and confirming it once more. The gauge made a biting hiss: a sound that portends an event, a percussion or a carnival whistle, but provided none. Lanze shuffled about like this. Threading stem caps and wiping sooted fingers in a rag. They'd stopped at a used and crowded Total station. A roadside layby with trucks and resting motorcycles, and a view cross the roadway of all the tanks and greasy plumbing of the petroleum commerce of Zeebrugge. Lanze studied the brakes through the wheel spokes and reviewed and grasped the planes of tire tread like melons. Beneath the hood, he turned and lifted caps and dipsticks and investigated belts and hoses and the place-state of every fluid: Oslo was unaware an ordinary automobile had so many. He imagined some must measure the others. He mused about the car while Lanze worked.

"Did you and the clearance official not do this already?"

"That was for damage," said Lanze. "This is for readiness."

Oslo moved to see him. "Is it special?" He moved again. Lanze stooped into the engine bay: dire reverence as body-posture. "Is it not the common type? Not the one of every traffic light in London?"

It's the—what is it called?—The Cellar Lounge, or some such. The Wine Cellar Venue? A cellar in the foundations of The Lanesborough. A barrel-vaulted brick basement in the footings of the hotel. A long table with formal chairs and many place settings—reduced now to four. Tablecloth and folded napkins. Vases and goblets and cut flowers. Lighted candles: they dance in a collective union. The room is absolute silence but for unseen ventilation which rushes with duct-thrum from the bellows of distant organs. Oslo sees himself there now, draws his timepiece from his coat pocket and fastens the strap. It says the time is fourteen minutes after one. This is where he is—this is where Manhattan enters. The door swings briskly. Manhattan moves to a chair not quite opposite. The door falls closed: heavily, with a formidable latch; vault like—thinks Oslo; interrogation-chamber-like—thinks Oslo.

Dean Denton received him from the affections of that far room of the far hall of the luxuriant quarters of the sparkling party. Collected him all up, and delivered him to The Lanesborough. Shared a drink with him at the bar, and shown him to his rooms—and then vanished into whatever type of fog he remitted to in off-hours. Oslo removed his coat and tie and washed his face and flung himself three-quarters onto the bed. One foot holding the floor for reference. His eyes closed: this is where the phone that summoned him had rung: An associate to see you, sir . . . A private room arranged . . . Someone to retrieve you—says the concierge. Outside the room is not Denton, nor staff, but some purpose-made version of a man stuffed through a jacket for the occasion. He's led to the elevator and through passages. Before a heavy oaken door waits something like a twin—if not of the same mother, then the same purpose: a loose tie over an unbuttoned collar and a jacket taut to the shoulders. He's shown this empty quiet room with dancing candle flames and four places and many chairs, and he waits here.

And when the door reopens with a fist of twins upon it, it is not them, but Manhattan who enters: him who was told to be Manhattan—that Manhattan of the party. The door is closed behind him. He moves to the table and drags a chair and settles into it. He does not sit at one of the place settings, but beside it. Oslo is not sure how long he is silent, with his darting animal eyes, but he knows he can hear his own watch counting it over the ventilation and knock of pulse in his temple. He moves to suppress it with pensive fingers. Instead, the thumping merely knocks from vein to thumb to elbow: it's the way roadway stutters up a bicycle tire to the chin, he thinks.

"Are you familiar with the Maastricht Treaty?"

"I've heard of it. But I doubt I'd teach it," says Oslo.

"Set of economic rules—they say: any eurozone member state must maintain a debt limit of sixty percent of gross domestic product, with annual deficits of not more than three percent of GDP. Do you know any martial arts?"

"I cannot say I do."

"Judo?"

"I know of judo."

"Holds and grapples, mainly. The essence of it is to capture your opponent's body weight and momentum; deploy it against them through redirections and shifting leverage. It looks nothing like karate or kung fu. It's gentle and receptive, and hard to see. And with it, the meek defeat the great by their own magnitude."

"I see," says Oslo.

"Perhaps you will, perhaps you won't. Are you a political animal, Mr. Oslo? Do you imagine you grasp the position? Simone will want you for her own causes: I will want you for her for this. And if I should have you—I shall have you for this."

"Maastricht?"

"In 2000 and 2001 the Greeks wanted into the eurozone. Like the Italians and others, their accounting was a mess. That everyone flouts Maastricht is beside the point: they differed only in that theirs was worse. They were unchaste. They required surgical help—our help. We provided that help. A confidential loan booked as cross-currency swaps. Simone negotiated the deal. Your predecessor engineered the products and pitched them to the Greeks: he made them and sold them. Simone brought to them the diplomatic urge of the pen. In consequence, they got into the eurozone—their deficits looked rosy; their GDP looked like they were goddamned central Europeans— they stayed in the eurozone. They were elated, we were flush: all was Mediterranean sunshine."

"Is the predecessor repositioned in the firm, or has he gone elsewhere?"

"He's no longer with us."

"Is there anything you'd wish me to discuss with him in preparation? Would you like me to reach out?"

"I've a headache. I'd ask you, but you wear yours. A bit like that perfume: is that purchased or rented? . . . A drink then? What do you take for headaches?"

"I'm fine. Thank you."

"Is it the Latin in the French, or the Norse, that makes him obstinate? Maybe it's just the peasant German substrate of him, I don't know—I only know it isn't French: there is no such thing. Not originally, anyway; now it's just a word hung on a recipe. No more than when Caesar governed the Gauls. Helena says you like wine."

"I do. It's common to the people of the word."

"So you would. I find it raises the headache I was trying to put down."

"Is the bar open?"

Manhattan rises and moves to a hutch. He examines provisions there. "Do you like rum? However precious, I find it always drinks like the liquor of the help—don't you? . . . Something medicinal . . . I'm having whatever this is. Whisky, I think."

Oslo makes a gesture that says: I'm having what you're having—and Manhattan peels a foil and pours into tumblers. He brings them, and he returns. "I'd apologize for the hour . . . but I think you've just got in. So I'll save my guilt for something else."

Oslo smells the glass: "Much of this and I'll be unfit for talking."

"None of that and you'll be useless in thirty minutes."

Oslo clears his throat: "It's a cunning strategy: interviews middle of the night."

"I've held the room for a week. You were up, and so was I . . . It's Simone's decision in the end. I just tell her what to do."

"Do you know what she will decide?"

"I've yet to tell her."

"Is she expected?"

"She wasn't up. Private time."

"Is there another matter with the Greeks?" says Oslo.

"Yes," says Manhattan. "Cheers."

X.

". . . Belonging. Belonging, is a thing for two, my sweet, it is verse-form for two authors; a poetry of two—and there is ever only but the one to read. One audience, one product, one voice of resolving stanza: one applause. One passion in revelation. One discretion: one forgiveness. And where it is necessary: one vengeance . . . for the vigilance of two.

"My sweet . . . I am our forgiveness—you are absolved of your indiscretion—you are absolved in our belonging, in the verse of our poetic union. But . . . there shall be no interloper spared. Belonging is a two-splendored form, that shall not be shared . . . or severed . . . or for any cause interrupted. Belonging is not dimensional, it is not manifold; it is binary . . . bipodal, and therefore singular in action. And so shall I be, my sweet. For our vigilance—the vigilance of two, shall I bring to bear four-fold vengeance upon these foreign strains—these wedges and virulent hurdles and festering impedi-ments—*impediments—impediments!* . . . of union: our union. Our union. And so shall I leave you now . . . for a time . . . to tend to this measure of vigilance, and seek the vengeful object; and bind those fissures of our union—and return. To you. My sweet, my love—my tender little swan."

Argos Argyros read this and lingered in this aura before the camera lens; and Mr. Lanze stopped the tape. And he turned off the camera. And Argyros turned the finger of whisky in his second glass, and spoke himself out from the fold of the strange relish which had taken him by his reading, and he said: "How was that?"

"Perfection itself."

2.

"What are these?" Argyros had asked, of the objects which Mr. Lanze had rest at the tableside.

"These," said Lanze, "are envelopes containing a certain quantity of fiat currency—which we will return to momentarily. *This* is an English travel dictionary, in which you may observe that I have taken the liberty of marking certain text to your attention: think of it as a concentrative aid; and this . . . is an alternate end to these scenes in development, which I'd like you to closely consider, while you enjoy your tobacco and spirits."

Argyros had smoked and loosely read, and turned over pages through the dust-fall of errant flecks of ash—and when he'd finished and looked up in his plaintive and expectant completion, Mr. Lanze had said: "Do you have it?"

Argyros nodded easily and sipped his whisky. And Lanze had taken away the pages then, and cleared the space of the table before Argyros: "Let us do this as well, then—while we are here. As before: from your *best* memory, Argyros, shall we?" he said, and retreated into the shade beyond the camera whose dim light had appeared once more: "In your own time."

And this is what he read—from the whisky-inflated apertures of *best* memory: this of the 'tender little swan.' This had seemed to please Mr. Lanze, who praised the reading despite its libidinous chemistry. He'd praised it, and then gone to pains reminding of his obligations to the role—once agreed to: that he would be well compensated in advance, but in consequence, must follow instructions to exacting precision with regard to matters of things and places and times: that he should not falter or deviate from these in the least. And then he'd presented the contents of the envelopes in fiat currency: "You must commit to be where you say that you will be, Argyros. Here: this is forty thousand pounds for you," he'd said. "This is thirty thousand pounds toward expenses—for which you must retain meticulous receipts: unspent funds will be collected at the completion of filming. Also this: copy this to your own notes," he'd said, and lay a typewritten slip of paper before Argyros. "This is a video camera—make and model as we've used today: buy one—and a package of tapes, and bring it when you are summoned to filming. Receipts. Purchase a few fresh suits. Have them fitted. We are a small crew so that the talent may be well paid—and these errands are the cost.

"And this . . . is twenty thousand pounds," said Lanze, and left his hand upon the envelope. "Do you happen to know where one might acquire hashish?"

"It is possible," said Argyros.

"You tend bar—and this gives me faith. My producer . . . he is a great enthusiast, and I've promised to fetch him some: get what you can for the money and we'll arrange to collect it later. Also—take one meal a day at the Wharf till I summon you."

"Canary Wharf?"

"Prefer Canada Square."

"It is quite expensive."

"As is all Canary Wharf—keep receipts. Prefer it: dinner; drinks; as you like.

This is your character. Observe. I think it shall be rather painless research. Each day until you are summoned," he'd said.

That night Argyros had sat on the floor of his kitchen, upon the brief linoleum patch, and he'd circled himself with the articles of his bounteous day: the video camera, as instructed, and tapes— and elective flourish of bag; receipts; order-slips from the tailor at Harrod's; a glass from the sink—washed three times in preparation for the whisky sent with him by Lanze—a most handsome carton, and bottle with strong-shouldered slope, and fluid the sanctified hue of trapped candlelight, and poured into his little bastard of scratched glass like honeyed milk: silken ambrosia—scented ancient Celtic truth. And he smoked the beautiful strong, Maduro-wrap ciga- rettes—the Shermans, and played with the delicate tissue of the box, and marveled at the luxuriant hermetic precision of its closure—the small decisive 'pfup' it made when the lid was dropped; and he ashed in a tray he'd cleared for the simple magnitude of the occasion, and he turned with a restless, intoxicated curiosity through the dictio- nary from Lanze: 'resolving,' 'revelation'—there, 'stanza'; 'verse,' there—'vengeance,' 'vigilance,' 'virulent,' there: each word set out in its own intrusive, swift, and exotic curl-mark of pencil. He did not know if they were questions or instructions—objects of meditation or revelation: he did not know if there were more. He leaved through, leant against the cabinet doors and smoked—delicious cigarettes from the elegant box and drank beautiful whisky from the scratched glass: a gemstone within its flaw; an inclusion-borne diamond—and he took stock of these things and this new-minted measure of self.

XI.

Chartres Cathedral is 'Acropolis of France,' says Rodin. Do I know this? No. How do I know this? It's present tumbling makes it so. How do I know that I don't? Do I know that I don't? No: I *don't* know . . . that I *don't* know this—thought Oslo, and squeaked through the portals of Chartres with his wet winter shoes and his damp cuff of pant. Sodden and squeaky—a bedraggled and disoriented confederacy of self: a flight and a drive and a delirium of fractured context of place change: yesterday; today; a plane; a train; a car; a country and home; an employment; an improvement—an improvement?

Proximity. This is first riddle of the labyrinth of Chartres. Proximity. It is not the way: it is that the way passes at first so close to the destination: the question just in forming, so close to its answer— and then far, farther; around, away. The pilgrimage. He stood at the mouth of the labyrinth of Chartres. What is this stone? He stooped to look: aged and porous and fractured, and partitioned—subdivided: the age and flaw and the becoming unbecoming of the stone. Rough worn smooth—or smooth worn rough? Which is the nature of the path? Does the passage of the pilgrim refine or abrade?

He stood at the mouth of the labyrinth of Chartres in the high dusk of a quiet overcast of midday. He was briefly alone with it: a lone pilgrim before a bit of ancient mandala etched into the breastplate of the world—mounted to the living masonry of the nave and transept and all its sanctified volume of space. An airlock. A cleanroom to study rare phenomena. A supercollider with a scanning tunneling microscope through its nose like a bone. We are so whimsical in our ambitions—he thought. A mountain reduced to the brick that proves it: the brick reduced to a mote of light—*ta-da!* Observe!—now, is but to prove the context which uses the proof . . . *Prove* the pilgrimage that makes the pilgrim chaste; prove the destination which receives him: prove that such a thing as a pilgrim may enter the mouth of such a thing as pilgrimage . . . That such a thing as improvement exists; that it may be laid on such a thing as is amenable to elevation. Is improvement additive, then; reductive?—is the dutifully smashed atom increased or decreased in the great labor-born act? Is there a charitable condition for the unantagonized thing? Is an unwashed pilgrim dawdling at the threshold, thing enough?—thing at all? Does he exist, who has not committed, is uncommitted, to the—?

Freddie Oslo was startled from reverie under hard braking. They glided through France in Lanze's speeding car. He had been since they'd set off, and now he slowed vigorously for a lorry waddling into the overtaking lane. He performed some dance with pedals and shifter and the car slowed with a drag chute physics—while Lanze looked neither moved nor surprised—and Oslo crushed breathlessly onto the belts, and the car seemed to stand on its nose. "Do you know, Mr. Lanze, the French police have little compassion for speeding . . . to this degree."

The motorway widened and crowded and lined with small, sharp-leaved beech and poplar, and rough-hewn untended cypress through villages and townships, and narrowed and lengthened, decongested and opened out onto edgeless plates of long May-green grass of wheat among France's unpopulous hectares.

"We are of few pleasures: we take them where we can, Monsieur Oslo."

At the Total, before Lanze had fastened the car for the wash, and Oslo had gone into the station to wait, he'd said: "... Where's it come from then? ... on your 'floating carpark' into Zeebrugge."

"From tuning."

"Tuning, where?" Oslo had said.

"California."

"That is a precious-long way for a service. It looks the one from every Mayfair park-up. It isn't?"

"You are repeating yourself," said Lanze. "With that you will make the day long for us both."

"Why should it be long? Are we leaving Belgium?"

Lanze had looked at him.

"Are we headed South?"

Lanze had looked.

"My home is in Chartres, Mr. Lanze—it would be wonderful to see."

"We are not visiting your home, Monsieur Oslo—rather specifically."

"And why so?"

"Do you imagine it is what your Helena had in mind for your holiday?"

"Perhaps I should speak with her."

"You have mentioned it."

"So, not south to Paris, then?"

Lanze looked.

"Not the A1, then?"

Lanze looked.

"If it is south, and not the A1, it must be the A26."

Lanze had shifted on his feet, and he had looked.

"How many litres is the tank?. . . of your beautiful automobile? . . .
It looks the thirsty type: is it thirsty? . . . How many litres is this tank
of your beautiful automobile?"

"And bewilderingly common, but a moment ago."

"Is it large?"

"May it please you: seventy litres, Monsieur Oslo."

"Do we stop in the evening? . . . Isn't that Dijon?" Oslo had said.
"Would that be a stop in Dijon?"

XII.

Jean-Pierre played on the floor with his cars. He played on his hands and knees, and with his soft bare feet, in pajamas. With his hair just in his eyes and a bracing palm against the cold midnight tiles. And his soft fingers against the chassis of an automobile in miniature speeding along the foreign planes of the coolly familiar. The silent television threw the room in strange matte and glimmering lights. And upon the soft cradle of sofa, the sleeping au pair.

Lila Torp arrived by hired car among the drive and terrace shrubs of her home in Chartres at 12:45 upon a mid-May evening, and watched as the car left before entering. It was not Lila Oslo, but Lila Torp—as she had been from birth. Who did not belong to her husband, but to her parents. Whose conviction in the maiden-strength of surnames was once intended to draw forth a dangerous and complicated persuasion: but Freddie Oslo was sympathetic and disinterested, and so she bore in womanhood the irritatingly unsatisfying childhood name. And when she entered, neither the boy nor the sleeping au pair rose to greet her.

The Spanish au pair was beautiful. It was no good for Freddie, but it was good for Jean-Pierre, she had thought—to be fortified, stimulated, to be in the admiring presence of such easy strength of beauty. While she was away. Lila had been to an opening and the ballet and a cocktail reception and the re-cocktailed afterword of friends with city apartments on the Champs-Élysées. She had talked gaily into the night of their handsome terrace above the glow of the long Morse-arterial throb of the heart chamber of Paris—until, having stayed already the night before, and the sparkle of Prosecco having brought chill to the terrace, they summoned a hire car for her, and she was shuttled sleepily home . . . to the boy in his flannelled midnight play and the Spanish au pair to be roused . . . from everything joyful in Paris.

In the kitchen the Spanish au pair lay her hair over a shoulder. She explained that she'd put him to bed hours before. She'd given him thirty minutes beyond bedtime to converse and play. He'd come down in the night while she'd slept, it seemed. But he'd been wonderful and quiet. Little Jean-Pierre. Independent, madame. She had explained this in the kitchen with her hair over shoulder. Drowsy. Dark, beautiful hair—that was good for Jean-Pierre to admire—while she was away: beauty, like a vitamin. -But there was a call, madame. She'd told her in the kitchen, combing her hair with the fingers of two hands. Madame. Someone had called the house phone—madame. Not mademoiselle. They had called in the monsieur's name—the Monsieur Oslo's name—the operator had said—and they had asked to reverse the charges. -And what happened? She refused the call. She refused the charges. Monsieur Oslo? Yes, Monsieur Oslo. Very strange. Yes, very strange. She had refused the charges though—certainly this was best; certainly this was correct. Oui? Little Jean-Pierre had paused from his play to listen—burning his last, bleary, clouded slick of lantern oil—that last, brightest, delirious, high-calorie flare before the tank pulls dregs; before the wick dries, and the light collapses into extinguishment. He sat cross-legged, listening, looking. Lila had smiled wearily from the counter, where she saw him. He bore the miniature car in his palm—a respite from its speeding explorations. And he blinked at them. In the kitchen. At her. She smiled, the rocking of the car ride, numb in her neck, in her hips—still—where she leant against the counter. And he blinked.

Later, when the Spanish au pair was not asleep in front of the somniferous strobe of television, but in the bed of her room, and little Jean-Pierre quietly, soberly under his covers, she had turned over the phone in her hands—taken from her purse to come lie beside her—to come occupy the full empty bed of the full empty house; to lay in wakefulness beside her while she had slept or thought of sleep—where the bedside lamp at last was turned to silence: where she had not called him in the night, but in the day that followed. And where he had not answered.

The emptiness had come in relief, then, when the call had tripped into the emotional anonymity of voicemail. The relief from present drama, from odd misfortunes or the tales of them—from confirmation of a missed call, from her absence to receive it; from her absence—like the action of a dropped receiver, declining to accept the charges. That emptiness which is not displaced: that silence which affirms the known. That had been the first call. So far as she had known, it had been first.

On the train Jean-Pierre lay his head in her lap. He could be reserved—distant often; he could be . . . distant—she couldn't think of the right modifier; the ones that came were all somehow off; incorrect. Dishonest. Somehow. It was uncommon just the same: Jean-Pierre's head in her lap—his brushed and bathed muddy-blonde turns. Off-blonde banana curls laying in his napping eyes; and she stroked them. Lila had thought Jean-Pierre might like the train: he said he did not mind it, but he did not like it. He liked machines, and so she had thought he might. He liked automobiles and spoked wheels and meshed cogs and padlocks and cut keys: he liked things with flanges and vents and flared wheel arches and clasps and triggering mechanisms: he liked made things—manmade things. And she didn't like it. She didn't like that he preferred forged and smelted and cut and stamped and flush-mounted, countersunk things. She thought he should like them born; formed things—made by rainwater and wind; sculpted in biology and erosion—things about mortality . . . she thought. Not high-carbon steel and aluminum alloy: not things about . . . immortality. Just the same, he did not like the train. He did not mind it, but he did not like it. He said it was ugly. He said it looked like a bar of soap—*une savonnette*—and she'd tried not to laugh. He said it looked like a bus on a guiderail. Something trapped— he meant. Something without liberty—he meant. She couldn't see the difference: a battleship, a fighter plane, a tower clock, a race car, a fresh-cut key—a bus; a passenger train. Metal, metal, metal: she couldn't see the difference. And she was suspicious: she saw the individuated in them; the particular, the exceptional. The distinguished . . . and she wanted to put it down—rub it out with bleach and water. She did not see the public, the common, the service—the steward—and it made her suspicious. Freddie liked wood and stone. There wasn't the least weapon-edge about him: he liked fabrics and stitching and leather tooling. He liked a watch, it was true, or a car from time to time: but he liked things he was supposed to like—he liked things upon which there was some elevating agreement—not things of themselves. That seemed . . . wrong. Not machines of their own. Was that good? Could it be?

It is an old farmhouse in Chartres. Freddie loves something in it: perhaps it is her and Jean-Pierre. She likes that Freddie loves the house. It is a reassuring sentimentality. It is good for men to be sentimental—diagnostic. A healthy fixation, that shows weakness and sensitivity. A goodness: like the beauty of Spanish au pairs, for her Jean-Pierre, when she's away. The house moves and talks at the poles of the season. It shifts and snaps. Heat and humidity and cold, make it talk. At empty midday; in the speculative wrap of night. Oak tenons creak. Old plaster cracks, and falls from nowhere to nowhere. Ghost sounds. Freddie is never at home when they happen, or he can never hear over the real-time progress of multi-monitor graphs, or he's buried beneath journal and wine pairings: the licked forefinger and thumb that clasp reluctant pages. The sharp rattle of the turn. The fragile noise of resting stemware. She wants the house to keep speech for her life in Paris: let it talk to her over curbside traffic and the café discourse tuned to rise above it: the din of impassioned civility raised to shout-down random chaos and the mechanical bellyaching of the world. Let it talk to her from there. The au pair, like Freddie—she is deaf to it. But Jean-Pierre—he will study the corners, the ceiling, when it talks. He stops his play to see it. He hears it. Storms will rumble off the October sea. The doors won't fit after a soaking rain. Not really. The downstairs bathroom won't latch one month. The next it will. In San Diego they don't make thunder. Not really. Doors are hollow, and they fit. One only pulls against an opposing force. There is no distemper of architecture there. Cabinetry glides; doors latch. When they cease to comply, the house is razed—exorcised—and they try again. The roads undulate; they rise up and down on smooth new pavement. All France rattles side-to-side on tight-fitting rails. Rails that apparently Jean-Pierre shares no sympathy for. They had a white bungalow in San Diego. Stucco and juniper bushes—an odd vault peak over the entry. When the car backed from the driveway to leave, her mother broke away for private crying: her father had stood there in the open garage. His arms folded. He adjusted his eyeglasses, and watched.

In the beginning warm, low sunlight falls into the car. An accident of cosmology that fires starlight through windows of the northbound leg of a French train. A mortal assault of the senses that bathes a national vegetation in gentle evening. Uprights and wires and station platforms wheel past the windows. Overpasses and underpasses. It moves along berms and troughs. Furrows and elevations, which peer into mossed and repurposed stoneworks, or out onto florid pastures. Patient, waiting fields. Rooftops in flight. Indecipherable clefts of forest which blur and blot out the light. While the distance moves at a stroll. Creeps at the edges. Why must the far hold its frame while the near, the immediate, is a-rush beyond cognition?—she thinks. Why shouldn't it be the inverse? The obverse, the verso? Why must the near wait for later comprehension, while the far treads forward in dignified clarity? The obtuse, the recto? If the past can be this way—why not the present? The future? What does it want from us that it must make us stop to see it? What is this indulgence it needs? Why must it have its way? What is this self-importance of the instant—what is this vanity of the now?

2.

They did not speak every day—Lila and Freddie Oslo. Not every week even. She put it to the nature of his work . . . immersed . . . diversified; residualized, interest bearing. But neither did she call him. She put it to him, but she capitalized on the space. She had called his office a few days later. It was the low-alarm measure over nothing. A call to a vacant phone. A call to an office. A call to an office assistant: Cygnet, who did not answer, but called back later. Days later. She moved from the building of a dance studio, across a wide brim of Parisian curb, and into a waiting car. Somewhere Parisian to go. Perhaps the Champs-Élysées apartments of her friends. Clouds had moved over Paris. They had cast shadow like floating citadels: a menace of bulbous woolen fantasy craft. A fleet of weather. She wore wraps over her dance clothes, and soft shoes. And the phone had buzzed and skittered in her purse when the car had pulled off.

"Oui, bonjour?" she had said.

"Ms. Lila Torp?—it is Rothman, London—office of Mr. Freddie Oslo: this is Cygnet, his assistant, returning a call." Her Ts were bright and her Hs breathy, and her vowels were all neat and declarative: not swallowed, but merely windswept; leant vaguely to the right—and Lila had wondered just what hamlet of Britain made that, or was it born anywhere at all, or perhaps just spliced in the laboratory of the middle-grades of high-finance: the sound of the A-Level prerequisites.

"Ms. Torp, my apologies, but Mr. Oslo is away from the office at this time: is there anything I can do for you?"

"I was concerned I might have missed a call from Freddie—that's all," she'd said.

"Do I see more than one call from you here?"

"I thought I might have missed a call: I tried his direct line before I tried you."

"You've tried his mobile, Ms. Torp?"

"I've tried his mobile—thank you, Cygnet."

"I don't have any messages for you, Ms. Torp."

"Sorry?"

"He hasn't instructed any message be delivered to you, Ms. Torp."

"I see. Thank you, Cygnet."

"Has he not been to Chartres, Ms. Torp?"

There was a bright silence then. There in the car with her. An instant with no horns or road noises. For a reason whose sharp edges she couldn't fully sense, there was just the hanging pause, and the slippery leather beneath her bracing hand, and the tunnel of light shown through the windshield: "No, Cygnet. He has not been to Chartres. Is there a reason he would be?"

"Oh, my apologies—I don't possess Mr. Oslo's current schedule—I merely thought to ask."

"Have I gone and spoiled a surprise?"

"No, no, Ms. Torp. I don't possess Mr. Oslo's current schedule. Shall I deliver a message for him to contact you when he checks in?"

"Yes, Cygnet," she had said. "Thank you, Cygnet," she had said.

They had wed in Santorini. It was on the high terrace roof beside the bell of a church hidden in the Escherian contrivance of architecture somewhere beneath. Freddie had wanted the South of France.

She always envisioned it on the beach—remembered it waterside with
toes curling volcanic ash—cuffs rolled and hems lifted. But it was not.
It was on a high white-painted terrace beside the shoulder-height
belfry of an invisible church—perhaps they stood upon it. But there
was no image of the ceremony, just the scene. The view into a beautiful water-laden caldera. It was not the South of France. Ships in the
harbor of an ancient goddess, vengeful and restless. Methane bubbles
drifting from her sleeping nostrils, somewhere unseen. They wore
linen, in bare feet. The terrace was hot. They had lifted their feet like
cranes. Alternated. The white bio-form, cubiform village, flung from
the sea as though barnacle riding a breaching whale. A callus on a
crocodile spine. There was nothing of antiquity about it. It looked the
wondrous mud-daubings of a separate species. She had thought of the
stucco vault above the door in San Diego. "Not everyone gets to get
married in Santorini," her mother had said. "Lila, not everyone gets to
get married in Santorini." Freddie had not paid for their trip, for their
travel, for their stay. They had not flown to California so her father
could: "Lila . . ." he had said, and she could hear his breathing in the
little office at the back of the house. His office. She heard the double
knock of the plunger of his pen. Breathing. The sound of light trapped
against a dusty yellowed blind; pressing: wind on the tines of a comb.
A thumb against the stubble of his chin. *Clack-click, click-clack.*

There is a carpet runner that makes the stairs quiet; soft beneath
the feet. It is the slow morning away from classes. None today—
none tomorrow. It is tea, and blended vegetables. The blender dial
like a rheostat. A volume knob of unmarked positions: persuasion,
emphasis, ecstasy. Deep stretches with the look of yoga to them. On
the carpet of the guestroom, not the living room in cold tile. Folded
on elbows between outstretched legs, reading Le Monde between her
knees—with a tracing finger, gently mouthing the French. A singer's

routine for off-days. The performer in toothpaste, paying weekend lines to a weekday mirror.

Tones On Tail played late morning. Early afternoon, perhaps. The house in Chartres was emptiness—down to the filament-hum of one. The first floor was hung with worthless miniatures of speakers. Tucked into ceiling corners. Disguised; concealed. An electrical embarrassment made for hiding, like a vestige of halogen track light. A dim votive to sound. Freddie kept the only decent ones on the desk of his office. An extravagance in electronics made permissible in company: monitors and cables and blinking, snicking computer drives.

The Spanish au pair was gone to market and to collect Jean-Pierre from school—and Lila took her music and a surreptitious margaritas-for-one into the remote privacy of Freddie's office. Upstairs, where she danced. Without thematic cause or punctuation: barefoot; drinking. Motion without teaching in it—a thing not for seeing, but to be performed in. A concerto for wearing . . . between all the prim white gable walls—beneath all the subjective industry of hand-cut timbers. That was the second call. The last call. When it came. Stealing music from an empty house: brief old joy, in an unsanctioned space. The house phone rang downstairs, from the pale tummy somewhere. Gurgling. A faint warbling beneath the grinding bass line, tri-bells and handclaps of "Go!" Between the 'ya-yas'—the foreign cry of rare digital fowl. A sound she had to stop to hear, to know. To clamber across the desk for the volume, and to listen. *Dring-dring*, say the French. *Dring-dring*.

Jean-Pierre walks on the palms of his feet. It gives him a gently cast forward look; tilted. He steps on their edges and toes, their thumb and the butt of their knuckles, shifting and angling as though he wore mittens rather than shoes. He touches the seatbacks of the train car for walking sticks, and peers down the corridor of each row, populated or not, as though it might open onto a gallery display. He takes his seat the way animations of stuffed toys do—shuffling and stiff. —Pooh and Piglet ride the train— He rests in a seat of the train car—a seat of his own. The windows are dark now, on this south-bound leg, reflective: one sees fleeting distant stars of light, or one sees themselves, gazing with weary sobriety into the obsidian mirror. Jean-Pierre looks there. He pretends to see into the racing night, but sees only the shapes of uprights and horizontal planes and the head-lights of roads snapping past, or the pale form is his own cheek. The soft snip of youth in drowsy silhouette.

The phone had warbled from the alcove near the kitchen: "Oui, allô?" she had said. She accepts the charges, she had said. She had leapt down the stairs, and peered into the alcove at the warbling phone, and coiled a strand of hair over her ear with a second finger. A hardline, they had kept for the Spanish au pair—the 'nanny phone' they'd called it.

"Lila? . . . Lila!" he'd said. "I'm on the continent."

"Have you lost your phone? I tried you at the office," she said. "I talked to Cygnet," she said—"Is everything alright?—are you working?"

"Lila—I have only a moment—he's washing the car, and I've just run in to the shop. I tried before," he said.

"Who is washing the car?—who is with you?" she said.

"The driver. We'll be in France tonight. Dijon, I believe—I think Dijon. Come see me. Lila, come meet me in Dijon."

"When? Tonight? Freddie? Tonight?" she said.

"Yes, yes, yes! Come now. Tonight—right away. I miss you—and Jean-Pierre—I love you. Come tonight."

"What's happened to your phone? Why didn't you call my cell?"

"I don't remember it—come tonight, Lila. I don't understand, really. I'm trying to understand."

"Who's with you, Freddie?"

"Simone's man. Helena's driver. I don't understand. I'm trying to understand, but something is *impair*; *éstrange* . . . amiss. Come meet me. Come tonight—I would feel so much better."

"Should I bring Jean-Pierre?"

"Come tonight, Lila. Leave now," he said.

"Take my number."

"I have to go. I have to go," he said.

"Take my number," she said into the dial tone. Take my number.

Jean-Pierre watches the compact where it comes out of the purse and makes its precious 'knock.' It has the sound of a landing tumbler, she realizes, the catch of a jewelry box, and opens a dusty mirror and brush and pad and powdered wafer—and the joylessly reflected enervated angles of the mouth and chin of Lila Torp. The lipstick tube lifts off with a candied 'pop.' A damp, cherry red sound. She sees this because she sees Jean-Pierre seeing it and she hears what he sees—the look of sounds she is otherwise blind to—long since deaf to the experience of. She applies the color and presses her lips and blots with a bite of clean tissue from her purse, and when she is about to hide it away, she gives it to the watching boy instead. Jean-Pierre unfolds it—like a cut-paper snowflake; a construction paper heart—a kiss for seeing. He considers the tissue. And he presses it against his cheek.

The wheels clatter and rumble over junctions. The brakes peel—a sound wholesome nowhere but with trains—and Jean-Pierre does not like this fact of trains either, and covers his ears with his sleeves. The train wends into Dijon and beneath its lights and wires—the things which can be seen from windows flush upon the night. They slowed and slowed, and slowed for the station—Gare de Dijon-Ville—where they collected themselves from their seats and stepped from the cars onto platforms, rain slick and cool. Her square-heel pumps play a flat, square-heeled sound down grey-brown corridors of stanchions and placards whispering their ways and wares with evening voices: none but the stray shuffling footfalls from a late train to call above: her erect-shouldered step and Jean-Pierre's vanishing edgewise tread, and the clutch of his fingers against her hand. They moved out through the high round terminal—a windowed hatbox of departure hall—onto the water-stained pavements, glistening and dark. And there they watched in waiting—travelers collected in circling automobiles, or dispersed to verges of benches or to enact the prepositional phrases of smoking—with a hitched shoulder and a locked knee—or to light their telephones in summons of conversation. And once Lila had unfolded her jacket. She had crossed her shawl. She had buttoned Jean-Pierre. She had watched the carpark empty its guts to the ambling taillights—evaporated into bedtime vacancy. Until Lila had begun to feel worried and foolish, and alone with Jean-Pierre. What had she expected: what *could* she have expected?—she thought. And then she too lighted her phone in summons.

Dring-dring, she thought. *Dring-dring.*

XIII.

Lila was thinking of stories when the taxi pulled up and shown its squinting headlamps on once painted wrought iron gates, and a single small tile marked: 8 –in a limestone and stucco-patch wall set before the Revolution. It was not a made or otherwise worried thought—there wasn't the least work in it. It was the sort of thought that blooms of its own into the dark of a car ride, like the sight of the moon. And smells of lilac . . . or honeysuckle. It comes to you. She was thinking of how her father and his engineer's training and his engineer's work were fitted snug as nesting dolls into the story of his father, and his father—his mother, and so. Reached off into imperatives of unseen past with the tireless urgency of upstream. The image seemed right to her, but it felt opposite her sense in the moment: that they all were connected adjunctly—her father, and his father, and his mother, and her—all conjoined by discreet umbilici of co-narrative. This seemed possible—went her thought—this seemed right. But it felt nothing of the kind: it *felt* a daisy chain of transmission signals reaching weakly backward from the receiver—streaming faintly from a taxi in France, outward from the present—outward from now. Whose story is whose? Which is which? What is one to another? It had the grit of mortgage; it felt like debt—and she didn't like debt.

"Oui . . . Oui, allô?" had said the Spanish au pair. She sounded breathless and sleepy. Did I wake you?—Lila had said—I'm sorry to wake you . . . Madame Torp?—she'd said—madame, no, no—I am awake . . . just resting with the television, she'd said . . . Were there any calls?—are there any messages? . . . Monsieur Oslo . . . he left a message, madame . . . Monsieur Oslo called? . . . Oui, yes, she'd said . . . For me? . . . Yes, she'd said . . . And you accepted the charges? . . . Yes, as you said, madame . . . He left a message for me? . . . Oui, yes, madame . . . And you waited for me to call to deliver it? . . . Yes, madame—she paused—yes, madame . . . And what is the message, then? said Lila . . . It is an address, madame—Monsieur Oslo said it was an address: 8 Place de la Mairie, she'd said . . . Yes, but where is that?—Lila had looked at Jean-Pierre—she'd lifted her hand; she'd shaken her head . . . Pichanges, she'd said . . . the monsieur said, Pichanges . . . But I'm in Dijon.

2.

"You are an English?" said the man through the low, arched postern gate.

"American," said Lila.

"Ah, so said the monsieur. He called to expect you—but perhaps you are later than what he thought." The man had shuffled into the night from the large provincial farmhouse, out onto the grounds in robe and slippers and a bedtime cut of bread. He tightened his belt sash at the gate and chewed, and the cords of light from the house caught in the silver grizzle of his jaw. Suit or bedclothes—she thought—the French beardage is a wire gauge all its own. "Bonjour to le petite monsieur," said the man through the bars. He clutched the bread husk in his teeth to unfasten the gate, and closed it behind them. "In the colombier there—you see?" he said, and pointed cross a dirt and gravel-stone patch of courtyard with a thrust of his chin, and again with his arm. "The . . . dovecote? You will find him there."

There were timber ceiling and stairs to another floor—a loft-like bedroom suite. There was a kitchenette with sink and small appliances. A hearth with heating stove. A side table and chairs, where Oslo sat with a bottle of Bourgogne Rouge and the glass. Stone floor and walls honeycombed with square and vacant pigeonholes—Oslo said they were *boulins*. There were small armchairs where she sat and Jean-Pierre sat. Occasionally, he sat. Or knelt, or hung over the arms, or stood and moved from *boulin* to *boulin*, inspecting them for size or depth or revealing artifacts—for doves.

He looks happy, she said. He looks tired, she said. Of course, she didn't say these. She thought them. But with the loud and distant formality of speech—and so they felt spoken. And he did: he did look happy, or something very nearly. And he did look tired. In fact, it was this mostly that seemed to weigh on his slow-smiling levity. He sat with the Bourgogne Rouge. He refilled his glass, he filled hers. A second bit of stemware he'd arranged as a predictive conceit, that had now the feel of wilting flowers and room-cool dinner—the rose pedal bath that's gone cold and drained away to suds. His stubble was trimmed and he looked bathed. Half-inebriated with sleep of bathing, evening, and local wine. He wordlessly and repeatedly beckoned her to the chair adjoining the table with him, but she did not go. "Each one contained a breeding pair," said Oslo to Jean-Pierre, and the room.

It was thirty minutes to Pichanges, in the dark with Jean-Pierre and his hands shimmed beneath his thighs, along the close village lanes to the unlighted gate, and the settled fare, and the rasping exhaust of the departing taxi—a sound that made her think of cards in bicycle spokes, and the phrase: *Souhaitez-vous attendre un moment s'il vous plait?* Would you wait?—*could* you?—she thought at the taillamps with the sidelong snap of casting stones onto water. Lila found a callbox and pressed the keys, and for a moment before the voice they stood in the brief unlit plaza before the postern gate, and watched the buzzing receding amber fixtures, looking every bit a lighted insect scampering into diminishment along the corridors of a maze.

The man had come in nightclothes and slippers, and let them into the *corps de ferme*—now a guesthouse, she understood—and they crossed the gravel court where a silver sedan was parked alone in waiting, security bulb blinking the cabin with sentinel pulse—fat-tired haunches and dew-glimmering deep-set rims. Jean-Pierre fixed upon it as they passed.

Oslo had embraced them and bade them in. There were kisses, and he'd carried Jean-Pierre about the whole of the suite—a silo once caked and white with runny pestilence, now chic, if rustic, *chambres d'hôtes* secreted into the lane-ways of Pichanges, Burgundy.

His jaw wrung into his knuckles and sagged his elbows. "Holiday," said Oslo, and palmed his gritted chin. "I am to be on holiday."

"And so you are. I didn't know whether to be worried missing your first call, or receiving your second. You look well-kept for a man reversing charges."

Oslo watched her let her hair down. He watched Jean-Pierre rubbing his fingers along the *boulin*, peering in. Moving along the wall with the attention of searching library shelves. "So I am," he said.

"You aren't at the house, Freddie? Why didn't you come, or give word? You might have had Cygnet call."

"I am to be on holiday," he said.

"Yes, and so you are, but—"

"I'm *to be* . . . on holiday. That I am . . . seems less clear."

"Oh, Freddie. It was a long trip to make last-minute, all at once. To race out with Jean-Pierre. I was worried. Jean-Pierre is tired. You said you would be in Dijon. I only received the message from the au pair at the station, Dijon-Ville. No one was there. Why didn't you call my phone?"

"I don't know the number. I remember the house phone."

"Where's your phone? Why the house phone and not mine?"

"I never remember to enter the house phone . . ." said Oslo, and slowly dialed his palm with his finger, "and so I never remember to forget it. My phone remembers the rest—which I do not have. I have no money, either."

"Where are your things, Freddie?"

"Où sont tes affaires, papa?" said Jean-Pierre.

"They are being kept for me, Jean-Pierre. Held in safekeeping."

"Who has your things, Freddie?"

"I missed you."

"Where are your things?"

"Monsieur Lanze. I mentioned him, I think: Helena's man."

"Who is this?"

"Helena's—Simone Helena's—*man*. Her driver, and security man—or one of them, I suppose."

"And why are you in France—not at home—on vacation with Simone Helena's *man*, Freddie? For the life of me this seems a simple place to be for such particulars: Helena's driver—no phone, no money—"

"No computer."

"No computer . . . Who is paying for this if you are not?—Helena?—Rothman? Lanze? Where are you going?—why weren't you in Dijon like you said?"

"Dijon was a guess. I didn't know where we were going—I don't know now."

"But, you're on holiday?"

"Helena asked me to take it."

"Right away?"

"Right away."

"And to take it with Mr. Lanze?"

"Rather, that he would take me."

"'My driver will take you on holiday—you must go right away!—give me all your things.' She said that?"

"She said, I must go—her driver will take me."

"Where?"

"On holiday."

"Sequestered holiday, more like," she said, and they drank Bourgogne Rouge, and Oslo refilled his glass.

"Yes," said Oslo.

"Yes?"

"They're having night terrors at Rothman."

"What over?"

"Pains of the common sort, they have conjured dark thoughts over. —Over little."

"Rothman or Helena?"

Oslo shook his head: "Helena, likely."

"Wants you sequestered?"

"Out of the office, I expect. Unavailable," said Oslo, and smiled a heavy-lidded grimace. "I didn't think you would come."

"And this is why *not* have your things?—to be unavailable?"

"The room is under a different name."

"No! Really? Over night terrors?" she said, as the door of the dovecote swung open.

"Ah, Mr. Lanze!" said Oslo, and stood with his glass. "Allow me to introduce Lila Torp, and Jean-Pierre Oslo, there—my lovely—"

"What have you done . . . Monsieur Oslo?" said Lanze, quietly from the doorway.

"We *just* were speaking—"

"WHAT HAVE YOU DONE!"

XIV.

Athens seemed everywhere vestigial to Freddie Oslo. A place of any and every moment but present; timestamped by architecture—a Doric, Ionic antiquity, and concrete-and-tile Brutalist middle-past; clad in faded paints or revisionist appliqué, Athens backways felt a people living among the graffito-ed standing ruins of near and far yesterdays: a landscape disarticulated from the future perfect tense.

Oslo sat at a café ten minutes ambling crooked stroll from Syntagma Square, with its parliamentary palace and administrative ante-buildings. There were roll-out awnings and colorfully cushioned chairs. The corner of Romvis and Klitiou was brick paved and slender. Automobiles crowded parking from stray verges and beech trees thrust from the street and into the slip of sky which held between multi-story buildings. It was fair and pleasant, and still, the nocturnal doings of man and animal had not been full-neutered by the slant-light of day.

He trained his own briefcase between his feet, and until Pappan Christakous arrived, he clutched the other in his lap. The satchel for the Minister was a fine, black, pebble-stamped Epsom leather Oslo rubbed beneath his thumbs: a flawless, crisp new Hermès, Kelly briefcase with belted clasp and palladium hardware, brought by flight to Greece in Oslo's keeping for Pappan Christakous, Greek Minister of Finance. The Minister, when he arrived, bore grey hair and a large-toothed ingratiating smile, his shoulders, the continual tension of someone resting elbows on a table, and he arrived with this lumbering posture and dark glasses and his suit jacket hung from his back by a finger. For a Greek he shown the unusual pallor of one who lives exclusively indoors. Oslo stood to greet him, but was batted down with a palming gesture.

The Minister hung his coat on an adjoining chair. "It is excellent to see you, sir," said Oslo. He sat; he ordered espresso; he shook his head in near imperceptible inquiry. "I have brought your satchel, Minister," said Oslo.

The Minister repeated the palming, dissuasive gesture.

". . . Sir."

"Indeed, you say so," said the Minister as he received it. He held it in consideration; he opened the clasp; he removed a folder, opened it on the table and leafed it through.

"That is a copy of the instrument for your records, sir," said Oslo.

The Minister performed the doubting shake again. He reopened the satchel and smoothed a hand along its compartments and inspected its pockets, until he produced a matching coat wallet: tall and wide, which opened to reveal four card slots with matching unmarked magnetic stripe cards, and a thick round key on a numbered fob. The key slipped from a note sleeve, and the Minster touched and replaced it. He closed and admired the wallet, and stowed it with the folder, back in the satchel. "Very nice," he said. "When is the signing?"

Oslo checked his watch on reflex: "Just under two hours, sir."

"Yanis and Milos are arranged?"

"The Deputy Ministers are also scheduled to attend, yes sir."

"It is lovely to see you, Mr. Oslo," said the Minister, and clasped Oslo between his two pale hands.

. . . Jean-Pierre was four then.

Now he was seven—a birthday hurtling toward them like the snatches of road sign calling out mid-breath to the whip-curl-bloom of engine note. Freddie Oslo imagined him the day he'd entered Athens. He imagined him climbing the short step of the school in his shuffling step. He imagined him received by the teacher—a guiding, coercive hand coiling his shoulder; he imagined him looking up in the reverie of distraction, through the schoolyard windows into a clouded day—he imagined pulling up in his car to collect him: an excited greeting with irrepressible smiles and wide-flung arms. An imagining. A vignette cast over a memory—deplaning in Greece, two briefcases in hand.

Now, just there, to his left, behind Lanze, fingers beneath his thighs leaning expectantly forward, seatbelt laced under his arm. There'd been no conversation in the morning. Lanze had entered in the night. He'd roared at them from the doorframe—stood there momentarily, wide-eyed, staring, teeth set. And then he'd left. Slowly, moderately, replaced the door, with his fist bulging on the handle, creaking like knotted rope. They'd rested and bathed. Lanze checked them out, as he had in Blankenberge—loaded the trunk with their things, and Lila and Jean-Pierre had studied Oslo's wan, Bourgogne Rouge-wearied face as they'd stood in the courtyard beside the dew-lapped car and he'd held the door for them—for Lila, for Jean-Pierre. He'd scampered across the seat; she'd folded into the front.

"Jean-Pierre has no car seat," she'd said. "French Highway Code states it is not obligatory for a chauffeur-driven vehicle, madame— as clearly this is," Lanze had said. And now southward at speed. The motion, lightly up and down over rises; an aeronautical undulating skip. The crisp sideward jolt of overtaking, the vicious deployment of throttle that lifted the feet and depressed the fluttering heart—that paid combustion into the cabin as dark music, and out, as an organ-pedal echolocation played back from bridges and broadside of trucks. And they rode in it; breath-holding, transfixed, and uncomfortably silent.

2.

"The reverse, perhaps," he'd said. Indian take-out tins lay on the floor beside their bags, chicken tikka masala, chicken saagwala, flatware from Harrods and barks of garlic naan. Bottles of Kingfisher they poured and drank from teacups. A housewarming in nipples, flatware and unmatched china. She'd leaned against the wall of the white marble floor and sat with her warm flesh and leaf of cloth against the cool tile and her suit jacket over formidable nakedness and a catalogue of furnishings upon her leg-crossed lap, and she smoked Gauloises and knocked ash with the hook of thumbnail precision. "Choice is a poverty," Cygnet had said. "Look at us here. On the floor of your luxurious flat: how much is it, your luxurious flat?"

"This is a privileged information," said Oslo. "Do you have clearance?—I am not allowed to know, so I have forgotten."

"We are beggars on Carrara," she'd said. "Impoverished in choosing. Bare feet to the soil—" she snapped her fingers and shifted the catalogue and recrossed her legs: "Peasants of potential!"

Oslo combed at his cheek and palmed his chinned beard of stubble. "I don't see that," he'd said.

"Choice is the equalizer," she'd said. "Survey your kingdom, and say so."

"A mere turn of simplicity, m'lady."

"A poverty in the trough of choice," she'd said. "A valley between mountains. Emptiness."

"The reverse, perhaps," he'd said, and folded elbows on his knees, and rubbed his calf and his lip with fingers and sharpened his Gauloises against a verge of naan. "A tower between yawning wastes. You are a woman of wonderous, surprising depth of naked curvature," he'd said.

She'd brought London Indian in high-fat sauce and handled bags; she'd brought teacups from the store—from disuse—from storage? His new flat with windows on Grosvenor Square—three months new?—four? He'd filled it with fine-hewn suits, monogram towels, timepieces and television; an extravagantly priced and sized bedframe, and bench to lace his shoes. She would bring the rest, cleavage and that great vacated interval peace, and area coverings and furnishings—find them by numerical markings in gloss-varnished pages, summon them, and they would arrive. Lila and Jean-Pierre would climb them for a visit or two: Cygnet, fade into the millwork of London enamel—the rooms of her own space; the apartment she kept for punctuation; commas and semicolons—the attendant ligature of the suspended clause. Tonight, tomorrow: in the morning she would leave in laundered things, clasp earrings in the lighted vanity of the bath, or Sunday in her four-poster wardrobe cross town to rummage for clothes. She rose and left early, arrived brightly, greeted from her desk, professionally, courteously. While he lay in. Watched through gaps for flat-lighted day; counted roman blinds by their fold, let the tortoise reel out its pretense of lead. But this was to come: the catalogue for them lay still on Cygnet's armature of hips. But Oslo could see it by memory—an epimetic sighting onto the past. Delivered by smooth-bore retroflexion onto the prefigurative moment: brushing Gauloises from the pages . . . turning them.

"May I interrupt, Mr. Oslo. I'm familiar with these mechanics. We've been leveraged against airports and airlines in the past. The

American 9/11 has made this costly for us. If you say that it should be Asian currency swaps pegged at 'historical' exchange rates, or if you say that it should be instruments backed largely by foreign military industrial conglomerates—these particulars themselves at this late date are of small concern. In fact, it is arguable how much is good to know. Perhaps the more challenged my attention the better," said Pappan Christakous, Greek Minister of Finance.

"The law, Minister, as it stands, permits it," said Oslo.

"No, Mr. Oslo, the law does not forbid it," said the Minister. "These are not the same, and merely made to seem so. When one says to the children, 'all of our silver in the drawer must be clean,' he has only not thought to say, 'therefore, you may not loan it to the sink, where it may remain dirty.' That Maastricht says—EU member debt to income must be X, they merely fail to say: 'therefore, you must not take loans you cannot hope to repay, used to buy commodities, and move debts into currency derivatives where it is concealed and where, one hopes, it will be reduced when the products expire.'"

"The Italians have had great success in this space—with our help, and the help of others. Do you have concerns about repayment?"

"Their debt remains near top of the Union."

"And they remain in the Union."

"With their debt they are inextricable."

"With the help of friends, you too shall be inextricable."

"Greece?—why so? To fail is to be absorbed by the Germans—Sudetenland South—or you imagine we are so great as to pull the whole tent down?"

The Minister shown his charming re-whitened teeth—his disarming smile—to Oslo. They sat at the immense smooth-lac-quered hull-shaped table—opposite each other by width of one of its unmarked narrow prows, so as to feign a conversational intimacy. They were in the high, private conference room of Rothman, executive floor, One Canada Square, where two unequal walls of glass

beyond them collected grey sunlit tears direct from the uncolored air
of sky—mourning drops straight off the weeping day—behind which
England climbed off in pavement mist and rooftiles, to the East. The
Minister wore a navy suit which glowed faintly in the sourceless light.
He stroked the knot of his tie as he might his Adam's apple, in overt
contemplation, and drummed ten fingers on the table to mark his
thought in conclusion. He leaned forward with his table-high-shrug-
ging shoulders, and reiterated his smile, but this time unaided by
teeth.

"Are those truly conversations you wish to have?" said Oslo.
"Perhaps you would like Helena for them."

"Not at all. But I would see what you have to say. Now that we
are here, I would witness your opinion."

"Respectfully, sir, it is Brussels, not Germany, to begin."

"The one is the bank of the other: they are the same," said the
Minister.

". . . And why should you bring the tent down?"

"Maastricht says not more than sixty percent debt to gross domestic product. It says deficit to GDP ratio of less than three percent.
We are twice worse than when we began, Mr. Oslo: two-point-eight
billion we give to you—to Rothman—debt moved off-book and into
currency swaps: two-point-eight billion euro, long-dated, illiquid
loan, you give to us. September 11 crashes interest rates and bond
yields: your instruments tilt your way. Now the number is five-point-
one billion euros in off-book debt. With your predecessor, we fix new
terms at new rates. With your predecessor the Greek National Bank
buys the swaps that hold the debt: with your predecessor Rothman
provides the instrument to finance the purchase. Now we have bought
huge sums of our own debt back, where it sits in our national bank
like fissile waste in a sieve of concrete vault: where we pretend it is
bars of gold. If your instrument should fail again—if it should tilt
again toward Rothman: to put the debt in a black bag, yes, this is

handy—but for the debt each time to come out profoundly greater—
who will buy it out?—your Brussels will do this? It goes in a sapling:
out comes an oak."

"Perhaps not a sapling—"

"They should kick us out, in that case! Mr. Oslo—do you not
think? Off the euro, and out of the EU."

"If so, you would renegotiate your debt on very favorable terms.
What they cannot do is kick you off the continent."

"Helena has said this too."

"Would you prefer to discuss the instrument package further
with her, Minister?"

"I have discussed what I have to discuss with her. We have spoken
earlier on this. No, I would not."

"No?"

"No, I would not. Besides, Mr. Oslo—she says that we must
discuss it: you and I. She says that you, Mr. Oslo—are expert in
this matter: that it is your *instrument*. Your product. That you have
designed it. So it is. And so it is I am curious for your expert view."

"We have secured you into the EU. You will remain in the EU.
And these will be the instruments to do it."

"Asian currencies and US military conglomerates?"

"Among others."

"We are, Mr. Oslo, to venture a phrase: too dear to burn? Is this
what you suggest? The Hindenburg was I recall, too dear to burn."

"Do you forecast difficulty with the debt component, Minster?"

"I do not forecast, I have people to forecast—I have you to forecast—it is merely that I think in long lines, and so I imagine adver-
sities like mirages on the horizon."

"My opinion, Minister, is that the EU could hardly afford to part
with Greece. You are not a Baltic state, respectfully. *They* could take
their corruption and debt back to Russia—where the wand should
be waved over it all—become invisible once more. But where should

Greece go? You cannot leave and certainly you cannot realign. There is nowhere to go, and nothing to leave from—because it cannot be afforded that you should part. Geo-political cohesion, trade, immigration, defense? Brussels should let you go over parking tickets, and have you draft your own trade and cut your own treaties? Go back to the drachma and shrug off a debt in euros? And who would follow? Italy? Portugal? Spain? France?"

"You say we would pull the tent down? I say we are an ant dancing on a stay-line."

"I say, Minister, they could hardly allow it."

"They would write down such debt?—worst come to worst: a bad weather end?"

"What is the alternative? Austerity?" Oslo smiled: "Minister, you cannot be that austere."

Lanze glanced in the mirror. He looked at Lila and back. The A6 entered the mouth of the Autoroute Du Soliel tunnel—where they would pass into the silk bedding of the soil and beneath the river Saône—and the green hills and the white buildings of Lyon passed from view, and Jean-Pierre touched the glass in looking out on white tile and strobe of orange lights and the close, suspended night which clung to the air like mist. —'Bring it to Athens. I shall sign it there,' had said the Minister. Oslo had pushed a copy of the product summary toward him, and the Minister had pushed it back. He rose, he buttoned his jacket, he stroked the knot of his tie; he inspected hands—palms and crown—for ink, for dirt, for misgivings: 'When your affairs are ordered—the contract prepared and sorted—Mr. Oslo—you shall bring it to Athens: there it shall be signed.'

He's tipped back in his chair now. Fallen back into the brace of it, and rubbing his temples. The room was long, thought Oslo—large, given context of objects to scale. He'd thought it as he watched the Minister leave—the long performative tread of dignity. A measure too long, he'd thought—a measure too large—without overheads and nothing but an illumination in ambient London grey: at last the door, at last the handle, crisp the final turn. A light like tweed.

He'd the room and window on pointillist day, briefly for himself. Fingers on his temples and body against the chair, before Helena. She enters with service cart, but being Helena, there's no stoop, but lording, rigidly above it as one might a shopping trolley.

"What does he say?" says Helena. Bottles and stemware and folded linens on the cart; Oslo lifts his hand to see.

"You'll wash that debasing labor from yourself," he says.

"Can you not see me licking my fur? What did he say?"

"Is it not premature to celebrate?"

"I come prepared," she says, and gestures the orange carafe, "to temper victory with the taste of defeat. In which case it should always have been mimosas for hangover, and nary a pretense to find. What, my dear Freddie Oslo, did . . . the Minister . . . say?"

"He says bring it to Athens; he would sign it there."

"Athens?"

"The signing should take place there."

"Naturally so!" says Helena.

Who to share this victory?—he thinks; his victory in potentia. Simone Helena beside her libational trolley: Champagne and sweating bucket. "Be a dear and pour us, would you. I'll summon Bretting," she says. Lila in smiling pause on the telephone?—nodding invisibly over numerical phrases, quietly through abstruse structural features—a praise to stop his talking. Cygnet?—inured already to vast numbers; Cygnet, for whom desk and bed are one—Cygnet, who relies on it; common as weekend breakfast; who blinks through Gauloises, brushes ash from billions with a B, like so much *Financial Times*. Helena then: it must be, even if only, Helena, he thought, as she gestures from across the room—up!—up!—on her phone, talking near the far door. She covers the mouthpiece with her hand: "He'll be along—pour!—pour, boy! Pour!" she says. And he moves to the service and turns the key of wire basket; and she casts four fingers at him from across the room; arms and pulls the cork—twists and tugs into linen, and he pours off flutes. Rising, excited, expectant, falling—some fractional fluid condensing of ecstatic liquid gas. He pours four flutes, and steals a sip while she's turned. But it's not Bretting he sees next, quavering at the threshold in his shoes like potatoes and his over-fat tie, but the first of a pair of toughs. First the one, and then the other—dark suits and broad collars. One takes exactly a step into the room, peers as a sniffing dog and retreats to the corridor where they both mill about in collective heel. Manhattan's twins, and then the man they presage: Manhattan.

He sweeps in, hands off his satchel to Helena, black and fine, and she ferries it to the service cart where she ends her call and trades it for waiting Champagnes. "When's the signing?" he says, sits with a back to the sky and Helena feeding a stemware into his outstretched hand, from which he drinks directly.

"À votre santé," says Oslo, with a wry lift of the glass.

"Bretting's to bring up a signature-ready draft from vetting. It's yet to be scheduled," says Helena. "We think, a few days."

"Are we so certain? Is there any concern they won't?" says Oslo.

"No, there is not," says Manhattan.

"You said as much, Freddie," says Helena.

"I conveyed what was said."

"He will sign," says Manhattan, and lays papers and fits reading glasses from the lanyard round his neck. "We're taking a substantial position in the euro," he says, and moves papers toward Helena. "This is the order."

"The short?" Helena lifts the papers to see. "Is this the Foal?" she says, and Oslo sees them exchange a look: Manhattan, a fleeting scowl over brim of glasses; Helena, a squinting wince she drinks, and turns to read.

"What is the 'Foal'?" says Oslo. His head shakes resigned, indifferently as the words emerge. It's a reflex to sooth the visible snare—an offering: Jean-Pierre, posing questions to quell unrest in deflection.

"Just words," says Manhattan. "Just words," he repeats toward Helena. "The *Belgian* Foal, is the foal in question—these are the words."

"What . . . is the *Belgian* Foal, then?" says Oslo.

Manhattan peers again over his glasses. He peers over them at Helena; over them at Oslo: "The Belgian Foal?—words ascribed to a package of arrangements."

"A short position in the euro, for example?"

"Among others."

"Among other positions."

"Among other arrangements. A strategy," says Manhattan. "Have you ever given name to an intention—?" he says, but is interrupted by Helena.

"Ian Bretting!" she says. "Dear Bretting!" She calls to him at the threshold speaking to Manhattan's twins. "Come, come! Let him through, boys. Bretting dear, fetch a glass, Freddie has poured for you. —Bretting, this is Manhattan, darling," says Helena, and guides him off with a hand against his shoulder.

He does as instructed: fetches his glass and moves to the table. Opposite Manhattan he set out papers and thinks to greet him, stands and thinks to reach a hand or round the table to engage the seated man—Oslo sees it in the cant of his hips and the hovering, uncertain fingers—but he's ignored, and the table is hopelessly wide here; a fool's crossing; and the deliberation spends the moment: "A pleasure to see you, sir," he says, and situates himself among his things.

Helena circles to Oslo—she wraps her arm round his waist: "Love," she says closely, "let us not introduce Bretting to the Belgian Foal, shall we: he's not a man of subtle meanings." She pats him on the ass and moves off to join the others at the table.

"What have I missed?" says Bretting to Helena, and flicks the foot of his glass. "My copies are ink-dry," he says, with a thump of his soft middle finger on his copies. "Are yours wet?"

"Bretting, you shall merely force Freddie to cork us another when they are: clearly the paper's not the only dry thing. Chin-chin, Bretting, the law is such a barren place."

Bretting passes his copies. He sets one for Oslo, he leaves untouched; for Helena, who reviews intently, and for Manhattan, who does not. Bretting leaves this moment of reading and not reading to its natural library sounds, and adds only the taking of Champagne. "Freddie?—won't you have a look?" he says.

"Bretting, I expect it's only what I put there, improved by cost of consequence."

Manhattan leafed through as though these were the sporting pages.

"Freddie, you'll want to review it," says Bretting.

"I'm with the second wave, Bretting; Simone is afforded right of first aggression."

"State your aggressions, Ms. Helena," says Bretting. "What is this?" he says, and indicates the papers already beside her. "Does it concern the signing documents?"

"No," says Manhattan. He reaches and slips them from Helena across to Bretting. "A position order."

"A short," says Helena. "Insurance."

Bretting takes the papers and considers them. "Insurance?" he says, and laughs. Manhattan straightens and folds his hands. Oslo sees him relishing, surprise or disbelief or conflict. His glasses are dropped on their lanyard. Oslo cannot see what's coming, but Manhattan seems to, and squares for it: he wants the swing.

"Isn't it?" says Helena.

"Insurance? Helena, you can't be serious. A six-billion-euro debt repackage to Greece, and this is insurance?!" Bretting laughed, and took half his glass at once, and laughed some more: a pinched, rosy, pained and joyless laughing. "This is your insurance? This is your short? Are we bombing it?!" He laughed again. "Insurance against the collapse of the currency, you mean."

"Oh, Bretting—"

"It's the biggest short I've seen," he says. He's incredulous—and now Oslo wants to see it too. ". . . Ever heard of . . . Simone?" he says. He looks at her. He looks at Manhattan. "Are you quite sure?" he says. Simone was standing now, angling away, shielding her drink from distasteful tonic. Manhattan sat placidly—relishing. "It's not a bet the Greek products will fail: it's a bet they will fail—*and* every geographic thing they're attached to: you're betting a collapse of the currency," he says, and finishes his glass. "Are you sure?"

"Well . . . I don't think it needs all that, Bretting . . . that would be outrageous," says Manhattan. He stands and tidies his pages, and slips them to the side, and buttons his jacket. "Because . . . it is gentle and receptive . . ." he says. He moves toward the door: "and hard to see . . ." At the threshold he turns: "And with it, the meek defeat the great by their magnitude."

XV.

When they all have gone—Bretting and Manhattan, and his doorway toughs, Helena refills them and they are alone in conference among the great hull-like table and the seats of its many stations at-oar, and the libational service cart Helena had deigned to drive alone. "Is it the law or his nature that makes him so tedious, do you think? —To you always, love," she says, and their glasses touch, and they stand with the table between them and terraced sweep of conquered lands beneath their window.

"Numbers of geologic scale, perhaps."

"Cosmological," she says. "Oh! Love, I nearly forgot," she says, and fetches a fine black satchel from the undertray of the service cart. "The Minister left this with me earlier—forgotten in my office—his satchel: be a dear," she says, and hands it. ". . . and bring it when you meet him: he's sure to miss it."

The second riddle of the labyrinth of Chartres . . . Here by car and plane and train and car: by snowy Range Rover—little black oxcart fluted down rutted tracks; little cart that trams and clatters but breathes illusive freedom at the low and hobbling catchments: cannot know it is merely a train for private purposes. . . . From London . . . To choose . . . His squeaking shoes and wet nape of cuff. It swung and slapped at the ankle—a swaying senser without smoke, but new-christening irony for those who cannot say yes; cannot say no: the pageant which neither instructs nor edifies, neither feeds nor warms—familiar and impossible as lost bigotry. The second riddle of the labyrinth of Chartres, he saw from the center now, lay all in mission. The pilgrims' faith is on the pilgrims' way. A pilgrimage that proves the pilgrimage, but no destination—kicks the can of it down the event horizon of meaning. What would you have?!—it says—who would you love?!—faith?!—or the truth that pulls it by the hair? Pleasure?!—or the reason for it? This rock . . . What rock is this now, so smoothed in love to wetness—Anointing? Shall he be taken from here? Direct through the roof. Perhaps to the desk in Paris. Perhaps, the house, seated upon the rivulet roads of Chartres. London, perhaps—gilded in carbon-steel timbers and de-stained glass, elevation by way of high-speed lifts. Faith rumbles in the surging tide, but the quiet eye is apostasy: the paradox of the labyrinth of Chartres is . . . having trod one's careful and scrupulous way, turning, turning, ever inward: shall he retread his step?—shall he escape from his goal down the same imagined corridors which led him?—or fell such walls as markers, denounce his former obediences, and step obstacle cross obstacle which never were . . . to flee them, and the uninhabitable eye, whose attainment flattens his way, lays waste to meaning, mocks devotion, vitiates the pilgrim by his chastity. An elevation to abyssal plane . . . flat, and far, far lower than beginning. London. London, then. Rothman—he'd thought. He saw himself standing thinking it. Center of the eye, and wet shoe leather. Shall he go? Shall they all? Uproot the field . . . for another—

"Papa."

. . . soil.

"Papa? Papa. Papa. Papa. Papa. Papa!"

There was light then. No somber monastic tones of Chartres interior, but saturation and sparkling incidence of eternal Cote d'Azurian solar noon. His eyes were open, as they had been, blinking in luminous and road-bound Gaulish south, but now, stepping from womb-lit reveries, it was bright, hot even—his arm, his face, in the window-borne sun.

"Papa? Papa. Papa. Papa. Papa? Papa. Papa!"

He watched Lila tip her head over: a quick sidelong glance to see Jean-Pierre—check the luggage, thought Oslo, and somewhere in the sight of it—'Say something!'—he thinks. 'Will you say something?' he thinks—'What!?'—he thinks—'Fucking Manhattan, and Helena'—he thinks, and the mandala of Chartres, and 'Bretting in his potatoes, and the Hermès Minister of Greece, and this mewling child' goddamn fucking child in his abstract warren of needs—What, child!? What! What!? What do you need!—and this Lanze, 'and this Lanze!' and his fucking boat and his fucking car and his fucking mayhem of my life in his secreting me away from Helena's mythical forces in the world, 'the touch of the law!'—and this fucking woman . . . 'this fucking woman!' who rolls over and blinks at the mewling child like I'm wet nurse on holiday, like so much luggage on her way—this fucking woman who wouldn't know I'd gone missing 'less I'd called to tell her: 'Say something!—say something!—say something'—and somewhere in sight of it, in sight of her dismissal, and the persisting assault of sound . . . his hand leapt up . . . violently to his side—leftward . . . where he caught it, saw it arrested from flight—in pause. —Where it unfurled then . . . from the elbow. A thing fumbled and escaped, and the length an instant, a line in sail—cast with no end . . . but water. Where it landed . . . against the supple cheek of Jean-Pierre: the lefthanded backward snap . . . of full ring, and knuckles.

And at first, he did not cry.

The silence which came—Oslo did not think, but felt—was belly-curdling; leaden against his scrotum, filling his socks with dribbling sick. Anger and illness, and distress. Disturbance, he thought. Disturbance. Rightful, he thought. Righteous, he thought—disturbance. He thought. And the car flung down the highway like a missile. It bellied and rebounded over the imperfections in glass . . . at such speed. And Jean-Pierre covered his face and sobbed—at such speed—a quiet, respirative sob. And Lila did not look. She did not check the luggage . . . for fit or wellness, for judgement or sympathy. There were just the eyes of Lanze . . . center of the center of the paradox of the labyrinth of Chartres—center of the rearview mirror—worked in steely glisten. Looking. Casting rearward, from some forward compartment, at him.

Oslo noticed the slowing then. Not so much a lift, but neutral. Gently at first, and brakeless. They drifted rightward. Straggled cross the centerline. Where they were caught. Eventually. Overtaken. Then in droves. A whirring traffic they once had escaped, now upon them—passed—passing—around them. And then drifting . . . with the rapidity of a flat-tire limp, ever rightward, onto the shoulder, shoulder, shouldering . . . Stop. And there they set for a moment, unstructured but for the sound of Lanze's refracted gaze. And then the doorlatch: not vague and residual, but sharp chorus of alto machine parts. And then he was out: trained his tie with a hand and buttoned his jacket, rounded the car, and the sound again. Hatchlike. Definitive. Ballistic. And he was out, with a hand from Lanze. Drawing; guiding; and the door was replaced: crisp, purposeful. Expressive. And he was taken by a bit of shoulder cloth, and pulled over the shallow drainage culvert, and he stood, back to the car, and to traffic, and slightly downhill to Lanze. And Lanze touched his lapels—lightly, gently, and drew back his hands. And there they hovered, in this place neither touching nor forfeiting touch . . . and he whispered then. Into his ear. Stepped across from where he stood. And Oslo thought it was like talking at the sea—quavering against the inaudible. And Lanze said: "I will drink your blood . . . and plant the parts of you for seed . . . if you should touch that boy again . . . in my presence."

XVI.

His nose whistled slightly as he breathed. His ears felt clogged in that way when you've been ill, or weeping. His face was wet and he wiped it with his hands. His hands, he wiped along the legs of his denim breeches. And then he covered not his eyes, but his face. Wet again. Dripping into his palms and orange darkness.

Everything was quiet but the engine and the air sliding along the windows. Maman had said—'He's hungry' when they'd returned to the car, and that was the last thing anyone had said. The man who drove—Mr. Lanze—the driver—had started the car and looked over his shoulder what felt like a long time, and then he pulled out and the engine made a sound that pleased and frightened him and everyone fell back into their seats and were held there as the engine grew louder and louder and then softer and then louder and louder again, and again. And this made everyone thoughtful and so they did not speak but concentrated out the windows on the sound and the sights of the world streaking by.

XVII.

A rgos Argyros had opened the case on the plane of his bed, bowed, as it were, on knees and elbows before it. The case was sturdy and perfect silver latches that unbuckled in release. The lid lay open on the days-old sheets of his boyhood bed, his boyhood room open upon his boyhood home, the windows opened onto this with air moving the scent of daylight melting bilgewater from the bellies of the knocking boats—once-lacquered hardwood forever wet and softened with fish parts and piss and the strange muck of boots—and the way the granite of the pier gave that nose of rain when the spray dried from it. He opened the case, and there lay the most beautiful object his boyhood eyes had ever lay upon. A deep amber viola fitted in royal blue velour: a bow in the lid; each piece hand-worked and glued and rubbed and polished and stained and polished and rubbed again. Impossibly light to hold; impossibly fragile. So delicate a thing in the care of a boy whose home sounded of television commercials and the tock of father's heirloom mantle clock and mother's wash and father's sleeping, or furtive attempts. It smelled of high varnish and resin and fresh naked woodworks: it was in every tactile and sensory dimension the sense of a museum piece entrusted to him. A bell glass lifted from a pedestal.

There were two other students at violin lesson—for which there was no other violin. They were attentive and they studied in a dark warm room in the interior of the school where the history instructor tutored them in rarified instruments. They stood at music stands and the bitter strings stung at his fingers when he plucked or made chords. And then they turned their pages and when he made mistakes he began again, and then they began to bow and when he made mistakes he began again, and plucked and pressed chords on the sharp strings and they bowed and turned their pages—in the warm dark interior room so near to the gymnasium that somewhere there was the heavy air of it. And one day the tutor said stop! Argyros, stop! And he wiped the bridge of his oily nose with his sleeve and replaced his glasses with the heavy gold rim and the strange bezel through the center of the glass—and he said—Argyros! I have told you—how many times have I told you that you cannot stop after each mistake—can you not stop?—it seems you cannot stop. And everyone had stopped. And their bows hung from their thumbs at their chest so they would not touch the floor—Argyros saw them in that odd posture suspending their bows from their sternums like as they were overlong strings. And he said—Argyros! Argyros, do you know what I am going to do—he fished two coins from his pocket and looked at them to see what they were and showed them to Argyros between his pinching fingers: Do you know who this is, Argyros?—he held out two coins pinched by their edge, and moved the one, and stooped before Argyros, heavy glasses moving along his nose. Everything moved in Greece, thought Argyros, like the curtains and the knocking boats—but for the air of this room where practiced their two violins and a viola. Argyros did not know who it was and shook his head. It is Aristotle. Do you know what it is?—no? . . . it is five drachmas. He moved the other coin—Do you know who this is?—no?—no?—it is Democritus. Do you know what that means?—do you know what it is then?—no?—no? . . . no? . . . it is ten drachmas. Argyros. Argyros, when you make a mistake . . . I am going to charge you five drachmas. The instructor wiggled the five-drachma coin to mark it out. And when you stop—Argyros—when you stop after you make a mistake . . . I am going to charge you ten drachmas. He moved this coin to show it.

Argyros sat in a folding chair at the back of the room. He sat with the viola replaced in its royal blue case for sleeping. It lay on his lap where he gazed on it to the end of class, when he closed the lid and buckled the latches and thrust it into the instructor's hands as he left.

He remembered the day his father had brought it home, and a jug and a fish in paper, and bread. He remembered his father presented it to him—the most beautiful thing that was not a violin—that he had ever lay his boyhood eyes upon. He remembered kneeling before it on his bed and touching the lining of the case. But he had never noticed until that day, arrived in rage and frustration, home from school, that the heirloom clock was gone from the mantle.

Argyros turned the foot of his glass upon a cocktail napkin upon his table, fourth floor, Canada Square, Canary Wharf, by the corners, by the pips of his pointing fingers. He'd set before a wall and roof of glass all enmeshed by elaborate stainless joints and tenons—looking out onto the dim, glass-captured shade of himself looking out: new bead necklace and open collar and new grey suit—onto the colonnade, green and loose and run to the foot of One Canada Square. A phalanx of lighted glass towers closed upon it by their ankles, in refractive discourse: blue-cast, white-lit volumes shown amber-trapped lives in their panes. Ten thousand lightboxes projecting transparencies of vacant desks and empty chairs onto a nighttime common, until they glow with the noise of stars. And it was here Argyros sat, in his cocktail and his phantom bite of strings once more in the pips of his fingers, and the rap of his wristwatch upon the table, and the smell of meats sounding frisson in their own oils, in a room lighted by all the lights of the gallery of other rooms.

"You are Argos Argyros, sir? Call for you, sir." The server had emerged from warbling obsidian conversation and bright flints of laughter, clasped his placket and tie in subtle bow to present the cordless handset.

"It is quite a bit of money, Mr. Argyros—you did obtain the hashish with it?" He recognized the accent immediately—Argyros thought he talked like one of the German army officers from the old films where they were always played by Britons—this was his sound: slightly distracted, slightly aloof, like a German with a British accent or a Briton with a German accent—slightly aloof, disdainful, and probably reading.

"Mr. Lanze!"

"Are you not hungry, Argyros?"

"How do you know I'm not eating?"

"You answered directly: no choked morsel, gnashing teeth, no last fork-full—no pausing to blot the corners of your mouth."

"My plates have been cleared, Mr. Lanze. I am on to fluids and a view." Argyros had fished a phone from his pocket to check it. "Have I missed a call from you, Mr. Lanze?—I see no missed calls on the phone you lent—the work phone."

"Technical issues, I'm sure," said Lanze,

"How did you know to reach me here?"

"I'd hoped you'd be at your studies, and happily, I see that you are: but it's lucky good, a lad such as yourself to be noticed, don't you think?—handsome, important Argyros receiving calls among the monied poshery of London."

"Canary Wharf."

"Indeed. Canada Square. So—the matter of the hashish?"

"Mr. Lanze?"

"It is for my producer, Argyros."

"Mr. Lanze—would you have me try you on the other phone, sir?" said Argyros, pressing ambient laughter from his ear with a finger.

"It is quite a lot, Argyros—you must imagine I'd be curious. You do possess it?"

"Mr. Lanze. Yes."

"It's in safe keeping?"

"Yes."

"I'd thought you might bring him a taste, but let's leave it be: collect it after production—on return to London."

"Return, Mr. Lanze?"

"Argyros—is this your bank card number?" said Lanze, and enumerated the sequence.

"Wait—let me check it—wait. Can you repeat it, please?" said Argyros, and Lanze repeated it.

"It is, yes. It is."

"You'll need to present it against incidentals, and to secure your room."

"Mr. Lanze, perhaps they'll be wanting the phone."

"The balance was a bit low. I took the liberty of advancing some funds: an account needs care and feeding, Argyros. Do you have a pen?"

"I have nothing to write with, Mr. Lanze."

"Well, this is the call, Argos Argyros—*your* call. I'll text the address to the work phone: let me know how long you require to get there—you may precede me. Bring your things, as we've discussed, and be there directly. Your passes will be waiting there under your name."

"What passes?—wait—Mr. Lanze?"

"What else, but the Grand Prix, Mr. Argyros."

2.

"Weayw, weayw!—look upon this hea'"—had said the barman when Argyros stood beneath the brass lamps and red ceiling, at the taps and red carpets of Crown & Sceptre. The Tube and two transfers had returned him to Streatham place, and he'd wondered the while why he'd not hired a taxi. The seared meats and truffle had given him a smart and restless stride—his heals clipped with the satisfaction of rolling timpani on street-side pavers—and so he'd carried his shine off for a few pints at the corner, in the gauzy, perfumed, pub-light of Wetherspoon's. "Oy, oy!" had said the barman when Argyros squared the tab: "ya gonna visit yo friens' when ya famous?"

"Why'd I do that?" he said. "Do parolees visit the inmates?" he'd said, and stepped off and out and down the short step and drew a cigarette from the brown box that closed with a 'pfup,' and lit his cigarette, and walked the half block home. He forced himself to slow, to breathe and smoke and smell the dark on the air like caramel—like char on the oak barrels of day; imparting clove and chocolate, coolant and rubbish; to taste the Maduro paper on his lip; to nose the diesel buses and to hear the rasping little transports that ferried people from light to light—to look on the sulking flats that would always have something coaled-up and water-stained about them, something that shrunk from him now in looking, as if moving slowly behind themselves. And when he stepped before his own apartment house he touched the sticky fingers of the hedge there, and smelled the humid private earth beneath it, and finished his cigarette down to the hot quick. And he sighed. And went in to collect his things.

3.

Place du Casino, 98000 Monaco, was an antique revolving door off a forecourt of exotic automobiles and hastening valets, onto a hall gilt-rubbed and columned and gleaming, glassed and high-domed of elaborate aquatic friezes. It was Argyros, moist socks and palms, and all his manner of luggaged things, British Airways two hours Heathrow to Nice Côte d'Azur, with his hands clasped tightly between his knees and the mother-daughter duo across the aisle engaging him by turns in some form of bald visual consumption, and the rippling Channel beneath the window, and all the May-tide green of unripe harvest of France, and coming down over the water as onto the deck of a grand aircraft carrier, the airport clung to the wet shoulder of Nice like as a pontooned appendage. By train then: you are in Monaco where the graffiti ends, when there are no sheets drying from the windows of high wrought iron balconies, where stray scrub greeneries grow manicured, where worksites for fresh pavements appear for near, untrod paths; and when the water is there—a plate in emerald blue, and swept and palmed, and buoyed and docked, and parked-up with yachts, lucent and imbricated as the warp of caravans at a campsite holiday.

It was a head valet on a comms and a man who might be security and a doorman on a stair under statuary nymphs—through a lobby as it might be for a museum or grand depot—all looking cut from a living marble cavern, and a pair of counters with stone and flutes and golden finials, and a cast dressed in tidy black suits like Milanese clergy—and his bags to a room on the fifth floor, and sconce lights and wood-and-carpet flooring, and scrollwork moldings, and a small terrace where he went and leant upon the railing and looked at the sea—and he'd said: "Is this Place du Casino, 9-8-0-0-0?" he'd said. And a concierge had lifted a phone receiver and checked her watch for time and spoken French, into the phone to a listener, and consulted a computer screen and made marks in a binder and replaced the handset, and said, "Yes, monsieur."

And he'd said, "I am Argos Argyros—a reservation is held in my name."

"Of course, monsieur—the last name please?"

"Argyros: A-R-G-Y-R-O-S. Argos Argyros: I am an actor."

"Of course, monsieur—let me find you, please," she'd said, and consulted her screen with the officious stroke of keys. "I have you here," she'd said.

"I am with a production: we are to be filming."

"In the Principality, monsieur?"

". . ."

"In Monaco, monsieur?"

"Yes . . . of course, in Monaco, yes."

"Excellent. Are you to be filming the Grand Prix, monsieur?"

"No. I don't think so."

"Well, you will have an excellent view of Massenet from your terrace, monsieur. Your rooms are paid through Tuesday, monsieur—but I will require a card to hold against incidentals—thank you," she'd said. "Would you prefer to have all expenses billed to the room, monsieur—very good. Suite, and communicating Exclusive room—sea views—with terrace: these are keycards for your room: you requested we hold the keycards for the other room at reception—do you still wish that, monsieur?"

"That would be fine," he'd said.

"Your guest will be required to check-in on arrival. Just a reminder that first practice is held on Thursday in Monaco. Friday is the rest day for Grand Prix—but there will be support series events."

"Very good," he'd said.

"This is the program for the weekend," she'd said, and pointed the dates on a brochure she'd advanced, with the tip of her pen. "And these are the circuit passes held for you—Monsieur Argyros—please enjoy your stay," she'd said. And he'd thrown his things on the mattress, and grinned at himself in the bathroom vanity, and turned the crisp-handled door onto the terrace, and leant lock-shouldered onto the balustrade and squinted into the tussling glint of sea air.

XVIII.

"I need you to listen closely," Lanze had said. Jean-Pierre had sat peering through the railings at the hot-flashing noise. Lanze had leant forward. He had reached forward and clasped her hands, he had looked her in the eyes with a ferocious urgency. He'd leaned close to speak over the turns of noise, like fighter jets coursing up the street in staggered formation and out of view.

2.

Lila furrowed herself against the open air. She'd carried an overnight bag for Freddie rattling with computer and charging gear, her purse and a small bag for herself and Jean-Pierre. There was comfortable breeze, high cloud had cut the glare, the pavements were smooth, the buildings were cheerful and affluent, but she was exhausted and stumbling, behind Freddie with baggage and carrying Jean-Pierre by the hand as he ambled like a hap-and-bowler-less Chaplin. Her brow hurt from pinching out the day and her body groaned from sagging postures of trains and automobiles, and the arch of her feet ached for ill-chosen, long-worn footwear. The city was crowded with sound and pedestrians and blazons calling everywhere in high-contrast corporate cartouches and proud stitching and placards and banners and ad-hoc barriers and suggestive catch fencing—and she longed simply to be some-where: to have a place; a declared state of arrival. This first was not a long walk: ten minutes perhaps, but canted ever upward or down, and never even. They trailed Freddie, a pair of garment bags slung at their biting hangars, and a phone, dialed numbly and repeatedly, wrong-handedly—peering into the screen, clutched to his ear, wait-ing—navigating by some sightless impulse, and they behind him. Eventually—under ironworks white as trellis struts—paused within the skylit Eiffel-domed lobby of the Hermitage, it was stowed, and he lay hands at reception to speak.

"Only registered guests may enter the rooms," Lanze had said. They had entered Monaco on a late afternoon Friday, by a narrow lacing road that had made Lila think of trimmings of Highway 1, where it writhed into and fled San Francisco—but with villas clung to it and decorative mortared terrace walls, and countermeasures against erosion: an old-money Mulholland Drive with ocean view, perhaps.

"What's in Monaco?" Freddie had said.

"Monsieur—your holiday, to be sure."

The road which snaked from the hills and into the city was alternately named for saints and princes, princesses and other terms of high-flung declaration. Lanze had followed this and the push-pull respirations of traffic, until he'd split off down a close, crowded, residential lane, and in a pause between a hedge of ornamental fruit trees and a cliff-face of fawn, looming apartments, he'd stopped the car.

"A room is arranged for you at Hôtel de Paris, but you've introduced a complication, monsieur."

"What accommodation?" Freddie had pulled himself forward by the seat shoulder. "Perhaps they can be added."

"Hôtel Hermitage. It's just there. A few blocks. Unlikely, and bound to be costly—but beside your hotel, monsieur, and a place to begin. —I think you would precede me on foot, given traffic."

"With what?—how should I secure it, Mr. Lanze?" Freddie had said, and wrestled into his jacket.

"Well, you may call first if it suits you," Lanze had said, and produced Freddie's phone and given it to him—and he produced his passport and wallet, and given those as well. "I'm led to believe your finances will match the occasion."

"You're giving these now?"

"Of course. You would miss them were they lost."

"I will ring Helena, I think."

"Of course you will. Just don't dither on the room—they can't have much, and it won't last."

It would be several hours before one became available. Much of it they had waited on a long sofa in the double-height Belle Époque lobby. Light sifted onto them through stained glass vegetation: flour; powdered sugar—she might lick it from her nose by the tip of her tongue, she thought—hear the click of the clumsy handle attached somewhere to the rivet-studded metal works. Freddie had paced about in his handsome new tailoring—his heals knocking with the distracted vigilance of a night-watch soldier. She sat cross-legged there, rubbing her instep with a straining thumb and peering into the voided cup of her shoes ranked on the floor before her. Jean-Pierre bounced and crawled on the sofa, and signaling some final capitulation, Freddie threw up his hands, and pocketed his phone, and joined them there with a defeated and full repose: "I can't reach her . . ." he'd said. For a time they sat this way, watching the guests leaving, or returning to leave, and the light settling like powdered sugar . . . that with her tongue she might taste.

She'd reached out her hand. Lain it on the sofa between them, a small consolational offering Freddie seemed entirely too coiled in himself to take: "You'll say something to Jean-Pierre? . . . Are you enjoying London? . . . Freddie . . . Can you be?" she'd said, but Freddie peered at the ceiling. The mezzanine. The staff. The counters. "You are on holiday," she'd said. "Are you on holiday?" she'd said.

"I suppose," he'd said.

"What did he say to you?"

"Who?"

"Lanze," she'd said. And Freddie traced the guests with folded arms. "We'll talk later. When we get back. But it was . . . You have to say something to Jean-Pierre. Freddie. It . . ." she'd said. She'd leant forward onto her elbows, onto her folded knees, and peered at the floor, and watched all the sugar slip from her nose . . . into her shoes—perhaps it will be smooth as talc, she thought.

Freddie had gone to his room at Hôtel de Paris after that. He'd taken his overnight and two garment bags, to freshen and repair, to check-in and to see what holiday-making arrangement it was that Lanze had prepared. He'd collected his things and lay a hand on Jean-Pierre's crown of hair, and pushed out through the door with a mien of trampled purpose, onto the utilitarian-looking service lane—Avenue de l'Hermitage—and it was sometime later a costly Diamond Suite, sea view, had been released, and they had been sent up—Lila and Jean-Pierre—and she'd sat with Chardonnay against the pillows and watched him, not on the furniture, but sitting on the floor of the open bedroom terrace, heels right to the railings, through rippling gauze of curtains, quietly, watching yachts of the harbor and streets made still to the violent overtures of racing.

3.

Bridgestone, Johnnie Walker, Helix: these are the words there on black and white and yellow. There is something called Armco—says Freddie on Saturday—it lines the Casino Square; he says it may be straight or curved—a crash barrier—but it looks quick low scaffolding for shouts of signage to Lila: what is a safety that cannot be brought to use? There are palms and cranes at the corner. The stand is filled with hats and heads—the heads are grey or sparse or they are suspiciously ordinary here in the B grandstand— the Casino Curve, Place de Casino, or the Casino Square—or whatever the name for this is because everything here is named. There are hats in different colors but the red hats belong not to a clique but an ethic: they are uniformed in red. This is Ferrari; these are its fans, Freddie tells her by telling Jean-Pierre. This is Qualifying; these are its sessions. This is Formula One; these words of the program are what I know of it. Freddie tries for answers as they come, but they make him tired, on top of the thin, blinking, brittle energy he brings; he serves out fulsome half-answers to halve the questions.

There is a screen opposite the circuit. In the square. It shows cars at other corners, at other moments of the circuit. An announcer calls out in mellifluous French, the names of drivers, and times, and sequence and order. If Olympus had an emcee, and he were French, this would be his sound—blown from unseen speakers into everywhere. The cars snap through, left and leftward and right, but in odd, exaggerated arcs: they are not loud, but stupefying as they pass, they cancel thought and ring somewhere in the optic nerve—they are felt at the back of the eye . . . where it connects to consciousness. Freddie says this is a 2.4 litre V8 that does this—that sound like tenfold colonies of bionic bees all weaponized against the middle ear at once.

"I don't know where to be," says Freddie, as they wander about the circuit—he might be talking about seating, she thinks, but maybe not. He hasn't meddled with the phone again other than to touch it in his pocket or check the screen at the end of a reflex gesture. He seems to be resolved on that point at least. For now. They wear lanyards with passes—these were waiting at reception, says Freddie, at the other hotel at check-in, he says—they look expensive and with them they move and enter where they please: two, and Freddie says that Jean-Pierre is five, and they look at him and they look at the passes and they wave them on, in, up, wherever they are advancing, they proceed. But Freddie is distracted: "I don't know where to be," he says, and they follow him, Jean-Pierre in her hand—as they had when they'd left Lanze's car, but without garment bags and the preoccupation of a conceptual 'other' end of Freddie's phone. Freddie tries to buy a hat for Jean-Pierre; she can see that it makes him initially happy to try. But they each say Vodafone or Petronas or Lenovo, or some other cluttery thing—Jean-Pierre wants a simple hat with a clean noble crest, like engraving on a breastplate—and all the noisy words and garish colors make him unhappy, and he won't have one. And this makes him imperceptibly more exhausted. There is a hollow at the cheek of his newly trimmed beard, and a stoop at the base of his neck, as though he is casting about for coins on the walkways, and there is something darting and removed in his look. They pass Grandstand B twice before they sit there—up high at the back, with earmuffs for Jean-Pierre, where he is five—and where they flee after only a few minutes—from Jean-Pierre's curiosity and Freddie's plague of restlessness. But he takes it with him.

"If I left London . . ." Freddie says. They are sitting in the living room or sitting room of their small home within the Hôtel Hermitage—their Diamond Suite. Jean-Pierre naps in the bedroom, and the French doors are open on twilit Monaco and the scintillations of harbor lights. The air is cool. Soon it will be too cool for a view through open doors. Freddie has returned from his other room—from Hôtel de Paris, where he spent the day—without his things. He says that he will bring them tomorrow—"If you like," he says. It strikes Lila as a thoughtless, lazy, backhanded superfluous provocation because she does not understand an alternative and cannot imagine one. He's not thinking what he's saying—she thinks. Freddie orders them bottles of wine and a bucket and he drinks chilled Chardonnay with her—for her: a peace offering of a bit, until he can stand it no longer and corks a Pinot he likes: "I cannot think of the charge for these," he says and grins cross the room at her from amidst the grips and turns of opening—"It would surely spoil the wine. It will bear a few hours of bad temperature, but not a moment of bad temper," he says. He lays fond looks on her. He returns to the armchair and fills it with his lugubrious and slouching mood. He is handsome. With his hook of nose and his effortless beard and his smile, his secreting grin, he breathes cunning charm wherever his image falls. He is smart and removed, and so indelibly foreign . . . even these years later. And, she thinks, he is a sometimes cruel, often leering shit. —Without the least intuition for Jean-Pierre. A shit. That she loves. That she loves? That she loves. That she loves. Like Jean-Pierre. That she loves. . . . When he is quiet . . . that she loves . . . when she's in Paris . . . that she loves . . . when he is compliant . . . playing . . .

preoccupied . . . not reaching out strenuously onto his own branches of being . . . that she loves. When he's sleeping . . . that she loves.

"I thought you might be in danger," she says. "When you called. When we came."

Freddie looks out the door, and rubs a hand through his hair, and puzzles his beard—the tidy, tidy stubble of his beard. "I thought I might be."

"And call a woman and a child through the night to save you?"

"Am I not worth saving? If in the night—if by a woman—if with a child . . . is that price too high? I am a life too far . . . for saving? For salving?"

"We came, Freddie."

"So you did. But not so you say."

"Are you in danger, Freddie?—are you on holiday?"

"I thought I might be. I couldn't understand."

"You might have called the authorities. Shared your plight with them," says Lila, to the taste of cold, dry Chardonnay.

"I didn't have my phone."

"But you did."

"I didn't have access to my phone. I did not possess my phone. Lila. It is difficult to explain. It would be difficult for you to understand."

"I thought you might be in danger. Are you in danger, Freddie, or not?—it seems like you have the crisis of a grumpy chauffer. Freddie. A slick and surly and taciturn, chauffer."

Freddie shifts in his chair. He grips the arms. He looks into his glass. "You came, and I'm grateful," he says.

"Didn't you say Helena instructed this? She told you to go? Sent you on holiday?"

"It was difficult to understand. You came . . . and I'm grateful."

He says this and he drinks, and he drinks again. She looks over her shoulder, back into the bedroom where Jean-Pierre lays crossways against the pillows, along the bed—dogwise. And they both look through the open doors, through which the cool air steps, out onto the sea and boat harbors and the quiet bursts of conversation, the errant shouts of motor, the lighted buildings from some quasi-factual style of time. And he says, "Lila . . . what if I left London . . . ?"

When he said it again it was Sunday wet and drizzled, raining, at a private table beneath a large parasol made parapluie by a mood of weather. "It's a question you ask like a statement," she said. They sat among plantings and greenery in the terrace garden, Hôtel de Paris, scooched and leant heavily onto their table so as to fall mostly within service of the umbrella. Jean-Pierre sat on his knees against the chairback, peeping over greenscaping toward railing and catchment fencing and the architectural precipice from which people had cleared to indoor comforts or to huddle beneath hospitality tents, and where the harbor was closed by chalk cloud and heavy day and great plumes of sound and water erupted from the unseen Massenet, and settled in rain-captured noise, back from where they came. "If you *did*?" she said. "Do you mean—what if you returned to France? Do you mean—what if you left Rothman? Do you mean—what if you found work in Paris again?"

Monaco rain was a mocking gloom. It is not like London or Paris—a restive blue melancholy so deep it casts its own resentful pleasures: it felt a false gloom, like all places bright-lit and holiday-made—even cold and moist it had somewhere the spot-lit and squinted about it. And already Lila had begun thumbing inarticulable misgivings of a Freddie Oslo returned to domesticity in Chartres—of boxes and church bells, of evening dinners and au pairs and Rover trips. —When the front desk had called up about a guest at reception. —It all had the spell of the matronly about it: expectations and obligations, and all the relational fetters cast off in vagary with his move to Rothman. —It was Lanze when they'd come down, Lanze all bladed down and glistening. He was warm and smiling. Gregarious even, in his extra-fine extra-dark suit. More Principalian pit boss or casino magnate than the flip-flopping, chicken-legged Slavs in audience—distended bellies and stripy peel-on tops: more Company than company. —Once, in the back of a Chevrolet Catalina—at a drive-in—all dark and movied-up, with another couple up front—all coital-ed and shimmying—a boy had been on her, and the threat of public and the crowded jostling car, and her, had made him ashen and still. Pained. Lips parted and shining: wet, while his tongue went dry. Lila thought of this when Freddie said it. He had the look when he said it. The pained thing.

Lanze bade them to Hôtel de Paris, next door—to a table on the terrace, arranged in their name—with service and hospitality and overlooking Massenet. He bade them, and they'd shuffled off, and she, tied to them as the walker to the leash. And Jean-Pierre strained and Freddie followed by his inward-cast amble, and Lanze said he would meet them. —No—she'd wanted to say. She'd wanted to shake her head and make the conversation lift. Tear this fiber out to the sound of shrieking racecars—Formula cars: like fighter planes, Lanze had said in some ante-room of conversation—in the car? in the lobby?— like fighter planes with poor lift and fixed landing gear, he'd said.

She'd wanted to thump his glass by the stem and say—No. Don't. Maybe, don't. It's fine the way you are where you are. Have your wine and vacation and a bath in Chartres and a good sleep and a flight to London, and it will pass like a gallstone. It will scrape and pinch . . . with an urgency of crisis—and then it will pass. Like a Christmas ghost, or a piece of bad potato. It will pass.

"There are things for me in Paris . . . after a rest . . . I'm sure," said Freddie.

"It will pass," she said. "Freddie. Like a bit of bad holiday," she said. And the rain eased then. And Freddie leaned out from the table.

Beyond the umbrella, where drops fell in his hair, and the features of his face, and he blinked in it. And people ventured cautiously from their hidings and back to the rail above Massenet, and the cars sounded up the hill again, and Jean-Pierre studied them eagerly for permission to go, and when he thought he saw it he scampered off for the rail as well. And the two of them watched him, in the pause of rain, until Lanze arrived.

"Fancy a bit of gaming while you're here, Monsieur Oslo?" He'd come and taken the damp empty seat from Jean-Pierre, and sat with sunglasses and adjusted his trousers at the knee and unbuttoned his jacket with a lefthanded snap. "No?" said Lanze. "When will you return? You should make some time for it. —I've had a call from your Simone Helena," he said, and Freddie turned to fix on him. "She's to call your room sometime in the hour."

"Did she say she'd missed my calls?"

"No."

"Did she say she'd seen my calls?"

"No."

Freddie leant forward again and checked his watch, and checked his phone. "Did she say the time?"

"She said she would be put through to your room. She said, within the next hour or so."

"What did you tell her? Did she give details?—convey the nature?"

"I said you would be waiting for the call," said Lanze.

Freddie tipped back again. Beyond the umbrella, with an upturned face and eyes closed. Turned up to the rain which fell there. On his nose and cheeks and flinching eyelids, as it had in his hair. "Alright," he said. He stood and touched her shoulder. "If it's soon,

I'll return here. Otherwise, afterward, shall I collect my things and take them to the suite at the Hermitage?"

Lila said nothing. She glanced at Lanze in dark glasses, and she turned up to see Freddie, and she looked into his waiting features, but no words came to her, and she didn't want to make them. He brushed drops from the edge of his nose and the plane of his cheek, and looked at her. And she looked off toward the railing, toward Jean-Pierre, toward where he must be. And Freddie left for his call.

The cars cycled up the hill and the spray fell several times before they spoke. Lila was filled with the same inertia—a much-ness, an over-ness, a state of being at angles to what is close, of wanting to spin again. She looked toward Jean-Pierre—toward where he should be. Through the rain . . . that was picking up. Was it picking up? Rain and settling plumes and coils of low ocean cloud . . . and the deafening scream of the cars . . . and she couldn't tell. Coming, coming, here, gone, now shrieking like harpies, rattling, distant, elsewhere . . . around the circuit.

Lanze said, "We do not see it from where we sit, but we are at the verge of Massenet. We overlook Beau Rivage. It is the uphill straight from the first turn, at Sainte Dévote. What precedes this is the start-finish straight, which itself begins in a kink, and a right-hand turn at Antony Noghès. This is near the pit entry. A short straight—barely a rest—precedes this, and a tight corner. Arguably, one of two, proper, acute-angle, low-speed hairpins. A small restaurant juts into the road here, and that restaurant is called—La Rascasse."

Lila had leant her chin into her palm into her elbow. And she blinked at him from a place in the table where her eyes fell.

"La Rascasse, is the name of that corner. It takes its name from the restaurant around which the road turns . . . *It* was named for a fishermen's bar which came before. It is a feature which alters the landscape. That it is a feature at the will and hand of man is no matter, it proves a feature nevertheless, which forms the landscape . . . and so we must drive around it. The turn takes its name from the restaurant, and the restaurant takes its name from the fish—do you know it?—have you had Bouillabaisse?"

Cars came up the hill and he paused to let them. And Lila shook her head and ground her chin in her hand, and watched the plumes rise . . . and fall.

"A stew—it is a provincial delicacy. Said to be difficult and time consuming: its name means, effectively—'to boil,' 'to simmer,'— *Presto, A tempo, Ma non troppo*—so much, but then, less. —Famed for its difficulty. Famed also for its key ingredient: the fish—La Rascasse. The *sine qua non* of Bouillabaisse. No? The scorpionfish. . . . No? Well—" he said, and waited for the cars whose plume he did not turn to see. "Well . . . I think some myth of the dish borrows legend from the fish. The scorpionfish is poisonous—deadly venomous spines— and it is said, that to fail to prepare it properly . . . with great care . . . may be fatal.

"Who can say if this is true. I for one am a layman in such matters as the toxicology of shallow-water, coastal marine species—but this is the legend."

Lila straightened out of her hand and onto her elbows. "The fatal preparation . . ." she said.

"No," said Lanze. "The innocuous preparation . . . of the otherwise, fatal thing."

"Are you hungry, Mr. Lanze?"

"No. I am not."

"Is this to tell me about Formula racing, Mr. Lanze?"

"It is as relevant there, but no."

"Then what is this . . . chinoiserie of place names and poison fish, Mr. Lanze?—this rufflage?"

"La Rascasse and Massenet, Casino—these are place names for turns. They are words for the landmarks of change. They are undeniable. To refuse them is to bait misfortune, is to hasten the end. To navigate them expertly, is success: The innocuous preparation of the otherwise fatal thing. To argue their validity is misplaced wishful thinking: it is a failure of apprehension."

"I don't care about your race, Mr. Lanze. If it weren't so loud, it would only be stupid. Petroleum and noise, signifying nothing."

"But it is not my race. It is your race too. You are also here. It concerns you . . . Ms. Lila Torp. Some truths are not elective."

"And Jean-Pierre is here . . ."

"Oh, yes."

"And Freddie . . ."

"Ms. Torp—what if someone told you, you were having the single most important conversation of your life? Most consequential. Most definitive. Ever. —Not when it would happen, or that it would happen, but that it was happening—you were in it—it was now."

She looked at him. He removed his sunglasses, folded them and slipped them into his coat.

". . . Do you think you would believe it? Do you think you could?"

Somewhere there were cars now, but further away—as though they no longer careened up the hill, but eddied about in the harbor, in the hills. She looked at his eyes and his nose and the dimples where his glasses had pressed. It was as though she had not noticed his eyes—never seen them before. They were odd. Not unusual, but uncanny. They were not unattractive, but still—as much the rest of his features. But they looked some earlier version—something couched in deep past—glinting from mossed escarpments, fern groves—lighted from cave mouths. They were green, strangely green, feral green—like grey wild dogs: tiger green.

"Why are we here, Mr. Lanze? Why did you bring us here? Why did you bring Freddie here?"

Lanze leant forward, and reached forward, and clasped her hands, and looked her in the eyes: "I need you to listen closely," he said. "This is that conversation."

"What do you want from me?"

"To listen. Closely."

"What, Mr. Lanze? You're frightening me."

"Freddie Oslo is dead."

"What! What?! No! That!—cannot be! He was just here. He was just here, Mr. Lanze!"

"And yet it is true," said Lanze, and leaned closer, and clasped her wrists more tightly.

"You are a madman! And you are hurting me. And I'll scream."

"Of course you will. And you will join your husband, and you will orphan your child."

"How can you know—this is a black and pointless story—how could he be dead?—how could you know?"

"Because I killed him."

"But you were here. He just left! You are a madman. Will you kill me and Jean-Pierre too?"

"No. Just you. And the boy will be an orphan—and he will tumble through all the charitable houses of France, and live a life of rough hands and coarse cloth, and suffer a rearing of great, great carelessness."

"I . . . will . . . fucking . . . scream."

"You won't. You will listen. Calmly. Quietly. Closely. Because you are having the most important conversation of your life."

"Freddie is dead, and you killed him?—you expect me to believe this?"

"It is essential."

"And you would kill me too?"

Lanze said nothing.

"You would kill a woman?"

"Why not? Now you are eligible to receive everything men gift each other—in their simple, stupid brutality—but the occasion of trust. Chivalrous deference? Don't you know?—we don't do that anymore. In a universe of equals, gentlemen condescend. You get to taste muzzle-flash just like the rest of us, Ms. Torp."

Lila freed her hands from his and pulled away and stood. "What will you do?! What will you do, Mr. Lanze?"

Lanze retrieved his sunglasses from his coat, and unfolded them carefully, and put them on once more. "If this is your decision, I will let you make it."

"I will go to authorities . . . Mr. Lanze."

"Certainly so. But it will not change the outcome. Restraint is elective, Ms. Torp—it is no obligation. If you void the predicate for that elective, you will not bar what comes. Those who cannot be strong, and yet, cannot be weak, inevitably become the captive of their enemy—there is no one to keep you from me."

". . . Why should I believe you? This is madness—you are talking madness."

"That you will believe me is inevitable. It is the timing that will make all the difference."

A server had appeared at her shoulder then, whom she noticed because Lanze spoke to him. "The lady stretching her legs is having the house Chardonnay. I am having an Oban, if you please," he said, and dispatched him. "I'm afraid I'm on a bit of a schedule this afternoon," he said, and checked his wristwatch, "so, presently, you'll begin staying, or begin going—I'm afraid I haven't much more time for it."

"What did he do, Mr. Lanze?" said Lila, as she sat again. "What did Freddie do?"

"I am not an arbiter for such things. Such decisions precede me. I have nothing but suspicions."

"What do you want from me? What do you want from us?—from Freddie and me? Is it me?—do you want me? Do you want his money?—do you want my favors, Mr. Lanze?"

Lanze laughed, and thanked the server when he came, and raised a toast to her when he left—"Let us be the dissonance, that precipitates the harmony, that resolves us," he said. And he drank, and with great hesitance, she drank too.

"White women, Ms. Torp—a novelty of some forty thousand years, and still, there is no one to tell you—No. I . . . don't . . . want . . . you! You imagine it's your beauty?—I'll rescue you for beauty?—because it's proof of virtue? You imagine I'll spare you for a bit of virtue I can wear like a condom? No. Mother. I think only for the boy . . . Perhaps, you will too."

After a long silence of engines and applause and rumblings of the body of Monaco, Lila spoke. "What do you want me to do?"

"It is simplicity itself—you will drink Chardonnay and listen to my instructions: In a few moments I will leave, but the terms of our arrangement will last the rest of time: this, the most important conversation of your life will be an explicit privacy, forever. —Forever. Say the word, Ms. Torp."

". . . Forever," she said.

"In a few days the police will contact you. I cannot predict the day, but when they do, you will know everything I have said is true—and it is only till then you will require faith. This is what you will tell them: You will tell them you met with your husband for an unexpected holiday. While on that holiday, he confided to you an illicit affair—"

"Is it true? Did he have an affair?"

"And on the very day—the very afternoon of the confession—the argument—you collected Jean-Pierre, and left straight away."

"And what will we do?"

"You will leave straight away. You will never dial Monsieur Oslo's number from any phone—you will not send him messages at any time. You are sick with grief of betrayal. When I leave, you will finish your drink, have another if you wish—do you have money to get back?"

"Back to Chartres? Yes."

"You will go exclusively, directly to your rooms at the Hermitage—you will collect all your things—you will check out of the hotel. You will take the train to Nice, and from there, back to Chartres as you wish."

"Just that?"

"Only ever that."

"And what would I say about you?"

"The monsieur was traveling by hired car when you met him, on the spur, in Dijon. You spoke with him very little."

"They will want to speak with the driver—they will find you."

"Seeking is not an argument for finding; it is merely the taper of intention. They may look to their content."

He drank from his glass, peered into it, through it to some other side. And she looked down onto her hands. Where they reached for her own, and where she stopped them, and where she saw the backs of them, and they looked withered and foreign, and drew them from the table to rest in her lap. To hide them there. "What you have said, Mr. Lanze—just these things? Just this."

"Only ever . . . this. I have already arranged for the bill. Please stay as long as you require. . . . Good day, Ms. Torp," he said, and stood, and he buttoned his jacket, and he finished the glass and replaced it, and he passed round the greeneries and plantings, and moved to the railing, where Lila could see Jean-Pierre when she leant to see—where Jean-Pierre hung by his hands from the railing in a space of rain by himself, and Lanze had moved toward him, and joined him at the fences, and knelt beside him, and Jean-Pierre had noticed him, and pulled down his muffs, and looked at him, where he knelt beside, and they had both looked past the circuit to the sea.

And Lanze rose, and he didn't touch his shoulder, and he didn't tousle his hair, and he left.

XIX.

Argos Argyros wiped the rain from his eyes. He stood behind the barriers at the Fairmont Hairpin and his formal dress was drenched right through and he considered the lined umbrellas and the laden balconies where pendants waved, and he smiled at his foolish sodden self. Buildings staggered uphill until they became raw crags and scrub green: buildings became hillside, hillside became mist of cloud—high enough and mountain, man, and the works of him were absolved in it. Rock wall and manicured trees lined the approach, and the cars in all their splendid shape of color pattern—little bits of high-octane origami toy—that wound their manic cries down to a mere idling boil, and their deep-grooved tires cast up a spittle of rain as they funneled ones and twos into the chute of the hairpin, and they didn't so much turn as pivot beneath the helmet, somewhere where brainstem mated chassis, they spun at the waist, like: a near gripless swiveling pirouette, where they shrieked off to the next corner and it made Argyros warm in his belly and happy and wet and vibrating with sound everywhere else.

Argyros stood with his fingers in his ears and his broad Mediterranean grin on his lips and he had a feeling of occupying three steps on the same stair in the same moment: of existing at three times at once. The sense was disjointed and odd, but not unwelcome. It tickled of the impending. In it the rain fell as spray of victorious Champagne, and the crowds of balconies were an ovation of private boxes. For him—as much as to cheer home some favorite-colored car. Argyros saw a staging for himself—a green room—and it was the spectacle of Monte Carlo, and it was a holding chamber, a door through which he had passed not to tarry, but to step swiftly once more—through yet another passage, a further passage, another door, no longer of entrance but exit, out onto a platform under crush of lights, before whirring cameras . . . and patient quiet approval—a love, the love, of arrival, of soundstage doors and backstage autographs and yearning begrimed glossies and aromatic pens: and he would be home. An arrival yet a gesture and a passage away. A motion inevitable as the automobiles which hurled into the fold of corner before him, and the gratitude carried there by the kiss of will, rose stems onto footlights, by this audience on high, heeled parapets. Merely an hour or so from now, and it would be nothing but fact-sewn truth— he thought. A reality pregnant with forthcomings. And he thought to check the noted time again: his text from Lanze. And he drew the work phone out into the rain to check, and saw it was little more than an hour away. And then he understood that it was little more than an hour away, from now—standing soaked at the Fairmont Hairpin—and so he hurried back to the hotel.

Argyros strode down causeways and lanes made narrow and crowded with cordons and guardrail. He skipped up the step, pushed through the revolving door, and through the lobby like a whittled vein of stone, and up to the fifth floor, to his room, and called up for a plate of lunch and coffee, and he bathed all the soil of common wetness from him with fine soaps and the sanctified waters of the polished spigots of the white marble bath, and he dried and he ate and he drank coffee in the open doors of his terrace. And he brought himself to a moment steadied and calm, where he waited for his call. —Where he stood at the base of a stair, and the middle of a stair, and the crown of a stair. And he thought he stood at the center looking up at him standing at the crown. But it was also hard to know. And he answered his phone when it rang:

"Good afternoon, Mr. Argyros, are you ready for your close up?" He had that sound of someone pinching a handset against their shoulder, he thought, and turning a gold coin over their knuckles—or perhaps he wouldn't care for gold. A monocle, and cigarette holder...

"I am ready, Mr. Lanze. Do you like a jacket for this or no?"

"I think a jacket will be fine. Are you rested and fed?"

"I am, thank you. I am well, and ready."

"Very good, Mr. Argyros. I am excited to work with you. Will you unlatch the communicating door, please?"

"What is the communicating door?"

"To the adjoining room," said Lanze.

Argyros slipped on his jacket and moved to the entrance: "I see three here: there are two additional doors beside the entrance. Which one, Mr. Lanze?"

"Unlatch them both." And Argyros unlatched them both, and the western door opened slowly and through it stepped Lanze with laden coat pockets and black rubber gloves and a shopping bag from which he drew a pair of shoes. "I think you may hang up now," he whispered, and Argyros hung up the phone. "Fresh polish on my hands," said Lanze, and raised a gloved hand to Argyros, "I'd hate to track it about. I'm told to wear the cloth gloves... best for the camera lenses. ... But I don't like them."

"You'd better to have put the gloves on first, Mr. Lanze. Polish: that will be on your hands for a week."

"I think you are right," said Lanze. "Will you close your terrace doors and draw the curtains," he said, and Argyros crossed the room and did this. And Lanze thoughtfully measured himself against the opposite entrance, and squared his back against it and knelt to fit and lace his shoes. And Argyros watched him consider precisely where to fit his shoes, and his opera dress and shopping bag and his eccentric gloves: was it Hughes—yes, Howard Hughes, he thought: and he wondered if this obsessiveness might be some peculiar key to Lanze's success. His effectiveness.

"Do you think that you'd threaten to tell?" said Lanze, as he rose and considered the shoes.

"Mr. Lanze?"

"Your character, Mr. Argyros. Do you think he would only menace, or also threaten to tell?"

"He is a very jealous man. It is hard to say. He might be capable of anything."

"I think you are right again. An uneven spirit. How much was already there and how much was borne of the fever—the jealousy, do you think?"

"It is hard to know where a man goes wrong. My father said, and I think he was right—that whether good or bad, you cannot build that castle of a man on nothing. Something must be there; and when you build that castle of him upon it, a road will go there to feed it."

"Did he say that?"

"Yes."

"And you find it true?"

"I believe it."

"What a wonderful creature you are, Argos Argyros: lend me your copy, and let us see if it is true," said Lanze, and circled in the foyer a few times and closed his opened door and moved into the room to a side chair at the coffee table. Argyros fetched his script from the bed and gave it to Lanze. "What do you think of this?" said Lanze. "Have a look." Lanze drew a pistol from his pocket and handed it to Argyros.

"It is quite handsome," he said, and offered it back.

"It's fine—I have the blanks. Keep it a moment. Berretta. I think it suits you," said Lanze, and leafed through the script. "It was either that or a Walther, but that seems a bit cliché. Here. Sit." Lanze indicated a bench at the foot of the bed, and Argyros sat there and cautiously examined the gun.

"What is that smell?" said Argyros, and raised it to his nose.

"Gunpowder. The paprika of ballistic compounds. Surely he would have test-fired it, no. He wouldn't have made it this far with a dry barrel," he said, and Argyros sniffed the gun again and sniffed his palm.

Lanze turned through the script and eventually found and removed a page, and folded the rest away in his coat. "I think there is some dialogue here, like this—from this position," he said, with a reciprocating gesture. "He's lured the rival under pretense: a baited tryst with the common interest. The initial test of confrontation. Here, some pretext of the cordial before it grows animated. Attempted negotiation, I would expect. –Let me see your phone a moment. —No, your personal phone," said Lanze, and Argyros produced it for him. Lanze removed his own, and seemed to copy a number from it into Argyros' phone, and called it. Argyros heard it ringing, and when answered, someone repeated 'hello' while Lanze slowly considered the time and hung up.

"Who was that?" said Argyros.

"An associate whose number I want you to have, but on second thought there's no time to speak with her just now." Lanze handed it back to Argyros and rose and moved now to the bedside phone. "You have your camera, as instructed, Argyros?—and your tapes? Collected them?"

Lanze checked his watch again and paused, then lifted the receiver and dialed. He held the phone lightly by his ear and watched Argyros with the package of cassettes. "*Put . . . one . . . in,*" he said quietly to Argyros. "*Into . . . the . . . camera.*" "Hello. It's just me," he said, when he was connected. "Have you taken your call yet? No. No? I'd have expected it by now. Say, I'm in the westward adjoining room. Yes. Mine is the next communicating room. Let me in. The next room over. Yes. Let me in." Lanze replaced the receiver. "Walk on the other side of the bed from me," said Lanze. "Let's see the look of that." Argyros carried the camera to the opposite side of the bed. "A bit more. Back and forth. Yes. –We'll do a full run through first," said Lanze, and collected the pistol where Argyros had traded it for the camera from the bed, and drove a clip and pulled the slide. "Then we'll move to the location . . ." he said, and removed a tube from his coat and threaded it slowly to the barrel. ". . . set with camera and lighting. Blanks are too loud for now, but you should have the action. We won't use this later," he said, and touched the tube, and placed the long pistol in the shopping bag.

"That is a fearsome business—attachment and all," said Argyros.

"Isn't it. It provides a sense of occasion. Shall we," said Lanze, and they moved down the hall to the eastern communicating door, which Lanze indicated, and Argyros found it opened freely, and followed Lanze through.

They entered by a hall onto a sitting room, where a television silently shown broadcast of the race. Beyond sliding double-doors was a bedroom where a man lay comfortably in socks and shirtsleeves and gazed, dull and listless, at the television in the next room.

"Jacket and shoes, Monsieur Oslo," said Lanze, "you are entertaining company."

"I'm not in a temper for company, Mr. Lanze," said the man—Mr. Oslo. And when he noticed Argyros he sat forward in bed: "Who is this?"

"You have a lovely suite. If only we'd know you had such an accommodating space . . ." said Lanze.

"Do you have a such a suite, Mr. Lanze?" said Argyros.

"I do. —We'll be brief, Mr. Oslo. This is the illustrious Argos Argyros. Mr. Argyros, this is the sought-after Monsieur Freddie Oslo—Mr. Argyros is a fan of your work. —Shoes and jacket if you please," said Lanze. "Don't you agree, Argyros?—surreptitious first impressions."

"Who is Mr. Argyros?" said Oslo, as he moved to the bench at the foot of the bed to lace his shoes.

"Mr. Argyros is the *rival amoureux.*"

"Mr. Argyros is what?" said Oslo, and looked up from his lacing. His mobile phone rang then from where he'd lain in bed, and he'd turned to look at it."

"That will be Lila," said Lanze. "I've just left her with cold, fresh Chardonnay on the terrace. But I'm afraid our task is pressing," he said, and Oslo finished his laces and moved to the bed and fetched the phone. "She's thinking of leaving the terrace soon. I'm to ask when you'll return. —This will only take a moment. She'll try back," said Lanze, and toss the phone on the bed, and collected his jacket and slipped into it as he stepped from the bedroom.

"What's the matter with your hands?" said Oslo.

"Shoe polish," said Lanze.

"He was just polishing his shoes," said Argyros with a smile.

Oslo looked down to Lanze's shoes, then to his own.

"They are," said Lanze.

"From Knokke-Heist?"

"Unfortunately, I find the size is not quite right for me. Have a seat," said Lanze, and motioned the chaise, and moved to close the curtains. "Argyros—you will sit opposite, there. Record from there," he said, and handed the sheet from the script to Oslo: "Read this, please."

"What is this now? These feats and ploys grow tedious, Mr. Lanze. Truly, I had thought we were done with this all once we arrived," said Oslo.

"Understandably so. A small bit of theatre. My final complication, monsieur. Once we have finished here, I will leave, and you will not lay eyes on me again."

Oslo looked at the sheet then, and Lanze moved out of frame, behind the side chair of Argyros—and touched him on the shoulder, and so he turned on the camera and began to record.

"'. . . My sweet," he read, ". . . I am our forgiveness—you are absolved of your indiscretion—you are absolved in our belonging . . . But . . . there shall be no interloper spared. Belonging is a two-splendored form . . . Belonging is not dimensional, it is not manifold . . . And so shall I be, my sweet. For our vigilance . . . and festering impediments . . . of union . . . And so shall I leave you now . . . to tend to this . . . vigilance, and seek the vengeful object . . . and return . . . My sweet, my love—my tender little swan.'—what is this?! This is nonsense."

And Lanze tapped Argyros on the shoulder then, and so he stopped the recording.

"I am not reading this!" said Oslo. "Be serious, Lanze."

"Perfection," said Lanze. "You have that?" he said to Argyros.

"Yes, I think so," said Argyros, and the gun swung round the chair before him and it made a sharp metal snap four times, and knocked the wall once on either side of Oslo and struck him twice center of his chest, and he fell backward against his head on the floor.

"'. . . And it was like knocking four quick times on the door of unhappiness,'" said Lanze, and rose from behind the chair to see Oslo.

"What is this!?" said Argyros. "My god, Mr. Lanze!—is he alright?—what has happened?" said Argyros, and began to stand.

"Sit, sit—you are perfect where you are," said Lanze, and crouched before the chair, and pressed the barrel against his sternum: "'Do not lament parting on any road whatsoever,'" said Lanze. "Tell me, Argyros—you are right-handed—"

XX.

The clawing gasp. It rattles up the throat. Ends as a breath trapped in a can. Deathlights of the eyes. Switched on in illuminated vacancy. In boyhood, a magic Hussar once had seen: a breath captured under a kerchief, dancing and plying for escape: a wisp of ghost made visible by the veil. A thing he might have heard, but only saw. As a fathom of stillness had fallen on him. Like a sunset from the color of flesh. An eruption finally captured in its own math, to rain back down in the pieces of its making. A volume which lay upon everything; pressed against it as weight on the veil.

Marek Hussar carefully unwound the suppressor—yes—he thought—the threads have been gently worked, you say; yes, there are subtle ballistic differences, you say . . . but you are the odd criminal of passion, Argyros, who plots his escape with his care of vengeance. No one sees you as the type. Hussar replaced the thread protector where the suppressor had been, and retrieved the work phone he'd issued Argyros from the pockets. He fitted the trigger loop over Argyros' thumb and lifted the arm till the hand held the barrel near the spot, and let it fall so the pistol tumbled into the lap and onto the floor. "Besides, we tend not to believe what we have no need to see." He straightened and examined his clothes for spoilage, and the soles of his shoes. He collected a pause with his companions and then the shopping bag he'd brought, empty but for surprise—and he left by the entry hall, and through the communicating door into Argyros' room, and stopped to clear the mouth and earpiece of his room phone with an alcohol wipe as a general caution, but not the grip—and in the small foyer he opened his own communicating door once more, and placed the shopping bag there, and stood with his back and heels to it, and knelt to unlace the shoes, and stepped out of them back across this threshold, and collected the shoes—Oslo's shoes—and stowed them in the shopping bag, and closed the door. And fastened the door. Hussar disassembled Argyros' phone and battery and toss them into one shoe of the bag, and slipped the suppressor in the other, and peeled off the nitrile gloves and wadded them into the shoes as well. He washed his hands and wiped dry the counter, replaced his own shoes at the bench at the foot of the bed, and he left the suite, and made his way downstairs to Le Bar Américain, where he met an open stool and took an elbow at the bar, and lay the crisp shopping bag on the rail between his feet, and ordered Oban, and lay out two Maduro-wrap Shermans on a folded napkin. From his phone he called registration, Hôtel de Paris—"I've had a number of cancellations—yes, cancelled guests," he said, "and those remaining will not, I think, care for the rooms I'm holding: please release my suites on five. I understand there will be no refund, but I no longer require them. —Yes, I still require the Diamond Suite, Sea View . . . Terrace: I have a vehicle at the hotel—please be sure it is correctly associated with this room. Yes. Yes, thank you," he said. And he opened a text on his phone which had read "(-)". And replied with a text that said "(.)". And he put away his phone, and he smoked, and he drank his whisky and peered into the frost-patterned mirrors and the bottle glass opposite him. And when he left, and sent his tab to his room, and he made his way with his shopping bag to the quai at the mouth of the harbor, and he stepped into one of the merely two Don Aronow "Bubbledecks" ever made—forty feet by the papers, and roused her fifteen hundred horsepowers, and cast off in idle till the port was clear, and then he woke her, and she spoke her angry truth to the water.

XXI.

There is a bamboo in a vase on the table. It bears fresh new shoots. Good luck. The promise of prosperity and personal growth. A damp little bodhi in a pot. Books purport to sell what it does with photons and the caramel luxury of time. They sell words with prohibitional wisdoms that pretend to atomic truths. A little green fortune, in an unused cup, on a table, under a window. A dark, midnight window. But the bamboo is unafraid. It has planned for this: it needs no other cleverness nor wisdoms. It has patience. It fizzes with the totality of creation. To prosper is to hold its form: increase. To fail—to have its intuitions in electron shells and the orbit of stars betrayed, is merely to fall apart. To decrease. To decay by cascading half-lives and return to source. To become one . . . again, from another. To return from having parted. This is the failure of bamboo.

There is a stony sound to the scene of this thinking: Charlie Haden—thinks Hussar—a pleading walking bassline which strides into growing minor magnitudes. It has the echo of truths so absolute as to be discomforting, and of the dark apartment, where burns the one lamp he will extinguish. The windowpanes are old and dripped as honey and look out onto coal, and the kitchen is cast with shadow, and this room has but this one light by which he packs and readies his things. It is a light for bamboo, by which he too is permitted utility. There are doors. Bedroom doors. One shows noisy with fringe of light. One which is dark—he opens: it is fragrant and floral with full night. The other, he reaches in and makes silence with a switch. And then he puts out the light on bamboo. There is a key laced in a sturdy bolt, and the bright fell of stairs. There is a corridor of Hamburg bent upon him, projected onto the windows of his thought as motion through a tube. And somewhere at the end of these corridors, there will be a cabin door, pressed-closed and lever-latched and sealed vault-like, and the electrical embers of night flight. –It is not a dream, but a memory hung rattling in one till it feels windswept and foreign: a dreamt and waking memory. Lucid undreaming. And it's what is in Hussar when his eyes open in the night.

Jugun Gebungeta Koma wanted fire. Werner Van Der Boor had already said there would be none, and so Koma had turned to the NPRC detail accompanying him—his guard. And he had shown him the earth pit in the sun and tread-worn clearing before the mission, the pit ringed with stones and limed with black ash of fire, and he'd told the guard to get the water of rain out of it so there could be fire. And the guard told him he had nothing to clear it with, unless with a shovel from the Rover—and in that silence one was not offered him. And so Koma told him, use his hands. And the guard had stood there in inertia of motionless disbelief. And Koma still kept his rifle—that rifle of his guard—and so the guard, that NPRC soldier, fell down onto the knees of his NPRC uniform, into the soft red earth before the firepit, and he bore his hands into that cloudy basin, and he scooped out water, like as if to drink. The water was milk grey and the earth was orange in the sunset and the sky was bleach-rubbed white of violet, and the shadow of the hills. Which leaned ever further over upon them. Until the soldier had made a pile of grey water beside the basin and Koma bade him collect things for burning and he'd collected refuse boards and stove wood and scrap lumber nailed through, and when Koma had gone to the Rover to fetch petrol Van

Der Boor had moved and lifted it from his hand and replaced it, and Koma had bade the soldier to fetch petrol in the dusk and he'd found it for generators beside the house of the priest of the mission, across the clearing and a footpath, and Koma had poured it and bade the soldier light it and he had and scrabbled out of the flames and Koma had stood before it in his damp linen suit and dark glasses and lighted a damp cigarette and watched it and smoked it, and once that fire had settled to licks of fume-stinking logs, and the dark of the hills had finally enfolded them, Kamadugu had torn the vulture wings from Hussar's pack where it lay, where they had sat on the stoop of the house of the priest of the mission, and had stormed to the fire and thrust in the wings and snatched up the petrol can and poured it over for watering and flame and sparks had lifted like flights of seed floss in riotous spring.

2.

When Hussar had opened his eyes in the night, from can-lit corners and green shoots and hard, travel-worn marble stairs, he saw instead the small dark room of the hut. The wide, gapped boards, the shadow-heap of things left behind in hasty abandonment—the barked trunk of roof-pier, eventually—somewhere above, a few feet from view would be the ribbed undulations of raw zinced-steel sheet. Through the doorway, Kamadugu on the few planks of porch. He hung from his knees against his rocking heels in crouch, and off across the footpath and the clearing, Kamadugu watched the firepit, aglow with angry choking coals—all the sunlight leapt-out and spent, and now reduced to fuel-less asphyxiating heat. And then Hussar noticed the boy. Jammed into an angle of the hut like a piled stray looking to vanish in a piece of sleep. And Hussar rose from his numb shoulder and his numb hip then to set out a bit of spare bedroll; but in the morning he could see that it hadn't been used.

It had rained till late-day when they'd come to Pujehun. Hussar and Kamadugu had been in the crashing noise of it, and had cleared the village door-to-door, hut-to-hut, and had paused to breathe and Hussar had wrung his hair with the edge of his hands and wiped down his brow and cheeks with both palms and snapped it from his fingers in the water-shade of the abandoned huts that smelled of refuse or wood-smoke of cool quiet stoves, or they smelt of wet steel and old-cut lumber and all the clove and mineral odors that emanate from vacant structures, when not overborne by scents of the body—breath and sweat and feet and unbathed folds, of food, of cooking, of humid oils taken up by porous timbers the way butcherblocks take up chicken. They paused in these places, where Hussar had thrown off some fractional wetness and Kamadugu had shaken his head—that the village was empty, and at Hussar clearing his face, as futile motions—and they had gone back out to draw barrels and strike on emptiness again. And again.

Van Der Boor and James Ngolo Vonjoe had sheltered at the mission and had minded the boys there, and Koma had sheltered there too, and the soldier had minded him. The boys were called 'Westies' Van Der Boor had said when Hussar and Kamadugu had finished in the village and the rain had cleared to patches of visible day. The one nearest the door had said this—"This little tiet 'ere," had said Van Der Boor, and marked out the smallest among them, a youth of maybe twelve—their chief and commander, Van der Boor had said, and found rising from narcotic bloom on the mission floor in beret and bandolier of 7.62, and company of Kalashnikov and sidearm, now a child in fatigue pants and soiled shirt, cross-legged in detention. "They talk to each other—he talks to us. 'Westies,' he says. RUF, I says. Rebels to be sure. King Westie—he says no. He says they know nothing 'a the priest and bodies—it was like this when they come—he says. Found it like this—he says. Sheltered from the rain—he says—miraculous bad luck the bodies an' the gore—he says—and all the dress and demeanor like RUF—he says. They're sympathetic—he says—NPRC irregulars—he says—he's good-guys, mên," said Van Der Boor, and laughed.

Hussar had noticed them but not noted them before: the mission held pews. They'd been toppled or turned before, but Van Der Boor and James Ngolo Vonjoe had righted and arranged them, shoved them out to make a clearing for the Westies in their penitential postures on the floor. But they were full, heavy, scrollwork pews—not rail-ties and bolted lumber, but four-abreast pews with woodworking and ornament, and they might have come from Freetown, but he gravely doubted it: they had some age and patina, scuffed and finish-worn arm rails, and he was amazed they hadn't warped and sat all, four legs to the floor—hardwood pews from an old and distant decon-secrated somewhere, put on a ship, he thought, and swaddled by the sea and craned off and fitted by coarse creole-secular-heretical hands onto a pair of trucks that drove the days here from anywhere, by scooped and rutted mine roads, just to leave them in offering beneath a stark, blue and humid covering at the nowhere foot of Kangari. A little pool of dry and cover and still-pungent odor of *dagga* from before, and Jugun Koma's cigarette smoke, where he sat at the edge of a pew in his high-boots and linen and black necktie, near the boy chieftain—soft-cheeked and maybe twelve, bearing an ageless and spiteful malignancy in the orbits of his eyes and the bite of his jaw. A full-worn Caesar in a miniature container, thought Hussar, and while they spoke Koma reached down, and served him a cigarette.

It was a bullshit, Van Der Boor had said: they'd run from the fireworks of the Kamajors yesterday—routed from the hills round Baomahun, pushed back and shaken out and they'd hid from the overflight of the Hind that morning, he'd said—the Hind whose flight had cleared a path of noise and sight, scared and scouted a way for the Rover that had laid way for Hussar and the Minister Koma, to arrive by rain that afternoon—and they'd hid in the mission, and the poor priest and the poor man and woman, he'd said—probably—he'd said—and when the rain had come they'd just sheltered to get high and drunk and fucked off—and got taken with their little tin-sol-dier pants down—he'd said. And when they'd sorted the mission he would radio De Bruyn and have NPRC, have a bit of army come and take them away—they were not holding prisoners on a mine-camp scout, said Van Der Boor. But Koma lighted his one cigarette upon the next and flicked the spent butt so it bounced off the opposite wall and rolled into the floor and he raised his cigarette-lighted hand to speak.

"Oh, what would happen to you then . . . ?" said Koma, and looked into the faces of the boys there—the leader of the Westies, maybe twelve, and his lieutenant, fourteen, taller, thinner, near him. "Oh, little Peter of the Westies; oh, little Andrew—what would become of you then . . . no cigarettes or wine then!"—he shook his head and crossed his high-boot leg over his knee. "A death of privation," he said. "What should happen to them then?" said Koma to Van Der Boor, and Van Der Boor's eyes narrowed heavily. "But Peter says—"

"This tiet is a Peter now?"

"What else could he be?—Peter of the Westies—"

"And Andrew, too?—this one, ja?"

"And Andrew, of course so—Peter and Andrew of the Westies: but Peter says they are irregulars—not RUF."

"He'd say he'd unfuck the priest 'bout now, too, hey?"

"He says he had nothing to do with this—the priest and the man and woman."

"They hacked themselves, hey?—in grief of loneliness, right?— and sprayed it on the walls—did it of their own, then?"

"He says it was here. Don't you Peter of the Westies?—say it was here."

The boy looked at him, callus; unseeing.

"You, Peter, say it was here—the priest—it was here when you came?"

The boy nodded his head. Slow. Bobbing.

"You see, your honor—the defendant denies the crime . . ."

"That's a bullshit, Koma."

". . . Minister."

"That's a hearty bullshit, Minister. Koma."

"What if it *is* the truth?"

"—"

"What if . . . *I* believe him? What if I believe . . . *them*?"

"Minister . . . Koma."

"I believe this Peter and Andrew of the Westies."

"We are to clear and secure your claim in grant, right? Stake your land-grant. We can not—we have no resource to hold them, right—anymore than we can stay to keep your grant for you, right. Ja? Right? I will need to radio De Bruyn, right? And the boys—the Westies—they will need to go."

"This ground springs corpses, Mr. Van Der Boor. In this war, they collect like hailstones. Why just on our way, Mr. Hussar saw one on the road—the sight of it gave him wings and a halo: already he has lost the halo," said Koma, and laughed so that he had twice to adjust his glasses on his nose. "My, Marek Hussar—what have you done with your wings?—have you lost them too?" he said, and shone the lot of them a great smile.

". . . Safely with my pack," said Hussar.

". . . Minister," said Koma.

Hussar looked at his boots and his smoking hand and his tie, and his glasses. And his glasses.

"They will be in my wardship," said Koma.

"They will need to go, Minister," said Van Der Boor.

"It is my grant—you said this."

"Yes."

"Yes?"

"It is."

"Pujehun. Yes?"

"Yes."

"And the mine fields, yes?"

"Yes."

"And the village—this too is Pujehun. Yes?"

"Yes. And the village."

"And the land of the village, and the trees of the village, and the resources of the village— This too, yes?"

"And this. Yes."

"And the buildings?"

" . . . "

"And the beams and bottles—the iron and fixtures, yes? Of the buildings, yes?"

" . . . "

"And their contents, yes? All they shall contain, yes? Yes! Yes? Van Der Boor, Mr. Van Der Boor!—yes?"

". . . Minster . . . Koma. You've no notion. You can not know. You cannot keep them."

"*Parens patriae*, Mr. Van Der Boor. I will mind them. You call your De Bruyn. And you tell him they came with the parcel, and they are mine to hold and to keep. You radio him—call Koning and Coevorden, and Van Lingen, too! You tell them: *parens patriae!*—Mr. Van Der Boor . . ."

3.

His head was close-shorn and round. His features were soft, and his eyes were walnut and amber through, and porcelain-white, and beautiful. Short pants and bare feet and thin blue shirt, as he'd had from the step of the mission where he was said to have spoken. He was across the red-sooted clearing and the footpath trail, and as they'd left the mouth of the mission he'd been set against the house of the priest of the mission, opposite the side of the stoop with Hussar's winged pack. And when the doors of the mission had opened he had fled from this compact folded pose leant against the house, and moved to the far corner where he could not see in. And when James Ngolo Vonjoe and Van Der Boor had brought out the man and the woman, and the pieces of the priest, from the mission, in that late day that held, to put them in the earth behind the mission, and Koma had come out onto the step to smooth his tie and smoke—the boy had fled the sight, behind the house of the priest. And that night, when the soldier had made Koma's fire with trash wood and petrol and Kamadugu had thrust the wings in it, and Van Der Boor had warned him from fires, and Koma and the soldier had stood near, and no one had dared venture to the Rover by firelight and the rest had sheltered away from it for risk of sniping, the boy had sat nearest of all to the furnace, and he had spoken to no one, and he had wanted nothing.

4.

The village lay against a streambed, on a wrinkled plain a thousand meters in all directions—where at sunrise columns of hill to the northeast and the southwest rose a hundred meters from the floor. And they felt like gates of Gibraltar onto the wide plate which opened westward there and fell encircled at the mountain foot. When Hussar rose the morning was already high with summer and even lying still he wanted bathing, soap and a fresh blade, and to step through a door to the sound of air handlers, and the sweet blue taste of refrigeration. To step through a door he would close behind him, and seal. Cool and eternal darkness.

Koma and his NPRC detail had already spelled Van Der Boor and James Ngolo Vonjoe from minding the Westies in the mission. They had camped out front and taken turns at wakefulness. Van Der Boor had radioed De Bruyn about Koma and the Westies in holding, and De Bruyn had signed off in the throes of battle planning in north Kangari, and left the matter in a demure of pause. And so he and James Ngolo Vonjoe had sat guard at the mission through the night. And Koma had disappeared into the mission that morning and his soldier had set to reclining on the step and clawing at the earth with the cleats of his boot, and Van Der Boor had straightened his weary roll of shoulders and staggered across the clearing to the Rover and across the footpath trail into the house of the priest of the mission, and there made coffee and foraged for cups and settled for the scratched and powder-white-beaten Duralex tumblers there, and

they drank coffee from these held by the rim, and Van Der Boor fortified them all with a splash of rum from the Rover—even Kamadugu.
Hussar had a magazine from a side table and a seated and leg-crossed
smoke, like as if in a train station or a metropolitan hotel lobby,
and there was the roll of the soldier and the sagging bed Koma had
taken, and beneath it, the weapons cache of the Westies, in a duffle
all safed away and poked and protruding with the secret enthusiasm
of Christmas fore-hoardings. Van Der Boor and James Ngolo Vonjoe
had prepared some feat of breakfast to pair rum-coffee and tobacco,
and by late-morning they had moved off to inspect the mines.

The large mine-bed of Pujehun was a kilometer-and-a-half from
the village. And that was where they found the boy. That they should
be called mines at all struck Hussar as a curiosity. They were not
burrows in the earth—tunnels and timber-frame supports. They were
not gold or silver mines with mole works blasted inch-at-a-time into
the noxious depths of mountain hearts, like the Americas. They were
not the salt mines of central Europe, dug into the forest-belly and
carved out like soapstone, with spoons. The alluvial diamond mines
of Sierra Leone were soft-soil streambeds of pits—ochre-bleeding
gashes scraped in the laterite wherever you please, and plucked for
faint stone berries the way boys hunt worms from clots of rain-soaked
field. One pierced the ground at their toes, and if they found the little
carbon flecks they continued—if they found stones, four stories might
be handily churned over on the spot: an impromptu strip-mine of
rain-pool-cess—a mine in its own tailings—of screens and probing
fingers and mud of grape-pressing feet.

When they had set to go, Van der Boor had sent Kamadugu
and Hussar instead—a scouting and return, he'd said—depending.
He'd looked off across the footpath trail and the clearing, to the
mission, and the soldier loitering on the step, and he'd stayed himself

and James Ngolo Vonjoe on some unstated cause, some squinted thumbing under his beard and removing his beret and wiping the band of crown—"No, you go. Bring what you see," he'd said. And they had gone out through that body of vacant village, and slipped down and crossed the bridgeless crossing of the deep streambed under tree cover, and up onto the scabbed and water-pocked plain sweeping west, a long blight of pilot hole worries following a sighing crease of ground. They had come down along the southern edge of the mine field—sixty meters round of scarred and raw-turned earth, of sweeping grooves and loose pits, and hidden depths of trench-works. Hussar gestured to them, and they both cast their eyes there, but Kamadugu continued south and upward into a canopied rise of the greater valley floor. He followed Kamadugu: his cabled knots of sculptural joints and his limbs of whole sinew, and his tool-worked unsmiling, bristling, lively, golem's face. And he felt his own straight, smooth, lead-plodding step. And he watched with envy, Kamadugu's supernumerous articulations spring and uncoil, with lightness and continuous press of motion. And on the peak, they paused to rest, and looking into the falling distance Kamadugu asked for the field glasses with cypher of his open hand.

Kamadugu looked and relooked. Set and reset with the glasses. He surveyed a wide arc, but was intent on half of it. It was a gesture like sipping, thought Hussar, tasting and savoring the landscape with his eyes—a mouthing sight. When he handed back the glasses he pointed just above west, and then again but further. Hussar looked. And there, was not a village but huts—ten to fourteen in a glance. And northward there was another mine field, a shallow unworked sprawl by the look. Footpaths, hard and dry, but for the recent rains: "Is it deserted? —It looks deserted," said Hussar. "—See anyone? Is this part of Koma's grant?—you suppose it reaches this far? . . . Why not give such a man the whole of Kangari . . ." said Hussar, and looked at Kamadugu. And with his gaze Kamadugu said—Is it for us to know what is in his grant?—would he be any more content with the whole of Kangari?—surely not. Shall we draw his lines?—surely not. —We shall assume it within his grant, we shall assume that he wants it, and we shall tell Van Der Boor it is here, said Kamadugu in the lights of his flickering gaze. And he gestured back, down the hill they had climbed, back toward the mine bed of Pujehun, and when they returned there for closer looking, it was there they found the boy.

He sat on a wet slip of ground in a trench basin of the mine. He sat in shallows to his hips, and with his hands between closed knees, and leant forward staring into the same cast of water in which he sat half-vanished. And Hussar could not tell if he was being born of the earth or returning. There was a screen nearby and dredge tin. To Hussar, the basin looked the texture of something chewed to digestion and disgorged in regret. And in this bottoms the boy sat still and peered into the perfect veil of water as though it were a mirror.

Kamadugu called to the boy in short Mende barks. He called with his hands round his mouth, and bent to a listening stoop. But the boy did nothing more than nod a fly from the porches of his nose. "Why won't he speak?" said Hussar, and called to the boy himself. And when again he would not answer, and Kamadugu shook his hat-tasseled head and gestured to leave, gestured back to the path and stream-crossing and vacant body of Pujehun Hussar slipped the stories into the pebble-mudded slurry and went to the boy and touched him on the shoulder. And still he did not speak, and still he did not move. And he looked up to Kamadugu, who spoke softly in his pidgin Mende, and gestured back toward the village with the edge of two hands. And Hussar removed two ration bars from his pack, and the canteen cup from his kit, and filled it with water from his flask, and left it there, and he clambered from the mud-greased flanks of the pit by hands and knees and the toe of his boots.

5.

That night Koma had the soldier search the village for what stores of palm wine there might be, and he fed what came to the Westies, and tobacco and what *dagga* they had left unspent, and they smoked these and drank Koma's share in found spirits, and the mission had rung with their hoots and cries and Koma and the soldier had stayed into the evening there, and retired to the house of the priest of the mission, and Hussar had sat his turn in watch this evening. He had watched their spare light echo off far rustling leaves, stray glistenings like first rain of a prairie edge, and had watched their shouts and claps of sound roll off to catch in the trees, and felt how the hot still night wanted a deep breath of motion, it wanted to be rattled to sharpness and attention by some work of crisp and foreign Octobers. And when he'd been spelled, and returned to the turgid darkness of the hut, the boy was there. In the spare bit of bedroll laid out for him. And the canteen cup, too.

6.

Van Der Boor had radioed De Bruyn again about the Westies and been informed there were neither men nor vehicles for several days, to hold or move or convey them, or anyone else. And he was in no hurry to press the matter while Koma claimed them absorbed in property. 'We're a force, right? Né? Not a government, mên. We work for a government. Right? The government that wants him . . .' Van Der Boor had recited from De Bruyn. The resources there, Kamajors and their small NPRC assignment, were in operations north, or minding the site in Baomahun, for putting down copters and supplies—for now there was attending the Minister, and waiting.

In the morning Hussar had risen to the emptied hut, where Kamadugu had taken to sleeping like a tilted vase on the step. He'd tongued the wet velvet of his teeth and rubbed sense into his eyes and clawed the itch from the cheeks of his half-beard, and he'd joined Van Der Boor and the others in these conversations, at the house of the priest of the mission, as what seemed a daytime tenancy of the house, where Koma and soldier had already parted for the mission. And they'd told him once more about the mine bed and the huts southwest. Kamadugu knelt in the doorframe and delivered gestures from the back of his hand and the knuckle of his wrist and he spoke at the back of Van Der Boor's coffee making.

"He says—he expects emptiness—as it was when they saw it. Probably it was fled and emptied at the same time as Pujehun—when the RUF moved on Baomahun. But it has the pulse of visitors: the kiss of snail silk. People have been there," said James Ngolo Vonjoe.

"He say dat?" said Van Der Boor.

"Yes, very much," said James Ngolo Vonjoe.

"Snail silk . . ." said Van Der Boor, and smiled a wide headshaking smile, and he poured their coffee's breakfast ration of rum.

"And it is not Kavoma?" said James Ngolo Vonjoe.

"Ask him again, what size?" said Van Der Boor.

"He says twelve or fourteen huts."

"Small, né. Kavoma is like as Pujehun, ja. Beside, it's like three clicks near south. This sounds two southwest, right."

"Is it in Minister Koma's claim—will it matter securing it?" said James Ngolo Vonjoe.

"Have you seen it?—you know its boundaries, right. It's no matter what it is—Jugungubungity's a hungry mên, right. It's big as he thinks, and no brick less. We'll go today. And we'll must be quick with it."

His collar looked soft-worked and oil-browned at the fold. His tie was stretched and the knot had the taut and strain-buffed look of a clove of shoelace. His jacket was off, and when he'd seen them kitted and moving he'd come out to smoke and true his glasses with the wrong side of his hand, and to call out to Van Der Boor.

"What needs you all—Werner Van Der Boor—the Polack and everyone?"

"Water and rations for the . . . Westies, in the house," said Van Der Boor. "Same as before. Have your mên serve them out," he said, and motioned the soldier.

"It is my grant, Mr. Van Der Boor—my land, minerals, my rights—and I mean to see it. So where do you go? Hey?"

"Survey . . ." said Van Der Boor, and hefted his pack to reset its straps, and approached him, "yesterday returned structures, southwest. I don't know if it pertains to your grant, but for safety of the Minister, and welfare of his deeds of real property, like—we mean to secure it. A brief visit should do."

"I want to see my mines."

"Nothing but mudpies to see, Minister Koma. I think you want to have them, and you do. You'd your turn with the Westies yesterday—mindin' them no dramas, I'm sure you can hang a stitch today, too, hey."

"You'll work them yourselves. Don't you leave Nigger Jim and the Polack in them. You hear me? You hear what I say," said Koma, and came off the step to say it.

"Mind the mission."

"Who'll watch the land, Van Der Boor?"

"We'll return, Minister."

"No. When you've gone. When we have gone. Who will see to my property, then?—when we have left here, Mr. Van Der Boor."

"That will be for the General—or talks of service with Coevorden, Van Lingen, right, Minister. We brought you, made an empty house for you—and locked the door, né. It is what we can do. It's what's done, and agreed. —Mind the store, hey!" said Van Der Boor to the soldier. "It's but a few hours pass, mên," he said, and marked it under with a thick two-fingered press. And Koma followed them to the body of the village, in his high boots and shirt sleeves, and a shuffling step.

7.

"Is a mine camp, sure," said Van Der Boor when they'd come the sixty meters down from where Kamadugu and Hussar had seen them, and finished clearing the huts of the circle of wood-and-scrub enclosure. And when they'd moved north through the thicket they'd come on to the mine bed they'd seen. And tucked into the brush and the lee of slope were more huts, they had not seen. "Is a mine camp, sure enough," said Van Der Boor, and they'd edged and staggered among the dredge basins—their waters sun-bleached tan—and they'd cleared these too.

"Much excitement Koma will be glad to know," had muttered Van Der Boor, as they climbed the hill-break back to the Pujehun plain. "Great good to decamp, that . . ." he'd said. And when they'd come down the other side and neared the mine beds of Pujehun, Van Der Boor had harumphed on in his plodding, laden step, and checked the fold of his beret with two sun-freckled, fair-haired hands, and Hussar had broken off into the mine fields to look for the boy, and Kamadugu and James Ngolo Vonjoe had fallen back to watch him. And Kamadugu had followed him into the field, to the very pit-edge where he'd stood before.

The boy was there. In the pooled depth. But he did not sit in the water today. But folded over his knees on the slip before the water. The scrim and tin were beside him, but unworked. Hussar called to him from the lip of the crater, and when he'd waved and called again, the boy had lifted his chin. Hussar waved him up. "Come up," he said.

"Up." And Kamadugu said something to Hussar, and he turned and looked into the damp-eyed inscrutable face, which spoke again, and danced the light and festive hat-tassel braids, and Hussar climbed down again to the boy. And set out his canteen cup and filled it from the flask. And he broke out a bar of rations, and left it there. And he took from his pack the pieces of crayon and the stone Koma had given him, and he took up the work-chaffed but soft and limp hand of the boy, and he put them there. And he closed the hand. And he climbed back out from the pit. And when they had rejoined James Ngolo Vonjoe, and the three had moved toward the village together, Kamadugu had spoken again. And twice Hussar had asked James Ngolo Vonjoe what he'd said.

"He says—you are a fool. And your kindness is a danger."

8.

When they arrived in the village Van Der Boor had preceded them. Koma sat on the step of the mission, and as they neared they walked into the smile he fed up to Van Der Boor beneath dark glasses, and his crumpled lapels from the coat he now wore, and his linen pockets from which he drew cigarettes, and knocked one free against his knuckle, and lit it with a sideways cant, and the soldier's machine gun which lay cross his knees. "Fokkol. Fokkol Koma!" said Van Der Boor, and turned to the soldier who sat across the clearing and over the footpath trail, on the stoop of the house of the priest of the mission. He did not look at Van Der Boor, but at his knees and his boots and the tough of ground beneath them. "What is this meaning, hey?" he said to the soldier, who looked at his dusty knees, and without his rifle, and with only his sidearm and his touching heels and his fallen shoulders, Hussar thought he looked naked. Naked and closed over his nakedness. "What is this about . . . HEY!" said Van Der Boor to the soldier, and he looked at the door of the house, and moved suddenly by a thought across the clearing and stormed through the door, and after a moment they heard him swear again. And again, and there was the crashing of furniture, and Van Der Boor appeared in the doorway: "They've gone! Right. Koma. You did this," and he came down off the stoop and moved toward Koma across the clearing. And near the Rover which set in the clearing, he stopped: "What have you done!" he said. And now they had moved so that they could see into the mission. And they could see that it was empty. And Van Der Boor stood in the clearing. And Koma smoked, and flicked ash, or tapped it off against the barrel of the rifle, and lit another from the coal and crushed the life from it beneath his toe, before he spoke again.

"They are my grounds. It is my land. And who will watch it when we've gone? Who will mind it, Mr. Van Der Boor? Sierra Leone has the General. The General has you. You have your Polack—right . . . Oxbridge?—to play your tunes. Where are my pipers, then? To play that tune I would have played? Hmm. Mr. Van Der Boor. My Westies. They shall. They will do it. They are my militia. My very own. For my very own kingdom. I deputized them. They are sworn to me. They are all my sheriffs, and now sworn, empowered and free. You have yours. Why not mine? I. I! I! Me! I!—am the Minister—Van Der Boor! I. Am. I!—am the brother to the General! I! am. Who are *you* . . . with your *this*, and your . . . *this*—that you, and your people, get them—and I should not? And I!—should not! You! You. You are nowhere. And I am here."

9.

There was the feeling of rain. That tickle of the inner ear. The way the air leans in. Feels charged with unseen promise. Vitality. Smells of cool streams in the hot day. Smells of earth on the tides of sky. But there was nothing but the white-blue of clear afternoon, from the shoulder of Kangari to the brown and yellow belch of Freetown, and the sea. And the bitter smirk of Koma. The automatic cross his lap like as it might be a trophy gun, and iced juleps. Van Der Boor, closing his eyes. Shaking his head, into the great space of the clearing. Into their buzz of waiting. At Koma; at himself. And this space had seemed large, and long to Hussar, standing where they stopped. When the radio of the Rover crackled with De Bruyn—for Van Der Boor.

The General wanted Koma, said De Bruyn. He wanted him for introductions in Freetown. For Ministerial posing and actings and, portentous, present-tense beings—thought Hussar. To appear at casting—thought Hussar. Van Der Boor took the radio with a foot in the sill, and a wincing, temple-rubbing mien. —The General wanted that Minister Jugun Gebungeta Koma's grant and properties should be watched. He wanted that he should be escorted under guard to Baomahun, where he could be fetched by Hind, back to Freetown for purpose. Escorted to the helipad clearing at the mine camp the General had visited, and spirited away to significance and safety. "Make it so, ja, right!" said Van Der Boor, "—make it so!"

Van Der Boor and James Ngolo Vonjoe had kitted with packs and magazines. They had laced their boots middle-tight, march-tight; had bounced their pack-straps to a smooth and fitted lay. Koma had dressed the rifle of the soldier on its sling. "What about the Rover? We should take it," he'd said. And Van Der Boor had smiled: "I think not, Minister. I think we won't. —After you . . ." he'd said, and swept their way with a large gesture, and the soldier had risen, and Koma had stared—aimed his dark spectacles at Van Der Boor—and they had all turned to go. James Ngolo Vonjoe had led, and Koma, and the NPRC soldier. And Van Der Boor had turned to them as he followed: "We'll be back, mên," he'd said, and tread off from the wide and dusty mouth of the road, into its narrow throat, and out of sound, and view.

Kamadugu and Hussar had waited out the remaining day, which finally had wearied with its own heat. They dined on butane flame and tin, and in conversation of utensils working in hollow, table-less plates—on the stoop of the house of the priest of the mission. They had made camp in the hut—in the flameless cave of night. And the far and restless hills turned and called to one another only quietly from their sleep, and lay, and listened to the low distant knock of munitions from the north, and the soft tapping phrases of rifle fire.

When Hussar woke. In the cloying heat-volume. The boy was there. Not folded upon himself in the corner, or on the mat of bedroll laid for him. He was against his leg. The rounded back against his knee, and his straight of shin. And he could make the form of the cup nearby, and there was the boy against his leg in the night. And he reached down and touched his head.

10.

When Hussar rose next day, he was alone. Bedrolls and barked roof-pole and the tumble of things, residual to the hut in its former life. In the day Kamadugu crouched where he pleased, and Hussar kept to the shade where he could. But it was of no use. The heat put off their appetites and they ate sparingly. Hussar paced at the clearing-edge under pass of cloud, or he and Kamadugu sat under cover of stoop, of the house of the priest of the mission. The boy had kept to his own. And Hussar imagined him off in the progress of mines in morning. And in the afternoon they'd seen him enter the mission. Appeared like a spirit, and slipped through the door. And there he had stayed for many hours. He did not leave it—not for food or comfort, and they left him to himself there. Many quiet hours. Into the pink-and-blue-brushed shadow of Kangari dusk.

Kamadugu heard it first. They had both sat far edges of the porch from one another. Hussar had rest heavily in his palms. Kamadugu's eyes had lighted. They had lifted and blinked. Moved and thought. And he turned up his head, and turned toward the road. And after a moment, Hussar heard it too. A shout. Cries. A motor. Motor. Shouts. Louder. Faint but clear, now: a vehicle on the southern road. From the direction of Kavoma. And then what had seemed distant was close. It was there. Breaking from tree cover of the southern road, at the far far edge of the clearing. A white Toyota. Laden, squatting, overhung with boys, like as they might be unfastened log-wood; flailing burdens of

grain. Shouts. Calls. Hollering gestures. It bounded into the clearing: winding, griding, mechanical, groaning, sagging, creaking leaf
springs. Circled the Rover once and pulled up at the mission. The
Westies. It was the Westies, Hussar could see. Three a-shoulder in the
cab, and the rest, standing, sitting, on the lip of the bed. Pounding
the roof, jubilant. Punching the air.

They hopped down from the bed, and from the cab. And it was
Koma's Peter of the Westies and Koma's Andrew of the Westies. They
had captured a truck, and the two wore new helmets. Used, green,
over-size NPRC helmets. And two others wore light dresses over
their fatigue pants, dark wet with stain. An RPG, extra rifles, and
jugs of the gasoline-colored wine. And the Peter and the Andrew of
the Westies saw them—Kamadugu and Hussar. On the porch. And
they climbed down. And they unloaded the truck. And they carried
their things. Through the door of the small, quiet, twilight-glowing,
pastel-blue mission.

Hussar stood then. He did not feel himself stand. He stood. And
he waited. And then he moved. He did not feel himself move. Slowly,
down from the stoop. Slowly. Slowly, across the footpath trail. Into
the clearing. And the noise had quieted. The calls, quieted. And then
quiet. Quiet. And Hussar moved in the clearing. Slowly. Crossed
the clearing. Then shouts. New shouts. Slowly. Shouting. Building.
He moved near the Rover. Toward the mission. Loud, angry shouts.
Cries. Sudden, whelping cries. And he was moving. And the door of
the mission burst open. And it was the boy. Clasping his forearm at
the haft. Like as he would hold it in. Stem the leaking, capture and
return it, with his palm. And he stumbled from the step. Running.
Stumbling. Across the clearing. Toward the body of the village.
Running. Toward the deep streambed, toward the mine beds and
plain, that opened there—between piers of hill like the gates of
Gibraltar. And he ran. And he clutched, and kept, and stumbled.
And Peter of the Westies stepped out from the mission, and shouted

at the boy. And they had poured out of the mission. In cloud of *dagga* smoke, and laughter. He shouted. And flung the blade into the boards of the step of the mission. And he threw the hand after him. Hurled like a bottle. And shouted. And Andrew of the Westies had come out too. And shouted too. "Thief!" he cried. "Thief! Basta'd thief!" And raised a rifle. And Hussar had made a sound. Shouted a sound. And Andrew of the Westies fired. And it missed in the dirt. Passed the running boy into the dust. And they had laughed smoke at the miss, and the running. And he fired again. And the boy skidded in the earth. On his shoulders. His chest. In the earth. "Don' fo'get the vote . . ." said Andrew of the Westies, and gestured, and there were shouts of laughter. And they turned to go back into the mission. And Peter of the Westies had taken something from his pocket. Looked into his palm, from the edge of the step. And looked up to see Hussar. Standing there. Middle of the clearing. And he'd looked at Hussar. And he'd taken something from his palm. And he'd thrown something down. Something small. Chaff. Into the dirt. Between them. And he turned. And he went back into the mission. And Hussar stepped forward. And looked into the dirt. And saw them. They were two. Crayons. One red. And one blue. And he felt himself floating then. Lifted. Not walking. Not climbing. Up, into the Rover. Using no force of the body to draw bolts of the M2s. To free the lock, tip up the barrels. No touch of thumbs to depress the triggers. And the guns erupted. Barking light and sound as though of their own. The Rover bucked in sympathy. A little boat in tight chop; in agreement. And the tracer rounds leapt from the barrels. Leapt out slowly, and then sped away. Punctured the cinderblocks. Powder-blue. Glowing in the dusk. Flecks and shards and fractures. Pierced with light. And the guns swung slowly. Cleaved and opened the walls. Roared in his hands. Snapped and jerked in his grip. His effortless, forceless grip. And the color crumbled from the walls. And they buckled. And fell. And the roof tipped in. Collapsed. And the phosphorus lit the dusk with streamers. Lanced through everything they touched. Until they sprouted lumber and palm-wine flame. Until the breaches coughed with smoke. And the belts stopped. And the triggers clicked. And hot brass filled the Rover-bed at his feet. Ceased its ringing in his ears. And nothing spoke, and nothing moved, and nothing laughed but flame.

And Hussar sat in the hot brass. And Kamadugu came to the Rover. Eventually, came to the Rover. With Hussar's canteen cup from his pack. And he reached in, and looked at Hussar, and set the cup. Set it there, atop the wheel arch. And poured from Van Der Boor's rum, into the cup. And looked at Hussar. And tore open fresh cigarettes. Taken with the cup, from his pack. And carefully, laid out twelve. And looked at Hussar. And one more. Carefully. In a row on the ammo box lid, there. Reached in to lay them out. Near him. At his boot. And he took the rest in their paper. And the bottle. And returned with them to the porch of the house of the priest of the mission. And they watched the fire there. And no one came.

He heard his breathing in his throat. Between cars he heard it, up his throat, into his ears, under the earmuffs. They made outside things quieter and inside things louder—his teeth touching, or his tongue or his jaw. Jean-Pierre hung from the railing above the road. It was cool and slippery and wet, and he hung from his fingers. He hung at the railing in a space by himself. Looked through the fence onto the road. Little diamond folds of metal. Peered through the little knotted links onto the cars. Hung from the rail beneath the falling spray. They kicked it up. And it came down like snowflakes in rain. They came up the hill, and he could not hear his breathing then. They sounded like cutting. From far away. And then it was the only sound. Then the cloud of rain. They threw it back into the sky, and it came down and touched like snowflakes. And then someone was near him. Beside him. The man who drove—Mr. Lanze. He knelt beside him, and he looked past the road to the clouds and the sea. And he could see that he was speaking so he uncovered an ear. And the man looked out at the sea, so he looked there. And the man was talking. And he said:

"To be with you . . .
To see you . . .
The things I would say."